# Garrett Joseph

Born September 23, 1995
at 12:21 p.m.

Weight - 6 lb. 12 oz
Length - 21 in.

Riverview Hospital
Heron Point, Oregon

Mommy & Baby doing fine!

Dear Reader,

The nature of a writer's work blurs the line between fiction and reality. We borrow elements from people we know, and breathe them into our fictional creations so that they sometimes become as real to us as any living human being.

And when you add the miracle of Christmas, the wonder of babies and the magic of romance, everyday reality is transformed into a place where love always triumphs and reigns over all.

What better place to spend the holidays?

I offer you such a place in Heron Point, Oregon, where Malia Rose from *Mommy on Board* and Chelsea Annabel from *Make Way for Mommy* came to life. In *Merry Christmas, Mommy*, Garrett Joseph is about to make his appearance three weeks early, to the consternation of his organized and systematic mother.

I'm glad you'll be there to greet him.

I wish you Merry Christmas and the blessings of the season, and love all year 'round.

*Muriel*

Muriel Jensen
P.O. Box 1168
Astoria, Oregon 97103

# Muriel Jensen
## MERRY CHRISTMAS, MOMMY

# Harlequin Books

TORONTO • NEW YORK • LONDON
AMSTERDAM • PARIS • SYDNEY • HAMBURG
STOCKHOLM • ATHENS • TOKYO • MILAN
MADRID • WARSAW • BUDAPEST • AUCKLAND

Merry Christmas to romance lovers everywhere!

ISBN 0-373-16610-9

MERRY CHRISTMAS, MOMMY

Copyright © 1995 by Muriel Jensen.

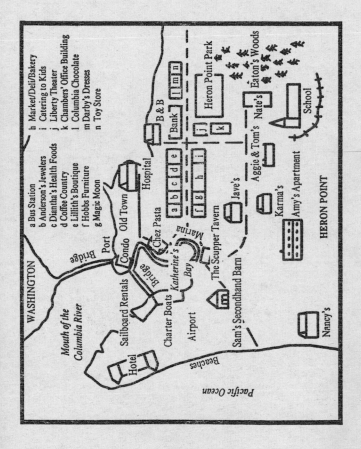

WASHINGTON

Mouth of the
Columbia River

Pacific Ocean

Beaches

Hotel

Sailboard Rentals

Charter Boats

Airport

*Katherine's Bay*

Bridge

Bridge

Port

Condo

Old Town

Chez Pasta

Marina

Sam's Secondhand Barn

The Soupper Tavern

Nancy's

Hospital

a Bus Station
b Anderson's Jewelers
c Diantha's Health Foods
d Coffee Country
e Lillith's Boutique
f Hobbs Furniture
g Magic Moon
h Market/Deli/Bakery
i Catering to Kids
j Liberty Theater
k Chambers' Office Building
l Columbia Chocolate
m Darby's Dresses
n Toy Store

a b c d e
f g h i

Jave's

Karma's

B & B

Bank

l m n

Heron Point Park

Heron Point

Aggie & Tom's

Nate's

Amy's Apartment

Eaton's Woods

School

HERON POINT

# Prologue

*Mother? What happened? Sounded like someone dropped a piano on the car. Are we all right?*

*Um... Mother? I think you're breathing too fast. And you're pushing on me awfully hard. You explained to me how this was going to work, but don't we still have three weeks to go?*

*Who was that? Where are all those voices coming from? What are the "jaws of life"? I don't like the sound of that. I'm willing to be born if you're sure this is the right time, but I'd hoped to be brought into the world by something that sounds more friendly.*

*Mother?*

*Okay. I don't like this. You're not answering me. I can feel your hand on me, but it isn't moving. You're hurt—I know it. Well, I'm staying right here until someone tells me that you're fine and will be there to welcome me.*

*I mean, we've planned this carefully. Labor was going to be induced on October the fourteenth, I was going to arrive with a minimum of fuss, we were going to enjoy a quiet night in the hospital, then spend the rest of our lives together doing tax returns, payroll reports, financial statements and all those other things that keep Endicott Accounting in business.*

*So don't expect cooperation from me. See there? I'm crossing my arms. Just try to get me out of here and see what happens. If I don't hear your voice, I'm not coming.*

# Chapter One

"Okay, I'm calm," Karma Endicott told herself in an even tone calculated to be convincing. "I'm calm. I think my left arm's broken, but that's okay—I'm right-handed. I'll be fine. I feel the baby moving. That's good. We're both fine. Good. I'm calm. I'm fine."

But the sound of her own voice didn't blunt the sound of rending metal, as she'd hoped it would. The giant pliers being wielded by several firemen were making sheet metal out of the Geo Metro on which she'd just made her last payment. And she couldn't help it. Her accountant's brain was calculating the loss, even with the insurance replacement. And she would just bet the rusty red pickup that had run the stop sign didn't even *have* insurance.

"That doesn't matter," she told herself as the driver's-side door was ripped off. "The baby's fine, I'm— Oh, God!"

A cramp tightened her abdomen in a grip that made her think the jaws of life at work outside the car had grabbed her by mistake. It was hard and lasted a long moment.

"No," she said, rubbing at the rigid mound of her stomach. "Baby, don't do this. It isn't time. We have the Butler Logging payroll due, and Mr. Fielding from Fielding Enterprises is coming in this afternoon for a personnel benefits consulta— Ah!''

''Hi.'' A young man with earnest blue eyes and a medical bag appeared where the door had been and pushed the steering wheel to its farthest position. ''Labor?'' he asked as he leaned over her and checked for injuries.

''Broken arm, I think,'' she said, wincing as he touched it and pain seemed to consume her entire body.

*MOM! Thank God! I'm sorry, I'm not really ready to do this, either, but it seems to be happening anyway. The walls are closing in here!*

''GOOD DIAGNOSIS,'' the medical technician said, turning to shout over his shoulder for a splint. He glanced into her eyes with a smile as he cut the sleeve of her white silk shirt away. ''Want to work for us? You seem to be good at this. Are you having labor pains?''

''No,'' she said as the pain in her abdomen subsided. ''I'm not due until October 14, when Dr. McNamara intends to induce labor, and I refuse to give birth a moment sooner.''

A second young man handed him a contraption that he fitted gently along her arm.

Under a glaze of pain, she watched the people clustered around her car. A police officer talking to a middle-aged man in coveralls, who pointed to the red truck another officer was pushing to the side of the street, firemen clearing away their equipment, bystanders trying to peer through her windshield as they stood beyond the flares placed on the asphalt.

She felt as though she were watching a scene from a TV show like ''Cops.'' This couldn't be happening to her. She'd planned so carefully from the beginning—the right moment in her life, the right sperm bank, a sperm harvest with a high possibility of producing a girl, the right obstetrician in the right hospital.

She refused to let it all go bad on her now.

"Uh-oh," the medical tech said. He was running his hands carefully along her legs and ankles.

Her eyes flew to his as he looked up at her, that same friendly smile in place. "What?" she demanded.

"Your water's broken," he said. "You *are* in labor, ma'am." He turned to his partner. "Tell ER we've got an MVA coming in with a hot baby."

The sound of sirens as the ambulance sped Karma toward the hospital deepened her sense of unreality. She never got hurt, she seldom got sick. Emergencies were unheard-of in her life because she was a planner. She hated last-minute surprises. Eighteen years with Daisy Dawn and Mountain Man had taught her more than she wanted to know about the spontaneity of life on the road without roots or destination. She'd loved her parents, but she'd promised herself she'd never live that way again.

And here she was, a victim of chance, speeding toward the hospital with a "hot baby." There was no justice.

"CAN YOU MEET THAT ONE, Nate?" Jackie Palmrose, Riverview Hospital's emergency room doctor on the day shift, peered around the curtains surrounding bed four and pointed in the general direction of the sound of a wailing siren.

Nathan Foster, just getting off the night shift, had already changed clothes and was shouldering a brown leather backpack.

He threatened her with a glance as the whoop of the siren grew deafening and finally stopped abruptly in front of the emergency room doors.

"As of ten minutes ago," he said, "I'm on vacation. The Canadian wilderness is calling my name." But he dropped his pack.

She shrugged, her expression blandly innocent under an irregular fringe of blond hair. "Sorry. This chest pain has us all tied up. That's a motor vehicle accident with a hot baby out there. Medic called it in while you were changing. You know how it's done. All we do is turn her over to OB."

Joanie, the nurse, peered around the dividing curtain on the other side and grinned at him. "We know how much you like babies."

"Go ahead," he said, moving toward the door. "Be cute." He lowered his voice as he pointed to the curtain. "You know that's a bad gallbladder and not a heart attack."

"But it's the administrator," she whispered back. "And he thinks he's having a heart attack. We want him to see us doing everything right."

"Fine. You can both forget the maple candy you asked for, *and* the bachelor Mounties."

"Just one Mountie?" Jackie whispered loudly as he opened the doors and stepped outside. "Joanie and I'll share him!"

Nate met the gurney. It held a very pregnant young woman with a tight knot of dark hair and big gold earrings. Her left forearm was in a splint. Pushing the rolling cot was his favorite pair of EMTs. Baldwin had taken a year off medical school to earn money to go back. He was capable and accurate and calm. Prentice was less experienced, but smart, if good-naturedly naive. He blushed purple at the nurses' teasing, and took the doctors' friendly abuse as a sort of rite of passage.

"We're having a baby," Baldwin said as they helped push the gurney into the ER. "You better get OB down here, or you're going to be delivering it." He grinned. "And we all know how much you like babies."

"If I want abuse," Nate said, "I've got Jackie and Joanie."

He leaned over the woman with his stethoscope. Her eyes were closed and her delicate features were taut with concentration as she breathed through a contraction. She grimaced and reached a slender hand out of the blanket, as though searching for something to hold on to.

He put his hand in hers, and she ground his knuckles together with more efficiency than Sugar Ray Leonard could have. He had to make a conscious effort not to wince. Baldwin and Prentice would have enjoyed it too much.

The woman opened her eyes. They were chocolate brown and filled with pain.

"Will you call Bert?" she asked, her voice breathless.

"Your husband?" Nate asked.

She shook her head. "My Lamaze coach. Roberta Dawson, at First Coastal Bank."

He nodded. "I'll get someone right on it. Dr. McNamara's on his way. Just hold on."

"I'm willing." She gave him a faint smile, but a tear slid from her eye down into her hair. "But the baby has other ideas. And she's three weeks early."

He squeezed the hand he held. "That shouldn't be a problem. Try to relax. You're in good hands now."

Her hand tightened on his again. "You don't understand. The nursery isn't finished. I was going to do that next week, after quarterly reports. I only have one box of diapers, no food in the freezer..."

"You'll have time to worry about that later," he said gently, thinking as she crushed his hand that it was a good thing he hadn't chosen to become a surgeon. "Right now, concentrate on relaxing so that this baby can make his big entrance."

"It should be a girl," she said. "I asked for a sperm harvest with a higher possibility of being female."

He blinked at her. "Say what?"

But Jackie called to him before he could make sense of that revelation. "Dr. Mac wants to know if we can bring Miss Endicott over. The arm will have to wait until after the baby."

"We'll take her," Baldwin said. He grinned at Nate. "Get going on your Calgary odyssey. And don't forget our maple candies."

Nate nodded to Jackie, then smiled down at the woman on the gurney. "These guys are going to take you to OB, and I'm going to call your coach—"

KARMA FELT her grip on him tighten. She couldn't have explained it, but she had some deep and powerful need to link their fingers inextricably, to keep him with her. He was tall, with longish blond hair, cheerful blue eyes and a wide-open smile. His grip was the only security in her world at the moment.

She could deal with any crisis, as long as she was prepared. But this was more than a simple crisis. This was— this was her baby's *life*. And it was coming into being three weeks early. Her plans weren't in place. Her schedule was decimated. She was terrified.

Admitting that, of course, was out of the question. She simply held on.

Nate tried to withdraw from her grip and couldn't—at least not without losing everything above the second knuckle.

Baldwin saw the woman's death grip and glanced at him with amusement curiously mingled with sympathy.

"Why don't I walk you over?" Nate suggested. He looked up to find Jackie nearby, also looking amused. Jackie was never sympathetic. "Would you call Roberta Dawson at First Coastal Bank? She's the patient's Lamaze coach. See if she can get down here."

"Of course." Jackie grinned widely and turned to the phone.

Baldwin pulled, Prentice pushed and Karma rolled toward OB, feeling as though her well-ordered existence was about to tumble out of control, like a piece of space debris.

All that could prevent that from happening was the solidity of the hand she held. It seemed to ground her somehow, prevent her from falling all the way down into the fear that yawned beyond the edge of the gurney.

"Well, isn't this a busy baby day." A nurse, who looked alarmingly military, met them at the juncture of the corridors. The EMTs wished Karma luck and left, and the nurse pushed her into a room that claimed her attention, despite her pain and anxiety.

It was lavender and blue, with flowered wallpaper and a coordinated print on the bedspread and curtains. She noticed oak details, and what appeared to be a parquet floor. Was she delirious already?

"This is one of our new birthing rooms," the nurse said, throwing the covers back and lining the gurney up right beside the bed. "Got two others like it. What do you think? Would you believe they're all in use today? Delivered two girls already this morning. This makes a veritable baby boom in little old Heron Point. Okay, let's get you in the bed."

Nate freed his hand to lift her from the gurney to the bed, with its delivery room refinements. He straightened, thinking he was free at last. But she dropped her arm from around his neck, slid it down his arm and reclaimed his hand.

The nurse fluffed her pillows, pulled her blankets up and gave her a maternal smile that belied her military bearing. "I'll tell Dr. Mac you're here."

"Ah—Beachie?" Nate called after the nurse's retreating figure. "Would you call ER and see if Jackie got through to Miss Endicott's Lamaze coach?"

"Right." She started out the door, then leaned back in to grin knowingly at him. "Afraid of ending up in the baby business yourself, Dr. Foster?"

His answering frown only made her laugh as she pulled the door closed behind her.

The patient gripped his hand as another contraction tightened her abdomen. Nate pulled the chair up to the side of the bed, resigned to being stand-in moral support until her coach arrived.

"Ah...okay," he said, trying to remember the little he knew about labor. It was ER policy to turn all such patients over to OB immediately. "You're supposed to be breathing, not tightening up like that. Come on. Short, shallow breaths—you know how. Puff, puff, puff—just like a steam engine."

"Yeah...I forgot." Karma complied with three proper breaths, then drew in and expelled a lengthy one when the contraction faded away. "Thanks." She turned her head to look at him, and winced when one of the pins in the bun at the back of her head poked her scalp.

"Another contraction already?" Nate asked anxiously.

"No." She even smiled. "My hair hurts."

"Oh." Nate considered that a great relief. He'd had the horrible feeling that they'd advanced to the delivery phase without warning. He stood to lean over her and work at the knot of hair at the back of her head until it was free. He dropped three pins on the small table and combed his fingers through the thick coil of hair. It fell over his arm like warm silk. The sensation seemed to run along under his skin, right straight to his heart.

He sat down again, his other hand still crushed in hers. She was watching him, curiosity covering the pain in her dark eyes. "Why does everyone tease you about babies?" she asked. "Don't you like them?"

He shrugged a shoulder, glancing at the door, wishing her coach would arrive. "I like children fine," he replied. "I just don't like to work on them. Or even help deliver them."

That seemed to surprise her. "Why?"

"Well . . . they're vulnerable," he replied, deciding that a surface answer was all that was necessary. "Because they're so small. It makes our job harder. I'd rather work on burly loggers or aerobics instructors." He tacked on that last part on a jocular note. Then, wanting to redirect the conversation, he asked, "What's your first name, Ms. Endicott?"

"Karma," she replied, then frowned. "Did I hear someone say you were going on vacation?"

He nodded. "Soon as I'm out of here. I'm going camping for four weeks in Canada."

She grimaced. "I'd hate that. I need electricity and a comfortable mattress. I'd like to see Canada, but from a hotel window."

Now he winced. "That'd be like watching a movie of Canada. Might as well stay home and turn on the VCR."

She nodded. "I spend a lot of evenings that way. Uh-oh."

"Another one?"

"Uh-huh."

*MOTHER! Could you send down a map? I thought this looked like the only logical road, but I seem to be at a dead end!*

"BREATHE. Breathe." He demonstrated, and she copied his huffing, holding tightly to his hand as the contraction crested, then passed.

She sank back against the pillow, already tired, though she knew this was just the beginning. That very thought brought the ever-threatening fear closer. She turned to him to have something else to think about.

"Your name is... Nathaniel?"

"Nathan," he corrected. "Nathan Robert Foster."

"M.D.?"

"Right."

"Married?"

"Wrong."

"Me either," she said. "All the men *I* found interesting were married, and many of the men who found *me* interesting were also married. So, I decided to have a baby on my own." She looked into his eyes. "I went to a sperm bank. Do you think that's awful?"

"I think," he replied diplomatically, "that you have charge of your own life."

Her gaze narrowed on him. "You *do* think it's awful."

He shook his head. "I think it's an option I wouldn't choose. But I can't hold you to my rules."

"I wanted to share my life with someone," she said, unconsciously rubbing across his knuckles with her thumb. "There's a lot about life I really love, and I thought it would be neat to give that to someone else." She sighed, the loneliness and frustration of the past few years crowding in on her as she held that sturdy hand. "But I couldn't find the right man. And I didn't want to settle for the wrong one. So, I thought I'd just skip that step, and have the baby."

That sounded a little antiseptic to him, but then, he'd never wanted a baby. At least not since Jimmy Cameron.

He smiled. "Some people consider that the most important step—or, at least, the most memorable."

She smiled back. "With the right man, I'm sure it is. With the wrong one, I can't think of anything to recommend it. So we settled for the invisible man."

"A handsome professional in good health?"

"Precisely. And he read Walt Whitman. That was what decided me. Uh-oh."

Nate, who was leaning forward, elbows on his knees, sat up alertly. He breathed with her through the contraction, then sat back in relief when it was over and Beacham peered around the door.

"Roberta Dawson," she reported apologetically, "is in Seattle at a district meeting. I guess she hadn't counted on you delivering three weeks early."

Karma closed her eyes, and groaned. She'd completely forgotten that Bert was leaving this morning for a special week-long training session. Was this Murphy's Law at work, or what?

Well, she could do this without Bert. She intended to raise the baby alone; she could certainly have it alone.

But the pain was so much more frightening than she'd anticipated. And the suddenness of it all, the lack of time to prepare, to plan....

Nate saw a tear slip out of her eye and into her hair. He tightened his grip on her hand.

"You're going to be fine," he assured her. "I know this is just dinky little Heron Point, but by some stroke of providence, we have the best collection of medical people here, bar none, and Mac's the best of those."

She sniffed and nodded. "I know. I'm not usually such a wimp. I just hate to be...unprepared."

"You're not unprepared," he said bracingly. "You have the baby and we have the doctor. It doesn't require anything else. You heard Beachie. We've already had two baby girls today."

"Did you help with those, too?"

"No. One of the fathers is a friend of mine, and the other was a friend of his. I met them at the coffeepot right after the second baby was born. One had hair, and the other one was bald, but pretty big." He grinned. "The babies, not the fathers."

"Well, girls like to be showy." She spoke airily, but he could see that she was demoralized by her friend's absence.

And he was too much the doctor to walk away.

"I'll coach you through," he said, taking a tissue from the bedside table and handing it to her. He could leave on vacation tomorrow morning. No big deal.

Something flared in her eyes—happiness, or perhaps relief—but then she said quietly, "But, you're on vacation."

"I'll leave tomorrow morning." He grinned teasingly. "Provided you don't have one of those interminable labors."

She sighed and squeezed his hand. "I'm usually very efficient. I'm an accountant, you know. Never a moment or a penny wasted."

"All right." He smiled up at Nurse Beacham. "Ice chips for the lady, waitress," he said, "and make mine a double espresso."

# Chapter Two

"Okay," Dr. McNamara said from his stool at the foot of the bed. "This push is going to do it, Karma. Give it all you've got."

Karma wanted to tell him she'd done that over an hour ago. She had no courage, no strength, left. But this had all been her idea. It wasn't the result of uncontrollable passion, or a romantic accident. She had planned it all herself. Except that she'd intended to have all her deadlines met, the nursery ready, everything in place for this momentous development in her life.

But fate had changed that, and no complaint or resistance could reverse the march of events. The baby was here. She had to welcome it home.

From somewhere inside herself, she had to find the strength. It was just such a surprise to discover that she wasn't the paragon of strength she'd imagined herself to be. She'd gotten through the past two hours on the courage of the ER doctor she'd literally dragged into OB with her. Had she really done that? Mortification tried to make itself felt, but there simply wasn't room for it amid the pain, panic and desperation.

All right, she told herself, pacing her breathing, getting ready. Maybe it's there, and I just don't realize it is. Maybe it'll surprise me. Maybe it'll come through for me, after all.

"That's it," Nathan Robert Foster's voice said calmly in her ear. She sat propped up against the angled head of the bed, and he stood beside her, leaning over her, one arm wrapped around her back. For an instant, everything else in the room receded, and it was just the two of them in the tight circle his arm around her created. "Build up everything you've got. This is it. Little Lady Endicott makes her debut at—" he glanced up at the clock "—12:21 p.m. Come on, Karma. A deep breath, and push! Push!"

*OKAY, stand back! Out of the way! Coming through!*

KARMA LEANED into the arm wrapped around her and gave the push everything she had left, and everything she was able to steal from her commandeered coach.

The world went red with pain and tension for one interminable moment, and then she heard Dr. McNamara's cry of triumph and her own body's exhalation of relief.

"And here she... Whoops."

"Whoops?" Nate straightened and looked over Karma's knees to the doctor. "What do you mean, whoops? Tell me you didn't drop her, Mac."

"Ah...no. Karma, you know that theory the sperm bank sold you about sperm being harvested at a certain time guaranteeing gender?" Dr. McNamara, his mask pulled down to reveal his wide smile, came around the bed to hand her the screaming baby. It was a boy.

She gasped in surprise. "I was so sure he was a girl." She hadn't even considered boys' names.

*GIRL? Who're you calling a girl? Do I look like a girl? Well, that's a fine greeting, I must say. After what I've just been through to get here. Someone had better make this up to me—and fast.*

KARMA took the screeching baby in her arms and absorbed the surprise of his gender, along with his physical perfection and apparent good health. She felt great pride, and nothing that even remotely resembled disappointment.

"You are," she whispered, putting her cheek to his, "the most beautiful thing I've ever seen."

*WELL. Hmm. Okay, then.*

"HE'S ALL RIGHT?" she asked in disbelief. "The accident didn't hurt him?"

Dr. McNamara shook his head. "He looks perfect to me. Let's clean him up and weigh him in."

Karma relinquished the baby reluctantly. "He looks all right," she said to Nate as the doctor took the baby to the scale on a table across the room. "Don't you think he looks all right?"

"He's beautiful." Nate helped her ease back against the pillows. She was pale, her hair damp at her forehead and temples. Her eyes were turbulent, and her smile was a little uncertain.

"How's your arm?" Nate asked, still holding her good hand.

"Starting to hurt," she admitted with a light laugh. "The good part about labor is that you don't notice other pain."

He smoothed the damp hair off her forehead. "I'll let them finish up here, then they're going to set your arm. I'll see you afterward."

"Thank you for staying." Her voice was thready, weary, and her eyes were focused intently on him. "You...kept the fear away."

Nate put his other hand over hers. "I'm glad I was here. I'll stick around until you wake up, to make sure everything's all right."

Karma shook her head. "I want you to go on your vacation. When you're sleeping under the stars, think of me and the baby. We'll be remembering how kind you were."

"No," he insisted. "I'll see you later."

"If the baby's all right," she replied with a smile, "I'll be perfect."

Dr. McNamara returned to the bed, the baby in his arms. "He weighs six pounds, twelve ounces. And had you carried him another three weeks, he'd have come out tall enough to play basketball."

Karma noted that the baby now wore a plastic bracelet. A similar one was placed on her good wrist. "Just so we don't give you to the wrong baby," the nurse said.

Nate frowned teasingly. "This is the hospital's most inefficient department."

Karma raised her good arm. "Can I have him back now?"

Dr. McNamara shook his head. "Sorry. We still have several rude things to do to you, and Dr. Dade, the pediatrician, has to give him a few tests."

Karma groaned and grumbled at the doctor as he handed the baby to another nurse. "You go through all this to have a baby, and nobody lets you hold him."

Nate rubbed her shoulder. "You tell 'em. I'll see you in a while."

She fixed him with a stern look. "Go," she said firmly, "on vacation." Then she waved, her dark eyes holding his for one extra moment.

Nate strode down the hallway, torn between a compulsion to run out of the hospital and race north in his car and an equally strong need to have a heart-to-heart with Mac, to stay within hailing distance, should Karma Endicott need him, and to look over her chart himself.

He was supposed to be on vacation, but suddenly that was the farthest thing from his mind.

He caught a whiff of coffee from the OB waiting room as he passed. Caffeine. That was what he needed. He detoured into the room and filled a paper cup and went to the window. It looked out onto the east parking lot. The big mountain ash across the street was just beginning to change color, its combs of green leaves tipped with gold, its branches heavy with clusters of bright red berries.

God. He'd just coached a woman through childbirth. He wasn't shaking. He was too good a doctor for that. But everything inside him was going at warp speed. It was just an adrenaline rush. He knew that. But deep inside him, beyond all the physical mechanisms he knew and understood, something else was happening.

He stood still, sipped caffeine and tried to analyze it. It took only a moment's thought to realize that he understood what it wasn't better than he understood what it was.

It was more than concern. He was a dedicated ER doctor; he knew all about concern. He felt it for all his patients, even the drunks who were ill or injured because of their own weakness, the women who drank with them, went home with them and invariably ended up in the hospital as victims of abuse, the druggies who claimed excruciating back pain that required a prescription for Demerol. He could see past their circumstances to the pain inside them that wouldn't be diminished by anything at his disposal.

He knew this was different, because he could treat all of them to the best of his ability, then walk away. He couldn't do that today. He wanted to, but he didn't seem to be able to.

He kept remembering a slender hand gripping his with a strength that astonished him, frightened and pain-filled dark eyes in a delicate face studiously set in calm lines. He remembered those same eyes following him as he'd walked to the door.

He felt as though a large hand had taken hold of his rib cage and squeezed.

"Nate."

Nate turned away from the window at the greeting. The voice belonged to J. V. Nicholas, Riverview Hospital's radiologist, and the friend he'd told Karma about whose wife had had a girl that morning—the one with the hair.

"You're still here?" Jave grinned as he poured coffee into a paper cup. "I thought you'd be on the other side of Seattle by now, on your way to the wilderness."

Nate had a little difficulty surfacing from his mental images of Karma. He smiled distractedly and sipped from his cup. "Ah...had a patient at the last minute with... complications."

Jave sat on the black vinyl sofa near the window. "The OB with the broken arm?"

Nate turned back to him again, frowning. "Your wife had a baby here today. You're supposed to be here as a civilian."

"You know a doctor is never a civilian." Jave angled one ankle over the other knee. He grinned. "Our inherent nobility prevents that. I happened to wander through ER while Nancy was sleeping and heard about the traffic accident and the hot baby." Jave looked into his eyes, his expression bland. "I thought you didn't like babies."

Nate knew what he was doing. Jave was everybody's big brother. Well, he didn't want or need one. His attitude about children was not a psychological problem, it was a conscious decision reached through a compilation of data and personal experience.

"Don't start with me," he said with friendly firmness. "I like babies, I just don't want one. I happened to get involved with this patient before the baby arrived."

"Involved?"

"The mother was alone, and I stayed to help."

"Ah." Jave nodded, resting his cup on his knee. "Watch yourself. That's how I married Nancy."

Nate laughed mirthlessly. Everyone in the hospital knew Jave's story. As the divorced father of two, he'd fallen under the spell of a single mother with premature labor who'd been sent to radiology for an ultrasound.

Nate had never been entirely sure what had happened—he found hospital gossip interesting only to a point, and that point didn't include his friends. The next thing he knew, Nancy and Jave had been married. That had been several weeks ago.

"I think," Nate said, "that you were more...vulnerable to a woman's charms than I am."

Jave raised an eyebrow. "Really."

"Yes," he replied, ignoring the amusement in his friend's eyes. "You had boys who needed a mother. You...you need a woman."

Jave's eyebrow lowered to meet the other in a frown. "Why do I need a woman more than you do?"

"You have a neat mom. You had a wife." When Jave's frown deepened at that, he added quickly, "Well, it had been good before she ran off. You're used to having women around you. I was raised in military schools."

"And you could probably never get a date."

"And I could never get a date," Nate agreed, then studied his fingernails with a falsely modest air, "because women are intimidated by my wit and my charm."

"Yeah, right. So why is it that Karma wasn't intimidated by your wit and charm? I understand she had a death grip on you when Baldwin and Prentice tried to take her from ER to OB."

Nate shrugged a shoulder. "I was there. Had *you* been there, she probably would have clung to you. How do you know her name?"

"She was in Nancy's Lamaze class. Anyway, that's not the way Jackie tells it. Or Beachie. They say it could have gotten very complicated if you hadn't been there to keep Karma going."

Nate dismissed the praise. "We connected. She needed help and I was there."

Jave gave him a considering smile, downed his coffee and got to his feet. "That's the epitaph of many a brave bachelor, Nate. 'She needed help and I was there. We connected.'" He tossed his cup at the basket in the corner. "So, you're off to Canada now?"

No. He wasn't. "Ah . . . soon," he said.

Jave clapped him on the shoulder and went to the door. Nurse Beacham stood there with a clipboard.

"Beachie," Jave said, putting an arm around the nurses' shoulders. "What's up? Looking for me?"

The short, square woman batted her lashes theatrically. "I've been looking for you all my life, Doctor."

He dipped her backward over his arm. "But it can't be, Medora," he said, his voice assuming a deep and dramatic soap-opera-doctor quality. "Because you're married to the famous heart surgeon Lefty Ventricle, and I'm dying of salmonella."

Nurse Beacham put the back of her wrist to her forehead. "If only someone had told me there's no such thing as *chicken* tartare."

"It's all right, my darling. I know you didn't do it on purpose."

"But I did, my darling. Because you're standing between me and the only man I want at this moment—Dr. Foster."

Jave straightened, the very picture of the wounded lover. "Medora . . ."

Nate approached them. "Beachie, this is so sudden."

She smiled blandly. "I know. I was hit by a car while sleepwalking, and now I have amnesia." She turned to Jave. "We need to be alone."

He placed a hand over his heart. "You're fickle, Medora." To Nate, he added, "Call me if you need help."

The door closed behind Jave, and Nate turned to the nurse with a teasing smile. "Where'll we go, Beachie? The supply closet? The nurses' locker room?"

Beacham put a hand to his chest and pushed him onto the sofa, then sat beside him. "I need assurance of your discretion, Dr. Foster."

"Beachie . . ." He leaned away from her with a wary look. "You're starting to scare me."

She rolled her eyes. "Dr. Foster, I do not crave your body. Although the nurses all think it's pretty buff. I want your advice on what to do about Miss Endicott."

"What do you mean?" he asked, stiffening in his seat. "What's happened?"

"Nothing," she assured him. "We're going to keep her for a couple of days because of her arm, but when we release her, she'll be going home to no one, with a useless arm and a brand-new baby who'll have her thoroughly exhausted in twenty-four hours. I want to have a health-care nurse look in on her, but she refuses. She insists she'll manage just fine. That's because she's never taken care of a newborn before."

"Arrange for a nurse anyway," Nate said. "Tell her she doesn't have a choice."

Beacham shook her head at him. "She does have a choice, Doctor. This is America. You were with her all through labor. I thought she might have mentioned a relative or a friend or someone we could call on to help her cope when she gets home."

He thought back. It was absurd, but they'd talked politics, music, movies, food—and they'd cheerfully disagreed on every point. But they'd never talked people. He'd gotten the impression she didn't have any family. And her only close friend—the one who was supposed to be her Lamaze coach—worked full-time, and was away for a week, anyway.

He drew a breath to tell her he didn't think Karma Endicott had anyone—then decided maybe she did.

"I'll get back to you," he said.

KARMA did not want an outsider intruding upon her first days with her baby. And nothing at home was organized. Another person, even someone intending to help, would just be in the way.

No. She would manage. With her arm set, she felt almost human again. She was terrified, but she would manage. She turned to the bassinet beside her bed and was relieved to see that her son slept soundly.

It would help if she could decide upon a name. She'd fed him only three times, but she knew he resented her calling him "baby." He was supposed to have a title that was uniquely his—a label, for lack of a better word, that told the world what he was about.

She closed the book of baby names she'd been studying and allowed her mind to focus on the man who'd seen her through labor. Nathan. That was what she would name her son if she could be sure she'd never see the ER doctor again. But Heron Point was a small town. Sooner or later they'd meet downtown, or at a party, and recall the very unusual morning they'd spent together once in a Riverview Hospital birthing room. And he would be bound to ask politely, "Did you finally settle on a name?"

She couldn't say, "I named him Nathan after you, because you're the only man I've ever met whose name, I felt, should live beyond him."

He might mistake it for a romantic gesture. And that wasn't it at all. She simply admired him.

"Karma?" Her name was whispered from the door by a figure in a flowered robe.

"Nancy?" she asked, thinking she recognized the woman from her Lamaze class who'd married the radiologist. She was writing a murder mystery; people had been talking about it at the coffee bar downtown.

There were two little boys with her, one on either side, holding her hands.

Karma sat up in bed and gestured to them to come in. "What a nice surprise," she said, genuinely pleased to see her. "Nate...Dr. Foster...told me two little girls were born today. Was one of them yours?"

Nancy nodded. "She's beautiful. We're so proud."

"Was your little girl the bald one," Karma asked, "or the one with all the hair?"

"The one with the hair."

She smiled down at the boys. "These are my boys," she said, holding up the hand of the older one. "Eddy, and Pete." She smiled down at the smaller one. "We've been checking out everybody's babies. Jo Arceneau had hers today, too, you know. The bald one.''

"All right!" Karma laughed. "A very large little girl, I understand.''

"She's *huge!*" Pete said.

Eddy poked his younger brother. "Pete's going to marry her when he grows up.''

"No way!" Pete protested loudly. "I'm going to be a pitcher and make lots of money and I won't go out with girls 'cause they're yucky!''

Nancy shushed him gently while smiling an apology at Karma. "We have to keep our voices down so we don't wake the baby. May we look, Karma?''

"Of course.''

Nancy and the boys tiptoed to the bassinet. The boys looked in, clearly fascinated.

"It's a boy, isn't it?" Nancy asked.

Karma nodded.

"What's his name?" Pete wanted to know.

Karma held up her book. "I haven't decided yet. I was expecting him to be a girl.''

Pete came to lean importantly by her bedside. "My dad does ultrasounds, so you can tell if it's a girl or a boy before it's borned.''

She nodded. "I had two of those. And sometimes you can't tell for sure.''

The older boy rolled his eyes. "He's too young to understand that the baby isn't always laying where you can tell.''

Nancy ruffled his hair. "Why don't you take Pete to meet Grandma and Willie in the cafeteria?''

The boys went off, the little one resisting the older one's efforts to keep him at his side.

"Stay with Eddy, Pete!" Nancy called after them.

She turned back to Karma, wincing. "I'm new at being a mother," she said. "And I don't just mean the baby. Those are my husband's boys, and... Well, I guess you know we just got married a couple of weeks ago."

Karma studied her in wonder. "Where do you get the guts? I'm terrified of that little baby. I can't imagine going home with a baby *and* two beautiful but probably smart and lively little boys. I'd be paralyzed with fear."

Nancy laughed. "They move too fast for you to remain paralyzed very long. I'm sure in a couple of days we'll both feel like old pros."

Karma couldn't imagine that. "I have one box of diapers, a crib, and that's absolutely it. I thought I had another three weeks to prepare."

Nancy smiled sympathetically. "A procrastinator? That's me, too."

Karma shook her head. "No. I'm usually very organized. But the time I had set aside to finish the nursery was the two weeks before delivery. I had a couple of big projects at work I wanted to finish first."

Nancy frowned at Karma's broken arm. "I don't think you're going to run an adding machine, hold a baby, and feed it, too, all with your good arm."

Karma shrugged philosophically. "I'm going to have to."

"Well..." Nancy yawned. "I work at home, so maybe we can get together once in a while so we don't go crazy. Or I can watch your baby so you can get some rest, or get some work done."

Karma smiled gratefully. "That would be great. And I could watch yours so you and your husband can have some time alone. I'm sure privacy will be at a premium for you for a while."

Nancy nodded and yawned again. "I'll hold you to that. I've got to get back to bed. I keep thinking I'm feeling stronger, then I practically fall asleep on my feet."

"*There* you are." Jave Nicholas appeared in the doorway, and came to take Nancy by the arm. He smiled at Karma over her head. "Congratulations. The boys tell me you have a beautiful son."

She agreed. "I'm willing to take all the credit. You're just in time. Nancy's about to fall asleep standing up."

He shook his head over his wife's wanderings and swung her carefully into his arms. Nancy waved at Karma over his shoulder as Jave carried her back to her room.

Karma watched them go, a wistful smile on her face. Yes. That would have been nice. A loving husband to coddle her and help her through the next difficult few weeks... months...years... But that hadn't been in the scheme of things, so she'd chosen an alternative. There was no point in thinking of what might have been.

She had wanted a child and now she had him and he was beautiful and healthy and everything she could have hoped for. And she wouldn't have to consider anyone else's opinion when she made decisions regarding him.

She could handle this. She could. She leaned into her pillow and closed her eyes, trying to organize the first few days in her mind, and promptly fell asleep.

IT WAS DUSK when she awoke. The baby remained asleep, her arm throbbed only minimally, and she felt a curious sense of comfort. She'd given birth to a perfect, whole baby boy, and that seemed like such a miracle.

She didn't let her mind move to going home with him. That would only cause her to panic, and she didn't want to do that now. She wanted to enjoy this nice mellow moment and stretch it out as long as possible.

Then she turned her head to look for the water pitcher—and saw Nate Foster sitting in the chair beside her bed, reading her baby names book. He looked as though he'd showered and changed. He wore a simple khaki-colored sweater over beige cords. Her reaction was equal parts interest and concern.

"I thought I told you to go to Canada," she said, pushing the button that controlled her bed so that the back lifted her to a sitting position.

He met her eyes over the top of the book. "You're used to having things the way you want them, aren't you?"

She smiled thinly. "Not precisely. I'm always trying for it, but everyone else usually has other ideas. Like you."

He looked down at the book. "Well, I'm going eventually. What about Dillon? It's Irish-French for 'like a lion.'"

"No. Too fancy."

He flipped a few pages. "Okay. Here. Mac. A Scottish or Irish surname prefix used as a given name. Just like Dr. McNamara, only as a given name, not a nickname."

She shook her head. "Too clever."

He looked surprised. "I thought the fact that you're using a baby names book meant you wanted something clever. I mean, you don't need a book for Bill, Bob and Mike."

"True. But it has to be just right."

"What about naming him after a man you admire?"

She shrugged simply. "I haven't admired many." Except you, she thought, but she kept that to herself.

He studied her closely. "Not even your father?" He'd seldom seen his father, but he'd admired him. It hadn't been his father's fault that fate entrusted him with the care of a child he had no idea what to do with.

"My father's name," she said with a grim smile, "was Mountain Man. Do you really want to do that to a helpless child?"

"Ah..." He narrowed an eye, certain he'd misheard her. "Mountain Man?"

"Yes. It had been Jeffrey Jamison Endicott, but he and my mother had such a revelation one sunny morning in the sixties, while camping at Big Sur in their VW bus, that he had it legally changed to Mountain Man. My mother's name was Daisy Dawn."

"Mercy."

"Yeah. I guess Karma isn't so bad, considering what they could have named me."

"They're ... gone?" he asked cautiously.

She stiffened a little and nodded. "An auto accident a couple of years ago at Big Sur. In their bus that did zero to forty in five minutes." A sudden wince negated the joke. "An oncoming truck hit ice, then hit them."

"I'm sorry," he said.

She lifted a shoulder. "They were very in touch with the life force of the universe. And they always wanted to go together. Okay," she said, her tone changing. She pointed to the book he held. "I did see a name I like. What do you think of Garrett?"

He considered that a moment.

"It means 'spear-strong,'" she said. "Too warlike?"

*YAWN. I like it. Long as you don't call me Garry. Sigh. I'll be glad when I learn to turn over. I have a kink in my neck.*

"GARRETT," he repeated. "I'm a peaceful soul, myself, but yeah, I like it. Middle name?"

"Joseph. The ultimate father, since he doesn't really have his own. Garrett Joseph." She smiled, warming to the sound.

Nate smiled, because she did. "Has my vote." Then he decided to broach the subject he'd come to discuss.

"Why won't you let the hospital arrange for a home health nurse to give you a hand?" He asked the question abruptly, hoping to catch her off guard.

"Because I want to do this myself," she said reasonably. "I'll be fine."

So, she was *on* guard again. Her vulnerability had evaporated with the arrival of the baby.

"You have one arm in a sling, Karma," he pointed out. "And with the other one you'll spend most of your time holding the baby. How do you intend to manage feeding, changing, cooking?"

"I'm sure I'll manage," she insisted. "I'm very organized and systematic."

That thought seemed to comfort her, but he saw it as trouble. He was a bachelor, but he'd spent enough time with married friends to know that sanity in a busy household required a tendency toward lunacy and a taste for chaos.

"Will you know enough," he asked, putting the book aside, "to call someone for help if you decide you need it?"

She folded her arms. She noticed absently how easy it was to do now that her stomach was gone.

"I grew up," she said, "in that Volkswagen bus, with two adults and an older brother. There was hardly room to change our minds, much less our clothes. Which was probably a good thing, since we didn't have many in the first place. When we could afford gas, we traveled around looking for work. Sometimes food was a day-to-day thing.

I *hated* living that way, but my parents and my brother were happy as larks.''

Nate wasn't sure how this related to her refusal to allow a nurse into her home, but he listened patiently as she went on.

"To this day, my nightmares consist of having anyone other than me in my house, and having empty cupboards." She shrugged self-deprecatingly. "I know I probably need a shrink, but that's the way it is. I have my life precisely the way I want it, and that's the way I intend to keep it."

"But you've purposefully chosen," he said, "to add another body to your household." He pointed to the bassinet and the sleeping baby. "How does that fit?"

"This is someone I've planned for," she explained simply. "Someone who'll take up very little space for a long time. Someone I've already learned to love."

Nate studied her worriedly. "You know," he said finally, "I don't have firsthand experience with this, but anybody with children can tell you that babies take up a lot more space than is filled by their size. Their needs and demands require a lot of elbow room."

"I," she said firmly, "will manage."

"Where's your brother?" he asked.

She rolled her eyes. "In a commune in Baja. We send each other birthday and Christmas cards, but he's a little too out there for me, and I'm much too establishment for him."

"What's *his* name?" Nate asked.

She shook her head, smiling. "Aspen." Then she held her hand out toward him. "Thank you for all you've done. I don't think I'd have made it through labor without you. But now you have to take off on your vacation, and I have to get on with my baby and my life."

Nate stood and took her hand. "All right. But do you plan to live the next sixty years like that? With your cupboards full and your heart empty?"

Karma looked into his eyes and felt them draw her to him as if with a physical pull. She had to yank her hand away to break the connection. She smiled bravely. "Have a wonderful trip. Drive safely."

He recognized a brush-off when he heard it, but her big dark eyes told a completely different story. He wondered if she even knew how badly she needed someone.

Well. This was best. His own life was chaotic, and he liked it that way. He didn't need to worry about a quirky woman with a baby, who would grow up to be a toddler eager to explore and vulnerable to all the world's dangers. He didn't have the nerves for it.

"Goodbye," he said. And because they'd shared something unique and special, and because those dark eyes held such a curious longing, he brought the hand he held to his lips and kissed it.

Her lips parted in surprise. Her eyes widened and softened.

He went to the bassinet and looked down at the sleeping baby. Garrett Joseph was full-cheeked, with a light dusting of dark hair on his head. His tiny fists opened and closed and his tiny bow mouth worked as though he were anticipating his next meal.

"Goodbye, Garrett," he said, touching a tiny foot through the blanket. "Welcome to the world."

Then he left the room.

*THANKS. Where you going? Hey!*

KARMA reached a hand out to the bassinet as Garrett shrieked with displeasure.

# Chapter Three

Karma had never heard any baby—human or animal—make such a noise in her life. It had come at the end of a thirty-minute screech, and was somewhere between a choke and a gurgle. She had no idea what it meant. She knew only that it sounded fatal. Heart pounding, lips forming an anxious prayer—"Please, please, please!"—she sat him up, and he stared at her silently for one long moment. His blue-black eyes were wide and weirdly serious.

Her rocketing heartbeat slowed. Thank God. Maybe he wasn't dying, after all.

Without warning, he screwed up his rash-covered little face and began to screech again. At 11:30 p.m. on a day that had seemed forty-eight hours long, she was ready to give Garret Joseph Endicott back to the Gypsies.

*I'VE CHANGED MY MIND. I want back inside. I don't like it here!*

SHE'D never entirely understood that old saying about giving a baby "back to the Gypsies." She'd always assumed it was a whimsical statement because Gypsies seemed like a magical and whimsical people.

But on day six of her baby's life—her third day at home with him—she saw it all so clearly. Gypsies kept no birth certificates, no social security numbers, no official records of any kind. Theoretically, one could give them a baby with whom one had failed miserably, and the terrible failure could never be traced.

"Garrett, please," she groaned, putting him to her shoulder and walking the floor of her small living room with him. "I'm doing the best I can. It isn't time to eat, you've been changed, rocked, walked. What *is* it?"

He screamed an indecipherable response.

*MY LIP HURTS, I have gas, I'm sleepy, and that thing on your arm digs into my ribs every time you feed or hold me! Where's that straw thing I used to have in my stomach that connected me to my food? I want it back!*

A BATH! Karma struck on the idea as though it had been divinely inspired. She'd resisted bathing Garrett because it seemed too difficult with one good arm and she was doing fine with a washcloth, but if she was very careful, it might quiet him. And she was desperate.

She let him scream in his crib for a few minutes while she filled the baby's tub with water carefully run to the right temperature. Then she undressed Garrett and carried his taut and screaming little body and poised it over the tub.

He became suddenly like a little helicopter, arms and legs swinging like wild rotors. His head and shoulders slipped right off her cast and into the water, and his face and chest were submerged.

She screamed and lifted him out. For a moment, he simply looked at her.

*WATER! That was fun! Reminded me of the old days, before you pushed me out into this cold, uncomfortable place. Well, where is it? Where's my water?*

GARRETT'S momentary silence ended abruptly with a loud, indignant wail that settled into the steady screeching that was about to make rubber of Karma's brain.

It was nearly midnight. If she called the emergency room one more time, they'd think she was insane. If she called Dr. Mac, he'd conclude she was incompetent and probably call Children's Services to take the baby away from her.

She considered calling Nancy Nicholas, then remembered that she had two little boys besides the baby, and if she was sleeping now, she well deserved to.

She thought longingly of Nate Foster and wondered where he was now. In his sleeping bag, probably, under some Canadian maple on the bank of a beautiful stream. She allowed herself to wonder what it would be like to be curled beside him, if she were not the rigid, orderly woman fate and life in the Volkswagen bus had made her.

Then Garrett's screeching forced her to deal with the matter at hand. She trudged wearily to the refrigerator for a bottle of formula.

The melodic sound of her doorbell stopped her in the act of closing the refrigerator door. She placed the bottle on the counter and went to the front door, thinking grimly that it was probably a neighbor, calling to complain of the incessant noise.

She didn't bother with the peephole, but simply pulled the door open, a ready apology on the tip of her tongue.

But it wasn't a neighbor—it was Nate Foster. She stared at him in openmouthed surprise.

KARMA WAS A MESS. Nate stood under the porch light, studying her as she gaped at him. She was pale, her dark eyes were red rimmed from lack of sleep, and the delicate skin under them was bluish. Her mouth, free of lipstick, was dry and puckered, and her dark hair was caught back in a disheveled ponytail.

She wore a pink robe and an air of utter exhaustion. Her broken arm was out of the sling, as though she'd been trying to use it like the other.

Against her shoulder, Garrett screamed like a banshee.

*THERE YOU ARE! Where've you been? She's pretty and everything, but she's not doing this very well, and I'd like to lodge a complaint!*

"WHAT ARE YOU DOING HERE?" she asked as she stepped back to let him in. "I thought you were..."

He nodded, wincing against the baby's piercing cries. "I was. But I couldn't leave. Car trouble. I've got a loaner while it's being worked on, but I don't think it'd make it to the edge of town, much less Canada. I was coming back from a poker game and saw your lights on. I remembered your address from your chart." He grinned. "One hundred Second Street. I thought I'd check to see if everything was all right."

Her lips turned up in an obviously forced smile. "Everything's fine," she said. Then her bottom lip began to quiver. He took the baby from her as she dissolved into gulping sobs.

He took a look around and headed for the kitchen and the baby bottle on the countertop. He ran hot water into a pan and placed the bottle in it. "You were just about to feed him?" he asked.

She nodded, following him as he sat at the kitchen table and held the baby up in front of him.

"But it won't quiet him," she warned. "It's not time for him to eat, and he's been changed, everything, but he won't stop crying. Of course, I'm sure it didn't help that I dumped him on his head in his bathwater..."

He looked up at her at that. Tears streamed down her face, and she looked as though she hadn't slept since she'd left the hospital. He propped his foot against the chair at a right angle to him and pushed it away from the table. "Sit down," he said.

She did.

He turned his attention to the baby. "Whoa," he said. "You look pretty rough, buddy." There was a blister on Garrett's upper lip, as well as a triangular red mark between his eyes, and his face was covered with milia, tiny white pimples caused by the working of the sebaceous glands. He looked almost as bad as his mother.

"The blister's from sucking," she said tearfully, "and the rash will go away. But I've already called the ER twice today, and I just noticed the red mark on his forehead this afternoon. It doesn't seem to hurt him."

Nate grinned at her and pulled the baby into his shoulder, where he continued to scream. "We call that a 'stork bite,'" he said. "There's a collection of tiny capillaries there, and his skin's so transparent at this age that they show right through. It'll disappear. It's nothing."

He stood and went for the bottle, then returned to his chair, tucked the baby into his arm and offered him the nipple. His movements were economical and confident. Garrett began to eat greedily. The room became blessedly quiet, except for the rapid sucking sounds.

Karma slumped back against her chair dispiritedly. "Tell me what I'm doing wrong."

PLEASE. *We don't have that much time.*

NATE SHOOK HIS HEAD, glancing up at her. "Well, apparently he thought it *was* time to eat. Or it could be that you're just not a guy," he said teasingly. "Your biceps are flimsy. Garrett's got a lot of aches and pains at the moment, I imagine, and he wants to feel secure."

Karma watched them jealously. Trust her to be one of the fractional percentage of women to use a sperm bank and turn out the kind of child who truly needed a father in the picture.

"Well, all he's got are my flimsy biceps," she said, her tone quarrelsome. "He's going to have to get used to them."

"He will," Nate assured her. "These first few weeks are hard enough for mothers who have fathers to help them, or some other kind of support system. I imagine for a single woman with a broken arm it's been hell."

She could have pretended otherwise, but knew it would be fruitless. "I didn't expect to be so terrified of him. He's so fragile. And he makes the most frightening noises. I was sure he was dying several times today." She frowned. "How come you're so good at this? I know you're a doctor, but you admitted that you give all the cases involving children to someone else."

He shrugged. "I don't know. It's one of life's little ironies, I guess. I did my stint in OB and pediatrics in medical school, just like everybody else. I liked it. Kids seem to like me."

She sat up, interested in his life story. "Why is that ironical? You told me when I was in labor that you don't like to treat children because they're so vulnerable. Is it just...too hard to see them in pain?"

He sighed and stretched his legs out, crossing his feet at the ankles. His leather tennies, she noted, were enormous.

"Yes," he admitted, smoothing Garrett's furrowed brow with the tip of his forefinger. Then he looked up at her, and she saw that it was more than that. That something personal had brought him to that decision. "But it's even harder to watch them die. I know, I know. A doctor is supposed to adjust to that, and I had—at least as much as you can when you care about people."

His concentration seemed to drift for a moment. Karma got up to get two colas out of the refrigerator, then came back to the table. She popped the top on his and handed it to him.

"Thank you." His long fingers closed over it and brought it to his mouth. "Good stuff," he said after a long swallow. "Poker's dry work."

He put the can aside and leaned back in his chair. Garrett had almost finished the bottle. "Anyway...I was an EMT for several summers while going to medical school, and we got a call one Saturday morning about a child who had something in his throat and couldn't breathe."

Karma wrapped her arms around herself as she listened. After less than a week with Garrett, she could easily imagine the terror of that child's mother.

"It was the ideal situation. The mother had called right away. They were only blocks away. We thought it was going to be easy. To open an airway, you just put a tube down the throat and feed in air."

His eyes, blue and solemn, stared at the past. "But the object in his throat was a big chunk of soft, fresh bread, and every time we pushed the tube down, the bread clogged it. We'd dig it out, but that took precious time, so we started cutting the ends off and feeding it in again, but we couldn't get through it. We lost him. He wasn't quite two."

Karma felt his horror, his frustration and his grief. All she could think of to say sounded trite. "I'm sure you did everything you could."

His eyes focused on her suddenly. "We did. It isn't that I blamed myself. But I'll never forget his mother, screaming that it was only bread. How could something as harmless as a slice of bread have killed her child? And it was right then and there that I decided I didn't ever want a child's life dependent upon me for protection."

She certainly understood his reluctance, but every parent in the world was up against the same daunting challenge.

"But imagine," she said, "if someone had been afraid to raise *you*. You wouldn't be here."

Garrett pulled back from the bottle, and Nate raised him to his shoulder and patted his back. He gave Karma a wry grin. "Someone was. My mother passed away when I was seven, and my father sent me to military school."

Karma's eyes widened. He seemed like anything but the product of a regimented life-style. "Why?" she asked.

"He didn't know what to do with me," he replied, with a shrug that said he'd accepted the fact long ago. "He worked on Wall Street. Checked out at forty-four with a massive heart attack."

"I'm sorry," she said, then remembered clearly the moment he'd said those same words to her, when she told him about her parents. They had more in common than it appeared.

Garrett burped.

Nate laughed. "A fitting punctuation to a life story. What are you going to do about a car?"

She shifted in her chair, adjusting to the change of subject. "Heron Point Auto is one of my clients. I'm getting a used Volvo."

He nodded. "Good car. Do you have a rocking chair?"

"Yes," she said, pointing toward the living room, which was in darkness. "In here." She led the way to a Boston rocker Bert had refinished for her and to which she'd attached a green-and-pink cushion and back.

"Great," he said, easing into it, still patting the baby. "I'll see if I can get him to sleep while you take a hot shower and try to rest for a few hours."

The notion was certainly tempting, but Karma found herself reluctant to agree. Her labor had forced them into an unnatural intimacy, but in truth they barely knew each other.

"I couldn't—" she began to protest.

"Sure you can. Go, before I change my mind." When she continued to hesitate, he grinned. "I promise not to ravish you in your sleep. I like to do that when a woman's awake."

She gave him a reproachful twist of her lips, but it didn't distract him from her blush. She saw his eyes go to her flushed cheeks, then to her eyes.

"Okay." He shifted the baby when he began to fuss. "I don't blame you for being concerned. But I assure you I can be a model of gentlemanly decorum."

She folded her arms. "You *are,* or you *can* be?"

He'd opened his mouth to reply when a strange beep came from the jacket he'd dropped over a chair when he came in.

Karma went to get it and handed it to him. He dug a cellular phone out of his pocket and answered it.

Karma heard a high female voice.

Nate glanced at Karma, guilt and amusement in his eyes as he laughed lightly. "Hi, Emmie. No, I'm not going to make it to the club tonight."

Karma sat on the arm of the sofa and shamelessly listened. She heard a lot of loud music and rapid conversation, though she couldn't distinguish the words.

Nate listened. The baby fussed. There was sudden silence on the other end of the line. Then Karma heard clearly, "What was that?"

Nate stood, the baby stretched across his forearm, his broad hand supporting the small torso, the little head nestling against his upper arm. "That was a baby," he said, pacing the living room. "No, smartie. He belongs to a friend. No, you'll have to party without me. Yeah, me, too. Say hi to everybody. Bye."

He flipped the phone so that it folded, then handed it back to Karma. "Would you put that back for me, please?" He looked into her carefully neutral expression and said, "And in answer to your question, I *am* a gentleman. I spent too long in a military environment not to revere the American flag and women everywhere."

She looked back at him innocently. "Emmie, particularly?"

He seemed intrigued that she approached the subject. "She worked in personnel at Riverview. Does a mean mambo."

She blinked. "I didn't know anyone mamboed in Heron Point."

He patted Garrett's back and earned another burp. "Good boy," he told him. To Karma, he said, "That's what you miss when you organize your life *not* to include the Scupper Tavern's Cuban night. Are you going to go take a shower and get some sleep, or do I have to get forceful about it?"

"I thought you were a gentleman," she challenged.

His smile was both sweet and dangerous. "A gentleman looks out for a lady," he said. "By whatever means are required. Will you go?"

A hot shower and a few hours' sleep were more than she could resist. But she had to get something straight.

"I . . . I'm very grateful for all you've done," she said, turning the end of the belt of her robe around her index finger. "But I like my life uncluttered."

He nodded, still patting the baby, who was now asleep. "So you said," he replied.

That didn't seem to get through. She tried again. "I mean that . . ."

He nodded again, forestalling her. "I know what you mean. I'm not to misconstrue this acceptance of my help as an indication of sexual interest."

She sighed, frustrated with his annoying way of distilling the facts.

She folded her arms, slightly discomfited. She was usually too prepared, too organized, to ever feel perplexed. It irritated her. "Yes," she said frankly. "That's what I mean."

"Not to worry." His assurance was amiable and heartfelt. "You're not in my plan, either. I was just being a friend."

"All right." She smiled gratefully. "Then I'll take advantage of that offer, and have a shower. I'll nap for an hour, then maybe you can still catch Emmie and mambo."

Karma walked away, turning back at the hallway to thank him again. But she found him watching her, a decidedly predatory look in his eye, a feral smile on his lips.

A sudden fluster replaced her gratitude, and she headed for the shower, her heart beating uncomfortably fast.

## Chapter Four

Karma felt sunlight on her face, and she smelled bacon. The high-heeled shoe on her right foot pinched her big toe.

Though she was just beginning to surface from sleep to wakefulness, she understood that the sensations weren't real. They were remnants of a dream that had been filled with color and music and a man who had danced her around and around an opulent ballroom.

Eyes still closed, she smiled, stretched her arms, then turned on her side and curled into her pillow, trying to recapture the dream for a few more moments.

But the sound of a baby crying was a discordant note, and the ballroom cleared. Even the man in whose arms she'd danced the night away slipped out of her grasp and disappeared.

She snuggled deeper into the pillow, trying to call everyone back.

"Karma!" a man's voice shouted.

"There you are," she said in a pleased and sultry voice, turning around and around in search of the man who'd spoken. "Just one more dance? Where are you?"

"Right here."

"Where?"

She couldn't find him, but his voice was close. He had to be within reach. She stretched out a hand. "One more dance?"

She felt his warm, strong hand close around hers and draw her near.

But what had happened to the music? The silence woke her.

Karma opened her eyes with a start. There *was* sunlight on her face. She *did* smell bacon cooking. Her big toe *was* being pinched, but not by a dancing shoe.

Nate Foster held it between the thumb and forefinger of his left hand. Her baby lay in his right.

She studied the sight of her toe in his hand for a stupefied moment.

"Sorry." He released it, grinning. "I had to wake you, and on the chance you didn't remember I was here, I didn't want to terrify you by getting too close."

"Oh, my God," she said with a surprised gasp. She wondered distractedly if her life would ever return to normal after her premature delivery. "What time is it?" She picked up the bedside clock, then put it down with a faint shriek when she read 9:12 a.m.

The events of the previous night began to come back to her. Nate had appeared when she was at her wit's end with the baby. He'd fed him, and quieted him, and sent her to take a shower and a nap.

That had been almost nine hours ago!

Color flooded her face. "I'm *so* sorry!" she said, throwing the covers aside and leaping out of bed—only to realize that all she wore were the panties and sports bra she'd worn under her robe the night before. As her color deepened, she resisted the impulse to press her knees together and cross her arms over her breasts.

Instead, she reached to the foot of the bed, where she'd left the robe, but her broken arm made putting it on difficult. Nate came to hold it up for her while she groped for the sleeve. Then the best she could do was hold it closed.

Thoroughly rattled, she apologized again. "I don't know what happened! One moment I was too tired to sleep, and the next I—"

"Please," he said with a smile. Was it mocking her, or was that simply her imagination? "Stop apologizing. Brighton Construction wants to know if they should bring their payroll information over."

"They called?"

"They're on the phone right now."

"Oh, my God!" She ran to the kitchen to pick up the wall phone.

"Miss Endicott?" Alicia Brighton, the beautiful and efficient office manager and wife of the owner, sounded impatient. Karma had never met her, only seen her photo in the women's section of the paper. She was always bestowing something or being awarded something. "I understand you've had your baby prematurely," she said, her tone patronizing, "and I imagine you'll need time to get your life in order. Why don't we take our payroll to..."

"I'll expect your payroll this morning," Karma said. Her voice sounded husky with sleep, but she hoped the woman would mistake it for a professional tone. "I have a remarkably beautiful son, but it's business as usual at Endicott Accounting."

There was a surprised silence on the other end of the line. "But, you've just had a baby."

Which I have to support, Karma thought. But aloud she said, "I have a bassinet in my office, and life goes on."

There was a small laugh on the other end of the line. "Are you in for a surprise…" Then, in a more serious tone: "And we can have the payroll by the tenth?"

Fifty-six employees on different pay scales, different insurance rates, with quirky deductions and always, always, a dozen last-minute changes. Ah… "Absolutely," she replied. "I have everything on disk. Just bring me your September hours and I'm ready to go."

"Thank you."

Karma hung up the phone, wondering how she was going to keep her promise, and came face-to-face with Nate Foster and the reminder that a strange man had just spent the night in her house.

At his speculative smile, she closed her eyes and tried to pull herself together. Big deal. So the man had spent the night with her. He hadn't even been in the same room. And only days ago he'd sat with her through four grueling hours of labor and delivery. At this point, he knew her pretty well—physically *and* emotionally.

She opened her eyes again to thank him with some semblance of decorum—and saw that he seemed to find her dither interesting. His blue gaze ran over her in a lazy appraisal, stopping with distracting suddenness on her hair.

*It must look like a hay bale after a wind,* she thought, remembering that she'd ripped out the rubber band that held the ponytail. She put a hand to it and felt the disarray. She never strove for a glamorous appearance, but she was usually well-groomed and carefully dressed.

Last night she'd been too desperate to care how she looked. This morning—with him looking fresh and fit in an Oregon Ducks sweatshirt and jeans—she cared a lot.

And her imperfections always made her touchy.

*"Gentlemen,"* she said, reminding him with a tilt of her eyebrow that he'd claimed to be one the night before, "don't stare."

"Of course they do," he replied, "when the lady is seductively tousled."

*Seductively tousled.* She repeated the words to herself as she glanced at her reflection in the window over the sink. He must have more imagination than she did; she thought she just looked messy.

"Gentlemen also don't patronize," she said, taking Garrett from him. She was thrilled when the baby didn't scream. He stared at her, his little mouth opening as though he were convinced she had a bottle hidden somewhere on her person. She nuzzled him, and kissed his silky cheek.

*Hi, Mother! He's cool. He rubbed my back while we watched the news, and we danced in the kitchen while we cooked. He says he's going to introduce me to some babes.*

"LADIES," Nate countered, taking the belt that dangled around her waist and tying it, "don't throw sincere compliments back in a gentleman's face. And while we're standing here arguing my credibility, your bacon and eggs are drying up." He pushed her gently toward the kitchen table.

He removed two plates of bacon and eggs from the oven. The eggs were gently over easy, the bacon was crisp and dry, the toast was golden.

Karma stared, still trying to adjust to having had his hands at the belt of her robe. Her mother hadn't been much of a cook, and space had been at a premium in the bus. Most hot meals had been cooked outside, and only if the weather allowed. Breakfast had usually been cereal.

Much as she hated those memories, she rarely cooked for herself these days, because she was simply too busy. But she knew that would have to change when Garrett began eating solid food.

She felt her mouth water. When she looked down and saw that her son had gone to sleep, she thought she'd died and gone to heaven. She hadn't had a peaceful meal since she'd brought him home.

"I'll just put him down," she said, going to the bassinet in the dining room, which she'd turned into an office. He didn't stir.

She went back to the kitchen and took her place, feeling suddenly guilty for being annoyed with Nate over *her* appearance. It wasn't even logical. And she *usually* was. She put it down to hormonal chaos after childbirth, and settled down to enjoy her bounty.

When she'd polished off her breakfast, Nate brought another round of toast and topped off her coffee. "Have you thought about hiring a nanny?" he asked, taking his chair again. His grin had an element she mistrusted.

"Can't afford one," she replied.

"Yes," he said. "You can."

She glanced at him suspiciously as she spread strawberry jam on a slice of toast. "How would I do that?"

"I'd work for free."

She'd taken a sip of coffee, and she choked on it.

"I can't go anywhere until my car's out of the shop," he explained, pushing away from the table so that he could angle one leg over the other. "And I've been bored at home."

Nate concentrated on pushing his plate aside so that she wouldn't see he was lying. There was nothing wrong with his car, and he'd never been bored a moment in his life. But he couldn't tell her the truth about why he was making this proposal, because he didn't *know* why. As he kept telling everyone, he liked babies, he just generally refused to take care of them. He also didn't like women who were distant and suspicious—as she was being now.

She'd just put up a barrier between them, as she'd done that night in the hospital. She was probably certain he was suggesting some lascivious alliance. The knowledge charged his sense of humor.

"So, what are you suggesting?" she asked coolly, an eyebrow raised, her shoulders stiffly set. "That you live in?"

He leaned toward her over his cup and met her judicious brown eyes with a practiced leer.

"Right," he replied softly, silkily. "Then we could chuck the accounting business, open a call-girl operation and have wild sex ourselves on a daily basis."

He saw the condemnation in her eyes change to indignation, then reluctantly to amusement as she read the humor in his.

"Aren't we clever this morning...." she observed.

"That's what you get," he said with a judicious look of his own, "for presuming the worst. I was going to make the perfectly civil suggestion that I spend a few hours here with the baby in the afternoons so that you can get some work done."

He looked back at her as she studied him, probably for signs of duplicity.

"You don't like to be around babies," she reminded him.

"Yeah, well..." He stacked up their dishes. "This one and I are sort of bonding. And by the time he's old enough to be a danger to himself, I'll be back to work and he can give someone else an ulcer or a heart attack."

She followed him to the counter. "I don't understand. What's in it for you?"

He put the dishes in the sink and frowned down at her as she pulled open the dishwasher. "Does there have to be something in it for me?"

"There's always a debit and a credit," she said.

He rolled his eyes and turned on the hot-water faucet. "Life is not a business ledger, Karma."

"The world is set up," she insisted, "so that everything is balanced by something else. For every action there's a reaction. What's debited one place has to be credited someplace else."

He rinsed their dishes and utensils, then turned off the water. She took them from him and placed them in the rack, then closed the door.

"Doctors," he said, "are less inclined than accountants to fix a cost on everything. There are exceptions, of course, but most of us do what has to be done, and worry about the cost—to the patient, and to ourselves—later."

She folded her arms and leaned a hip on the counter. "That's because of health insurance. For us, there's no such thing as 'loss insurance.' We have to keep the books balanced."

Nate shook his head at her. "So, you're saying you won't let me help you by spending a few hours here in the afternoon, unless I insist on payment of some kind? That your emotional books will be out of balance?"

She thought that over, and wasn't sure that was what she'd intended. He went on. "Fine. So, let's retain the part of the plan where you and I have wild sex on a daily basis."

Karma sought escape from the thoughts that suggestion provoked by giving him a dose of his own medicine. "As charming as that sounds," she replied, "I've just delivered a baby. I'm out of commission in that regard for a good six weeks."

"Oh, gee," he said with bland surprise, "how could a doctor like me have forgotten that?" He narrowed his gaze on her, his scolding tone underlining his words. "Unless my intentions *were* nonsexual. What about if you fixed me dinner before I left in the evening? Or is that too much bookkeeping? I mean, are there separate entries for meats and fish? Do you break down vegetables into green, yellow, tubers, cruci—"

"Oh, shut up," Karma said, torn between annoyance and amusement. She frankly felt a small degree of pleasure at his suggestion. She loved to cook. She seldom did, though, because it wasn't very satisfying to cook for one.

She looked into his blue eyes as she considered, and saw an element of danger there. It wasn't necessarily aimed at her, it simply existed in the depths of his eyes. He was carefree and flirtatious. He liked to mambo with a woman named Emmie.

No, she thought resolutely. It wasn't a good idea. She *would* need help with the baby, but it would be safer to find some reliable older woman, or a day care that took infants.

Whoever heard of a nanny—even a part-time one—who was a handsome man in his prime? And a doctor, at that? It wasn't logical. And she didn't trust anything that wasn't.

She opened her mouth to answer, but was interrupted by the ringing of his cellular phone directly behind her.

Nate, at the sofa where he'd left his jacket, called out to her, "Would you answer that, please?"

Karma raised the flexible antenna and pressed Phone. "Hello?"

There was an instant's silence. Then a husky feminine voice asked abruptly, "Who's this?"

The mambo queen? Karma wondered. Something about the demanding tone annoyed her. "Hillary's House of Harlots," she replied. "Who's this?"

Nate, shrugging into his jacket, snatched the phone from her with an expression that was half grin, half scolding frown. He found it interesting that the sweet courage in her that had appealed to him had a sharper, less predictable side.

"Hello," he said. There was an excited exclamation on the other end of the line. "That was Hillary herself," he replied with a punitive glance at Karma.

Karma dropped a curtsy as she passed him to wipe off the table.

"No," he said after another spate of excited conversation from the caller. "A friend. A very nice young woman I met at the hospital. I came to help with her baby." He listened for a moment. Then he shifted his weight, looking mildly impatient. "Yes, it is early." He listened again and then said evenly, "Yes, I did spend the night."

Karma looked up from her task, waiting for him to explain. But there was a stubbornness about his square-shouldered stance that told her he didn't intend to.

There was silence on the other end of the line. Then Karma heard the voice again. It was quieter now.

Nate glanced at the clock. "Hold on a minute, please, Hadley." He held a hand over the mouthpiece and smiled at Karma. "Am I employed?"

Karma was tempted, and that alarmed her. She couldn't have done without him when Garrett was born, but now he presented a complication she didn't need when she had a life to reorganize.

"Thank you, but no," she said. "I'll manage."

He studied her long enough that she almost changed her mind. "You're sure?" he asked.

The very fact that she wasn't made her tell him she was. "Yes. I am."

Without apparent disappointment, he turned his attention back to the woman on the phone. "How about if I pick you up in fifteen minutes?"

After what must have been an affirmative reply, he pressed the End button and pocketed the phone.

"Was that the mambo queen?" Karma asked, tossing the sponge at the sink.

He shook his head. "Hadley. She's an outdoorswoman. We had a date to climb Camel Mountain today."

"Is Hadley a first or a last name?"

"First. Hadley Brooks."

Karma walked him to the door. They stopped on the foyer rug and turned to face each other. "Shouldn't you have explained about spending the night?" she asked. "Just to ease her mind. She sounded upset."

He shrugged a shoulder. "I'm a free agent, and so is she. We hike together. That's it."

Karma had a feeling that wasn't the way Hiking Hadley wanted it. "Does she know about the mambo queen?"

Nate folded his arms and smiled down at her. "I don't know. For someone who's afraid to have me around, you're very interested in my social life."

She raised an eyebrow. "Afraid?" she questioned imperiously.

"Deny it," he said challengingly. "You're terrified of me. That's why you won't accept my help with the baby."

She rolled her eyes heavenward—mostly so that he couldn't look into them. "Terrified?" She laughed. "You're the gentlest man I've ever met, and I acquired that information under rather intimate conditions. Why would I be terrified of you?"

He caught her chin between his thumb and forefinger. His bright blue eyes looked into her dark ones, and she felt a tremor somewhere deep inside.

"Because you know that isn't all there is to me. And you're afraid you'll find something else you like." Then he leaned down and kissed her quickly, chastely, on the lips. "See you."

Karma stood for a full twenty seconds, eyes closed, heart fluttering, lips tingling. Then she marched to the computer and brought up Brighton Construction's file.

Nate Foster was absolutely right and there was no point in pretending he wasn't. She *was* afraid of becoming any more interested in him than she already was. She had a business and a baby, and that was all any woman in her right mind should tackle at any given time.

A husband, of course, was different. That, presumably, was a known quantity. But a boyfriend, a beau, a . . . an other—significant or otherwise—was a questionable factor. And she liked sure things.

"YOU MEAN," Tom Nicholas repeated slowly, carefully, "that you decided *not* to spend four weeks in the Canadian wilderness with no one to answer to but yourself because of a . . . a woman? One you'd just met?"

Nate stood several feet away from Tom, who was spreading redwood stain on the railing of the deck he'd just built onto the back of Nate's two-story A-frame at the edge of Eaton's Woods.

"Yeah," Nate replied. "You think that's out of character?"

Tom gave him a grinning glance as he continued to work. "You *have* no character. You keep more relationships going at one time than 'The Love Connection.' So, what's this all about?"

Nate thought about it a moment and shrugged. He waved the coffee mug he held in a wide arc. "Beats me. She was delivering early, her Lamaze coach was out of town, I was there..."

Tom gave him a frowning glance this time as he shooed him backward and swept the brush farther along the railing. "Karma Endicott, my tax accountant. Nancy told me she had her baby. You hate babies."

"I don't *hate* babies," Nate said defensively, "I just don't like to take care of them."

"Then you don't want to get serious about a woman with one."

"No," he said distractedly. "Of course not."

"So... consider yourself lucky."

Nate knew he should do just that. He'd changed his mind several times before finally going to check on Karma and Garrett that night. Then he'd offered to help with the baby only because she looked so tired, so surprised by the enormity of her new responsibilities.

They'd struck a rapport during the birth of her baby that had brought him closer to her than he'd been to anyone since his mother had died. He hadn't realized how much he'd missed that heart-to-heart connection until he felt it again. He wanted it back with a desperation that astonished him.

But he'd wanted a lot of things in his life he hadn't allowed himself to have because he knew they weren't good for him. Like the Porsche. And the yacht that had once belonged to a first baseman for the Boston Red Sox. And the harlequin Great Dane puppy.

The Porsche would have encouraged speed, but it was important in life to enjoy the passing scenery. The boat would have encouraged indolence, and a body needed exercise to remain fit. And the puppy would have been left alone much of the time, and that would have reminded him of his childhood. And he wouldn't have inflicted that on a dog.

No. He shouldn't pursue Karma Endicott, no matter how interesting or appealing he found her. That would encourage him to open up to the possibilities—and most of his feelings were in a vault.

"Move it, or get it stained Ripe Redwood," Tom warned as he advanced with the brush.

Nate backed up a few paces. "What about you and Amy Brown?" Nate asked, needing to divert himself from the futility of his own romantic interests. "Saw the two of you at Chez Pasta a week or so ago. What does Riverview Hospital's PR director see in you?"

Nate wished instantly that he'd used more care in picking his words. He was kidding, of course, but since the fire that had taken the life of Tom's friend, and put Tom himself in the hospital for several long months, his friend considered himself a diminished man. That had been almost two years ago, and he was taking the long road back.

Not that Tom ever spoke of it. But his brother, Jave, the radiologist, who'd warned him that his bachelor days might be numbered, sometimes shared his concerns with Nate, who'd been on duty the night of the fire. Tom had been brought in by his fellow firemen, smoke-blackened and blistered, with fourth-degree burns on his right leg.

"What everyone sees, of course," he replied as he pushed him farther back. His glance was filled with the wry humor that had gotten him through physical and emotional therapy and the birth of a new career in carpentry. "Wit, intelligence, charm, good humor, impeccably good ju—"

Nate interrupted him. "Please. My stomach's a little delicate."

"Big surprise. What did you and Miss Big Biceps have for lunch on your hike? Pinecones and bark dust?"

"Clever. If you had a little respect for your body, it wouldn't look quite so much like a Dodge truck."

"That's muscle." Tom had reached the end of the railing, and he turned back to check over his work.

"I thought we were talking about Amy."

"You asked a question and I answered it. What more is there to talk about?"

"When did you two start going out? Do you plan to see her again? What do—"

"Whoa, whoa!" Tom capped the can of stain and put the brush in a bucket of turpentine in the big wooden toolbox in the corner. "Did my mother hire you to spy on me?"

No, Jave had put him up to it, but Nate wasn't about to tell him that.

"Just curious. Everybody at the hospital loves Amy. And since no one likes you, we're naturally concerned."

Tom's eyes surveyed the finished deck. "I bust my butt to finish this for you so you can sit on it in October and watch the leaves turn, and you want to talk women and harangue me?"

Nate clapped him on the shoulder. "Good job, Tom. For which you're being well paid, I might add. The lady was looking at you with adoration in her eyes, and as your friend, I just want to know what it's all about. I mean, should I be planning a bachelor party, here? Should I send my tux to the cleaners? Should I—"

"You should mind your own business," Tom said amiably. "And the next time my brother tells you to try to get something out of me because I'm not sharing with him, either, tell him where to go."

Nate was not surprised Tom had seen through the plan. Espionage was not one of his skills.

"I can't do that. He's a department head. Just tell me you and Amy will be seeing each other again, so I can report back to Jave, and there'll be peace and harmony all around."

Tom drew a breath for patience and collected his gear in the toolbox. "I am *not* seeing Amy again."

Nate could see that he was pushing the bounds of privacy. He'd intended that, of course, but he also knew he couldn't expect Tom to like it.

"Why not?" Nate asked, following with the can of stain as Tom headed down the steps and across the driveway to his truck.

Tom set the toolbox on the ground and lowered the tailgate. "Because I . . . I don't know." He put the toolbox in the bed of the truck and turned to take the can from Nate. "I guess I'm just not ready."

"For what?" Nate asked brutally. "For her to see your leg?"

Nate gave him a lethal look and lifted the tailgate into place.

"Or aren't you ready," Nate went on, "to admit to yourself that it wasn't your fault, that you did what you thought was the right thing and your friend died anyway because that's life and it often stinks? You could be happy if you could let yourself admit that. Is that what you're not ready for?"

Tom walked around to the driver's-side door. Nate followed intrepidly. Tom yanked the door open and glared at him. "I thought Singleton was Riverview's shrink."

"I did my psych internship," Nate said. "I can try out my skills if I want to."

Tom shook his head. "Try it out on somebody who has faith in your diagnosis."

Nate caught his arm and stopped him from climbing into the cab of the truck. "I'm right," he said quietly, steadily. "And you know it. You've been carrying that night on your back for almost two years, like some sort of penance. Let it go. You aren't responsible."

"I'll bill you for the deck," Tom said, shaking off Nate's hand and climbing up into the seat. He pulled the door closed with a slam and glared down at his friend as he turned the key in the ignition and jerked the truck into reverse.

"The advice," Nate shouted after him as he screeched backward out of the driveway, "was free of charge!"

He watched the truck disappear in a swirl of fallen leaves and wondered what the hell he thought he was doing psychoanalyzing Tom, when he'd canceled a long-awaited vacation on a moment's notice, and couldn't shake the mental image of a woman with dark hair and eyes and a squally little baby covered with a rash. Seemed his own sanity was suspect.

"OH, Karma! Oh, God, I'm *so* sorry. I can't believe you delivered early! I mean, I *prayed* I'd get out of being your Lamaze coach, but I never dreamed it'd really happen!"

Karma held her living room door open and stood aside as a young woman with blunt-cut brown hair and emphatic blue eyes stumbled inside, arms loaded with packages. She dropped everything on the sofa, then turned to take Karma in her embrace.

"You *know* I'm kidding. I really wanted to help you through this." She stood back and stopped talking for a minute to frown at Karma's arm. "You had to have a bone set *and* deliver a baby? Was it awful? You look like it was."

Karma laughed lightly. "You'll have to try it yourself sometime. There's nothing else quite like it." She pushed her friend onto the sofa. "I'll get you some coffee."

Roberta Dawson caught Karma's arm. "I don't have time—I'm on a lunch break. But I brought a few things for the baby, and something for you. Where is he? Can I see him?"

"Try and stop me from showing him off." Karma gestured to Bert to follow her into the bedroom, where a nightlight illuminated the baby sleeping like a cherub in the crib beside her bed.

"Karma, he has measles!" Bert whispered as she leaned over the crib's padded rail.

Karma stroked the tiny head with her fingertips. "It's just a rash. It'll go away." The sight of her son sleeping peacefully filled Karma with a satisfaction that went deeper than anything she'd ever known. "Isn't he beautiful?"

"Oh, yes." Bert put the tip of her index finger to his tiny hand. "Good work, Karma. You didn't even need me."

"Well, you were off being Miss Career Woman. I had to cope without you."

Bert straightened to grin at her. "I understand," she said softly, "that you bullied the studly Dr. Foster into taking my place."

Karma rolled her eyes and led the way out of the room. She pulled the door halfway closed. "I can't believe you've been home all of about twelve hours and you already know that."

Bert smiled smugly as she fell onto the sofa beside her packages. "There's a candy striper at the hospital whose older sister works with me. She told me this morning. Everyone's interested, you know. This is a small town, and you can't expect something like a sperm-bank pregnancy to go undiscussed. Particularly when the delivery involves the handsome emergency room doctor who delayed his vacation to see you through labor, then completely changed his mind about going.''

"Jeez! He had car trouble. It's in the shop." Then Karma analyzed Bert's statement. "Am I being watched?"

Bert nodded. "Of course. Oh, not literally spied on. But I'm sure you're being observed. Everyone wants to know how it's going to turn out."

"Turn out?" Karma frowned. "It *has* turned out. I've *had* the baby. That's the outcome I wanted."

Bert shook her head pityingly. "Karma, this is small-town America. It hasn't 'turned out' until they know what happens to you romantically."

Karma blinked, stunned. "Why would anyone care?"

"Because they like you. Because, although you're just a little more reserved than the average Heron Pointer, you've earned a reputation since you reduced Diantha Pennyman's tax debt and helped her invest her money. She tells anyone who'll listen how good you are. You contribute to community projects, *and* you always look nice. If a little..." She stopped and waggled her hand descriptively. "You know."

Karma looked down at her cotton slacks and sweatshirt. "A little what?" she asked. "I have a new baby."

Bert shook her head. "I don't mean those. Actually, they're an improvement. But your work clothes are... stodgy."

"They're professional."

"They're gray and blue and tailored. When you head for work, you look like somebody's lawyer."

Karma sighed dispiritedly. "Fine. Is your lunch break over yet? I don't think I can take much more of this friendly visit."

Bert glanced at her watch and smiled. "I'm afraid you have me for ten more minutes. So—are you seeing the doctor?"

Karma decided she could play the same game. "As a matter of fact, he spent the night earlier this week."

Bert's eyes widened, then narrowed. "What?" she asked flatly.

"He spent the night," Karma repeated, studying her fingernails. "With stodgy little old me."

"Oh, no." Bert's voice portended doom.

Karma straightened indignantly. "What do you mean, *no?* He did."

"You couldn't have..." Bert waggled two fingers together in a gesture Karma interpreted as suggesting a joining.

"No, we didn't. I did just deliver a baby, after all. Why? Does the idea seem impossible to you? That the handsome doctor could be attracted to stodgy old me?"

Bert frowned, obviously confused. "Well, nothing's *impossible*, but I thought you'd decided there isn't a man worth having, and Dr. Foster has a reputation for... um, my mother used to call it 'playing the field.' Be careful. You're kind of an innocent."

Karma put a hand to her eyes. "Bert. I'm twenty-seven, I have a business, and I have a baby. I know a little more than you think I do. And anyway, Nate just came to see how I was doing and stayed to watch the baby so I could take a shower and have a nap. He was here all night because I was exhausted and didn't wake up until nine the following morning. He performed a kindness. That's all it was. I tried to make it sound like something else just to rattle you, because *you* seem to think I'm a sexual nonentity."

"No, I don't." Bert reached for one of the packages she'd brought. "I just know you're afraid of men."

"I am *not* afraid," Karma told her emphatically, wondering what on earth she'd done to give everyone that impression. "Why does everyone say that?"

"Karma, your baby was fathered by a sperm bank."

"Because I wanted a baby and I was single. I didn't know any man I considered worthy to be my baby's father."

"Don't you ever wonder about the sperm donor? Particularly now that the baby's here?"

Karma didn't even have to think about her answer. "No. The very nature of the process confirms that he'd just as soon remain anonymous. And as far as I'm concerned, the baby's *mine*. And he's all I want."

"What about when he begins to wonder where his daddy is?"

Karma had considered that a concern since the moment she'd decided to use the sperm bank. And now that Garrett was a living, breathing reality, she wondered even more often how he would react to the way he'd been conceived. But he was here and he was wonderful, and she had far more immediate concerns to cope with.

"You know," she said, fixing Bert with a firm gaze, "if you'd been there when he was born and experienced the miracle of it all with me, you wouldn't be asking so many questions. You'd just accept him for the wonder that he is and let tomorrow take care of itself."

Bert stared back at her in surprise. "I only asked because you've *never* been one to let tomorrow take care of itself." She smiled suddenly. "Maybe the baby's changing you already. Well. I've got to get back to work." She stood, and pushed Karma back down when she would have followed her. "I'll let myself out. I'll call you about dinner one night this week. I have to check my calendar at the office.

I'll bring something over, if it's too hard for you to get out."

Karma smiled at her from the sofa. "Thanks, Bert. That would be wonderful. I am getting a little tired of my own company."

Bert blew her a kiss and was gone.

Karma pulled the lid off the box and found a small card on top of the folded tissue.

Thought you might need something to make you feel glamorous after the very unglamorous work of producing a baby. Love, Bert.

Karma parted the tissue and found a turquoise silk slacks set with a big shirt top and full trouser legs. She made a soft sound of approval, knowing it would feel wonderful on.

Another package contained a one-piece suit for Garrett with ducks on it and a blue polka-dot tie that matched the romper pants. The last held a musical plush bear that played a lullaby.

Garrett loved it. Karma watched his eyes search for it as she cradled him in her arm to feed him. She'd placed the bear on the arm of the sofa and sat in the corner close to it.

*HEY, I like that. Where did it come from? I used to look like that once—hair all over. 'Course, I wasn't out yet. I can't make music, though. You don't think I'm slow, do you?*

SHE FELT curiously selfish, enjoying this moment all by herself. She wished there was someone she could turn to to say, "Do you see that? Isn't he cute?"

But there wasn't, and that was the way she'd wanted it. It was a new world, filled with single-parent families. But staring at her beautiful baby, she couldn't help but wish he had someone else to admire him, too.

"You know what?" Karma said aloud to Garrett. "We are going to be the happiest mother-and-son team since . . . since . . . oh, what's her name? In *So Big*. I know you've never heard of that. It was written by Edna Ferber, and it's about a mother and son who keep their land against impossible odds when the father dies. And they work so well together that eventually they build a great empire.

"We're not going to do that, exactly, because it's hard to build an accounting empire unless you're H & R Block, and taxes really aren't my favorite part of the whole thing. But I'm just trying to tell you we're going to be fine. I think I'm over the blues, or whatever that was that made me melt all over Nate Foster when he came, and everything's going to be great for us. I'm sure of it."

*ME, TOO, Mother. But I do like him. He can hold me in one hand. Can't we invite him back?*

# Chapter Five

Karma awoke the following morning to the sound of the baby screaming—and to an emotional relapse.

She patted Garrett while she paced the kitchen, waiting for the milk to warm. She felt blue and hopeless, and the portion of the payroll she'd managed to work on last evening while Garrett slept seemed so small a part of the overall project. She had to finish it in the promised time to maintain her professional credibility.

What had she been thinking? Whatever had made her think she could maintain a business *and* raise a baby?

I'M VERY HUNGRY, *Mother. How long is this going to take? My rash itches, and I* really *wish I could have one of Nate's massages.*

GARRETT QUIETED after taking his formula in the company of the musical bear. Getting herself ready with one good arm took Karma until midmorning.

Garrett on her shoulder, she went to check the mailbox, hoping for sweepstakes winnings, or the appearance of a misdirected Mary Poppins.

The box contained neither, but she gasped at what she did find.

A bouquet of red roses protruded from the mailbox attached to the front of the house. There were no distracting ferns or baby's breath—just a dozen brilliant crimson, just-opening roses wrapped in florist's paper and sticking out of the old black box.

"Oh..." Karma heard her own whispered, protracted exclamation. The beauty of the surprise made her heart thump, then her entire body soften as though she'd been patted on the head or stroked. "Look, Garrett. Roses!"

She transferred Garrett to her wrapped arm and pulled the roses out of the box. She held them to her nose, then to the baby's. He stopped crying and flailed a hand.

"Can you smell them?" she asked.

*WOW! I bet it's a pretty color. Can I have one?*

KARMA held the stems away from him, feeling the thorns through the paper. "They're red, Garrett. Aren't they wonderful?"

*UH-HUH. Yes. I bet* he *left them.*

KARMA SUSPECTED Nate was responsible for this whiff of heaven.

She looked up and down the street, wondering if her benefactor had waited for her reaction. But she saw no one. Most of the cars in the neighborhood were gone, their owners off to work. All she saw was the battered blue truck her neighbor used to haul wood for his woodstove.

"Well. We'll take these inside," she told Garrett, "and call Nate and see if he did leave them." She felt curiously excited, and was surprised to discover she was pleased to have an excuse to call him.

Karma looked up the number and placed Garrett in his carrier on the counter. She played with his tiny hand while waiting for Nate to pick up.

"Hi. You've reached Nate Foster," his voice said cheerfully. "I'm out. Leave a message after the beep and I'll call you back."

"What do you think, Garrett?" Karma asked the baby while the series of beeps played musically. "Should we leave a message?"

*YES. Isn't that the polite thing to do? Tell him I said hi.*

"POWER-PUNCH, please, Devon," Nate said to the young man behind the counter at Coffee Country, Heron Point's premier coffee bar. "With amaretto cream. And can I use the phone? I won't be long."

"Sure." Devon handed him a cordless phone. "Take the back table. I'll bring your coffee."

"Thanks. How's Jo? I hear she had a girl."

"Well ... the baby's fine," Devon replied, his expression wry. "But she's caught in that weird situation, you know. Surrogate for her sister, her sister dies ... and she's left to deal with the baby and the banker-father."

Nate raised an eyebrow at Devon's tone. "What do you mean? Ryan Jeffries is all right. I know him."

Devon shrugged and reached for a mug with the coffee bar's logo on it. "He acts like he owns her."

"Maybe he's just acting like he owns the baby. It is his."

Devon put the mug under the hot pot labeled Power-punch. "I guess. None of my business, anyway."

Nate stabbed out his number and wondered if Heron Point had always had so many unorthodox relationships and so many babies, or if he just happened to notice them because he'd been somewhat involved in one. Baby, that is. Relationships weren't really his forte—except friendships.

It occurred to him to wonder why he'd left a dozen roses in Karma's mailbox, if that was true, but he dismissed the thought. Analysis took all the pleasure out of spontaneity.

His answering machine picked up, and he pressed the keys to enter his remote access code and listened to his messages play back.

"Hi, Nate. Alexa. The reception I told you about for the Chilean sculptor is tonight. I heard your car's in the shop and you're still in town. Want to go? Let me know. I'll pick you up."

A beep ended the message.

"Nate, it's Emmie. Tango tournament at the Scupper. *Tell* me you'll be there. If I have to dance with Robert Botsford, you're a dead man. Thought you deserved a warning."

Nate smiled and waited through the beep.

"This is Hadley. Low tide tonight. Want to go clamming? Call me."

Devon brought his coffee. Nate thanked him and handed him a bill. He sat back and sipped at his coffee.

"Nate?" The voice was quiet and hesitant, and brought Nate instantly upright in his chair. He held the cup away as its contents sloshed onto the table. He heard baby sounds in the background. "Ah... Hi. This is Karma Endicott. Did you...I was wondering if you...left roses in my mailbox?" There was a pause. "If you did, thank you. They turned my day around. If you didn't...thank you again for everything else you've done. Garrett says hi. Bye."

"Yes!" Nate said in a quiet, triumphant whisper as he stabbed out Karma's number, then dropped napkins on the puddle of coffee.

KARMA SAT at the computer with Garrett in a front pack, lolling contentedly against her, eyes looking up at her with flattering fascination. She had a handle on the Brighton Construction payroll—even though she could only hold it in one hand—and she was now making encouraging headway. It was lucky, she thought, that the number pad on her computer required only the right hand.

She'd placed the roses on a table at her elbow, and their fragrance enfolded her as she worked.

She was amazed by how positive they made her feel. She wondered if it was their color, their fragrance, or the simple fact that someone had thought about her, that had boosted her morale and helped her out of her hormonal slump.

The phone rang, and she reached for it absently as she reviewed the figures on the screen. She guessed it was Bert, calling to suggest a night for dinner.

"Hello?"

"Hillary's House of Harlots?" Nate asked.

Karma felt herself smile. She also experienced a sudden shortness of breath. "Yes, it is. You sound healthy. Hadley didn't push you off the mountain for having spent the night with me?" She closed her eyes and put a hand over her mouth when she heard her own words.

Nate heard her involuntary intake of breath and grinned. "No. She did try to walk me to death, though. I'm a foot shorter than the last time you saw me."

"Aw... I have a dozen more roses than the last time you saw me. Did you leave them?"

"I did," he replied. "I figured you probably already had enough letters and bills. Your message said they turned your day around. Were you having a problem?"

"Probably postnatal depression. I thought it was a myth, or that work would keep it at bay. But..." She sighed, putting a fingertip to a silky red petal. "It seems to be very real. One moment I'm thrilled at the possibilities of my new world. And the next, I'm overwhelmed by my responsibilities."

"I think that's a pretty typical reaction to childbirth—even for women who have help. You're sure there's nothing I can do?"

It would be so easy to say yes. She was managing to get *some* work done, but she'd have to accomplish a lot more before she could feel that Endicott Accounting was really back in business. In fact, Garrett was beginning to stir and fuss. That was all it took to make mincemeat of her productivity.

And she *wanted* to do this alone. This attraction to Nate Foster was probably the result of her body's hormonal riot since she'd given birth, and she couldn't change plans in midstream because of it.

"Thank you," she made herself say. "But I have Garrett in a front pack, and I got a little work done today. I just have to learn to cope."

"Why," he asked quietly, "do you have to learn to cope *alone?*"

"Because I am alone," she said.

"By design, not by destiny."

Karma gripped the phone, momentarily without an argument. "Does it matter?" she asked finally.

Of course it did, but he doubted there was any point in arguing that now. He tried another tack.

"So, if I understand things correctly, every debit requires a credit. Am I right?"

She sensed a trap, but she couldn't deny the facts. "That's right."

"Then, if I debited roses in your mailbox, you're required to credit my dinner table with your presence."

"Ah..." Karma considered that curious accounting maneuver with excitement and trepidation. She'd love it, but she couldn't afford to love it too much. "The currency is a little fuzzy, but I think that's two debits. A debit is a placement, a credit is a removal."

"Piece of cake," Nate said. "We credit your house and debit my dinner table."

She had to laugh. It was all so absurd.

"I appreciate the invitation," she said, "but I haven't really lined up a sitter yet, not that I'd want to leave Garrett this soon any..."

"That's what diaper bags, infant seats and those nifty wooden high chairs that can be turned upside down to hold them are for. Chez Pasta has them. I'll pick you and Garrett up at seven."

"But—"

The line was dead. Karma smiled at the squirmy baby. "Well," she said. "We have a dinner date."

*I'M PLEASED ABOUT THAT. What'll we wear? I have that new outfit. The ducks are a little frivolous, but the bow tie is a sophisticated touch.*

"Hi. Are you... Whoa!" Nate stopped just inside the door, with a hand to his heart. He'd never seen Karma wearing makeup and with her hair combed. The sight of her stopped him in his tracks.

She was gorgeous. Her long, dark hair was straight as rainfall, and swung past her shoulders like a shimmering jet curtain. Thin bangs skimmed naturally dark eyebrows over thickly lashed brown eyes. Her cheeks were pink, her lips a darker shade of cherry.

She wore a pants outfit in a turquoise color that at first glance disappointed him. It was oversize, and though he knew the look to be fashionable, he shared most males' preference for the also-fashionable snug mini.

Then she crossed the room, beckoning to him to follow, and he saw that the voluminous silk moved seductively around her, flatteringly molding itself to her curves, draping tauntingly into the hollows. The color darkened her eyes and brightened her cheeks. Even the bulk of her wrapped arm in the left sleeve did nothing to diminish the impact. His breath caught in his throat. He had to clear it to speak.

"You don't look like an accountant," he said.

Karma felt every tendency toward common sense she possessed warn her to tell him she'd changed her mind.

Nate wore a simple pair of jeans with a white shirt, open at the throat, and a black linen blazer. His golden brown hair was side-parted and combed into order, a small wave at the side already resisting his good grooming.

She watched his blue eyes look her over—and approve what they saw with a masculine tilt of his eyebrow that spoke volumes. She knew she was in emotional danger. The self-protective instinct to tell him that she'd changed her mind, that Garrett felt feverish, was very strong.

But the impulse to face danger head-on was even stronger. And she couldn't quite believe that, because she'd never been a thrill seeker. She'd always avoided the unknown, the ungovernable, knowing they would only wreak havoc upon her orderly existence.

*Childbirth has done this to me*, she thought absently, as he took the step that brought them within touching distance. *Having a baby has made me crazy.*

He cupped her head in his hand and lowered his until their noses touched. "I *have* to kiss you," he said.

He smelled like the ocean on a windy day. "Well, if you *have* to..."

Karma felt his other hand slip around her waist, warm and strong and confidently competent. It held her against him as his mouth closed over hers, slowly, tenderly, expressively.

She counted her heartbeats, because they were so loud—and because counting was what she did. Then she lost count and got confused. Her heart beat fast, and everything else inside her seemed also to develop a pulse.

Mild panic began to develop. She pushed gently at his shoulder.

Nate drew away at the first sign of resistance, frankly surprised he'd gotten that far. Not that he was calculating his advance, but he knew how reluctant she was to let a man get close. He wondered if he did indeed have some appeal for her, or if she simply wasn't as reluctant as she thought she was. He considered it his masculine duty to find out.

"You look gorgeous when you're not in labor," he said with a grin. "Where's Garrett?"

Karma went to the overstuffed chair on which she'd placed the infant carrier. Garrett, all bundled up in a quilted baby blanket in shades of blue, gurgled at him and made wide, uncoordinated gestures with his hands.

*HELLO! How've you been? I missed you. I hear we're going to dinner. That's great. I'll have what you're having.*

"WE CAN'T STAY very late," Karma said, pausing to lock the door as Nate waited for her on the top step. "I'm working on the Brighton Construction payroll. I have only three more days to get it to them."

"Karma," he said gently, chidingly, holding the carrier in one hand and reaching the other toward her to help her down the steps. "You know what happened to Cinderella when constraints were placed upon her evening."

"Cinderella didn't have a baby."

"Only because no one troubled to write the sequel."

## Chapter Six

"Oh! A brand-new baby!" Two waitresses greeted Nate and Karma as the host saw them to a table by a window. The young women placed one of the wooden high chairs Nate had talked about upside down at the side of the table and placed the infant carrier on it. "Aren't you just adorable?" they cooed over Garrett.

*Hi! Yes, I guess I am kind of cute. Or maybe it's the tie. I'll have whatever Nate's having.*

A BAND OF FOG invaded the sunny evening, clouding the sunset and enfolding the dusk like a tulle scarf. The lights that marked the ship channel were visible, their glow magnified by the prismatic effect of the fog. Karma watched the serene view as Nate tried to show her how to roll pasta onto her fork.

She turned her attention to him. "Is this a skill one would *want* to perfect?" she teased.

He seemed surprised that she'd asked. "We have contests in the hospital cafeteria. Try it."

She did, then shook her head over her awkward efforts. "Aren't you supposed to do it on a spoon? Maybe that would be easier."

"No," he said in disgust. "Spoons are for sissies. Just pin your fork to the plate and turn it."

Karma tried again. Several strands of pasta flew off her plate, and the rest refused to adhere to her fork. She dropped it in disgust.

"I give up. I don't have one drop of Italian blood in me. It's probably ethnically impossible for me to do this. Did you have an Italian grandparent, or something?"

"Roommate in college," he said, holding up his fork to show her, with a superior glance, an expertly rolled ball of pasta. "Antonio D'Oro. Loved opera. Got all the girls."

"*All* the girls?" she questioned, resigned to cutting her pasta into manageable pieces. "Is he the one who taught you your charm with the ladies who mambo and mountain climb?"

"Somewhat," Nate admitted with a grin. "At the heart of my success is the fact that I like them. And most women—most people—just want to be liked."

"But in romance," she said cautiously, "isn't it awkward to...like...a lot of women? I mean, what happens when the mambo queen meets Hiking Hadley?"

He shook his head, sprinkling more Parmesan on his pasta. "Nothing. They're not serious. And neither am I."

"You mean," she asked with a puzzled frown, "they want to be liked, but not seriously? How can that be?"

He thought about that a moment and shrugged a shoulder. "Well, Emmie's just a happy free agent. Alexa, too, I think. Hadley would like to get serious, maybe. But she's seeing an anthropology professor, too. She'll have to get serious with him."

Karma stabbed a bite of red pepper. "Alexa? That's a new one on me."

"Sorry. She's my cultural connection. Loves galleries and museums and theater openings."

"I didn't realize there were that many in Heron Point."

"A few. But she lives down the coast, and spends a lot of time in Portland. She's a decorator."

Karma leaned her chin on her fist and studied him. "How many more are there? And how do you keep them all straight?"

"Ah . . ." He narrowed one eye as he appeared to calculate. "Maris is a lawyer who also happens to be a weekend sailor, and Barb's a reporter for the *Herald*. Loves to go to movies and talk politics. They're all interesting and good company. We just fit into each other's schedules when we can. They all know I see other women, and I hold no claims on them."

"And you don't feel special about any particular one?"

He made a straight-line gesture with his fork that Karma interpreted as a no. "We all know it's just for the moment, and that's comfortable for all of us."

She shook her head, still confused. "Why would it be comfortable," she asked, "to not be special? To just be one of five or six?"

He frowned at her. "Maybe they consider it preferable to being alone. You may prefer solitude, but not every woman does."

"But too much company," she argued reasonably, "is not much different from too little. I mean—it ends up the same, doesn't it? When you're finished being temporary— you're alone again."

Nate examined the logic of that and decided he didn't want to touch it. "Can we talk about something else?" he asked. "Tell me about your business. About your plans." She smiled suddenly. She glanced at the baby, found him still fast asleep, and reached for a breadstick. She snapped it in half and offered Nate a piece.

He was sure the gesture was unconscious, but he enjoyed it all the same.

"I'd love to have an office one day," she said, her eyes losing focus as she thought about it. "Outside my home, I mean. And I know just where."

"Where?"

"In the Chambers Office Building, fronting the park. I can't afford the rent yet, but someday. There's an upstairs office with a skylight." She lifted her shoulders in a gesture of happy anticipation that made him smile.

"Is there room for a crib?"

She shook her head. "I'll probably have to hire a nanny when I get to that point." She reached out to touch Garrett's sleeping form. "I love him to pieces, but he's already very vocal. I don't think I'd get very much done with him around." She grinned at him. "And *you'll* be back to work by then."

"There's an older woman in town who takes care of babies," he said, searching his brain to try to remember the name. "Jo Arceneau at Coffee Country was going to use her, but she changed her mind. She could give you some details about her."

Karma nodded. "I'm determined to try to cope for a month, then I'm going to have to get serious about work again. Is Jo back to running her business already?"

"No. Devon's spelling her for a while."

"Right. The student." She smiled speculatively. "I think he has a thing for her. I mean, I don't know either of them very well, but I've seen him watch her, and I think he has more than business on his mind. But then, I think the baby's father does, too. In our Lamaze classes, he always seemed so intense when he touched her."

Nate laughed lightly. "There are a lot of convoluted relationships in our little town."

Karma laughed, too. "And *you* have most of them." She put her coffee cup to her lips as he stopped chewing a bite of his breadstick to give her a scolding glance.

KARMA WAS DETERMINED not to invite Nate inside, but the phone was ringing when she unlocked the door, and Garrett, frustrated because the comforting motion of the car had stopped, was screaming at the top of his lungs.

"Get the phone," Nate said. "I've got the baby."

It was Bert. "Where have you *been?*" she demanded. "I was beginning to get worried. If you didn't answer this time, I was going to come over there with the police!"

"To dinner," Karma replied calmly, aware of Nate taking Garrett out of the carrier and pacing across the living room with him. She turned her back to him.

There was a surprised silence on the other end of the line. "With whom?"

"Nate Foster." Karma strove to sound nonchalant. "And he's here. Can I call you back?"

"Is he staying the night again?"

"Bert..."

"All right, call me back."

"My friend Bert," Karma explained to Nate from the kitchen, where she ran a bottle of milk under warm water. "She was worried because I wasn't home."

Nate came toward her, the plump, fussy baby held in one arm against the preppy elegance of his blazer.

That picture of him had been imprinted on her mind since the time he'd shown up at midnight to check on her. She loved the one-handed confidence with which he held Garrett, his manner relaxed despite the baby's cries.

Well, if I were a doctor, she thought wryly, I could be relaxed, too, instead of thinking my baby's always at death's door.

He leaned back against the counter beside her, holding Garrett right up to his face and looking into his big-eyed stare. The baby stopped crying.

*OKAY, okay. I like you, too. But if you leave again, I'm going to be upset.*

"So, what's the problem, buddy?" Nate asked. "Or are you trying to establish a nightly routine of mental anguish for your mom?"

*WE WENT TO DINNER, and I clearly remember ordering whatever you were having. But nobody brought me anything.*

"IT ISN'T OUR FAULT you slept through dinner," Nate said. Garrett's brow furrowed as he concentrated on his face. His little mouth worked into an O. "But we appreciate it. You gave us time to talk."

Nate reached a hand out for the bottle. Karma handed it to him, thinking that she shouldn't. She should thank him politely for a lovely dinner and explain that she had to be up early to deliver the payroll.

But there was that pleasure in watching him with the baby. There was something artful and touching in the long, lean muscles wrapped around the helpless little bundle, the big hand that could cover Garrett from ankle to chin.

She was surprised by the emotion it stirred in her, the little niggling of pain she felt at the thought that this was simply a momentary thing, that the man Garrett studied in fascination didn't really belong here.

Nate looked up from feeding the baby and surprised a look of... He wasn't sure what it was. There was a wistful smile on her lips, and a paradoxical combination of pleasure and sadness in her eyes.

It confused and unsettled him. He liked to think he understood women. He was always honest with them, and he appreciated it when they were honest with him.

Karma had told him she wanted to be alone. He'd suspected that wasn't as true as she thought it was, but that look in her eyes seemed to confirm his suspicion. She looked very much as though she wanted...him.

But *he* didn't want that. Did he? At least not in that way. He'd have enjoyed seeing desire in her eyes. But need? That was something else again.

Still, he felt an excitement he couldn't understand. He should be feeling panic.

Karma took the baby from him and ignored Garrett's loud protest.

*I WANT him. How many times do I have to... Oh, what's that? Food. Okay.*

KARMA BOUNCED HIM in her good arm, her injured one holding the bottle. He began to suck greedily again.

"Thank you, Nate," she said. "I enjoyed dinner very much. And I'll keep practicing that spaghetti roll."

Nate noticed a curious finality in her tone. The panic he should have felt a moment ago, he felt now.

"What are you doing tomorrow?" he asked.

"I'm working on Brighton's payroll," she said briskly, "then I might call Jo Arceneau about the sitter."

"I'll bring dinner over tomorrow night," he said.

That sounded wonderful. But she knew better than to believe it could be. "No. That wouldn't work."

He raised an eyebrow. "Dinner wouldn't work?"

She frowned at him. "You know what I mean. *We* wouldn't work. You're content with just-for-the-moment relationships, and I now have a baby to think about. I can't do anything just for the moment. So I'm going to follow my original instinct."

He studied her evenly, then asked, "To remain alone, you mean?"

She angled her chin. It was her decision. "Yes."

He nodded as though he understood. But something about the jut of *his* chin told her it wasn't going to be so simple.

"Well, that's certainly the easy way out," he said.

She shifted the baby's weight and asked coolly, "Easy way out of what?"

"Whatever's going on between us."

"Nothing," she replied, "is going on between us. I'm just...longing for *cozy* things I can't have." She gave the adjective a disparaging emphasis. "Because my hormones are in a tizzy. And, let's face it—" she looked him in the eye "—you're just looking for a woman to fill the sixth night of the week, and I don't think I'd like a class-action relationship."

"I explained that none of the ladies is serious about me, or me about them."

"So, presumably, I'd be expected to see you on that same basis. No."

He folded his arms. "Well, if you're intent on remaining alone, doesn't that suit your purposes?"

Hmm. She chose to sidestep his logic. "I'll be too busy for recreational dating."

He smiled. He couldn't help it. He saw that it annoyed her, and took a certain satisfaction in the fact. "Recreational dating," he repeated. "What a phrase. What do you call the kind of dating that's serious mate hunting? Acquisitions associating? Marriage marketing?''

She glared at him. "Maybe it's time you said good-night.''

He held his ground. "First I want to know what kind of 'cozy' things your hormones are longing for.''

He thought for a moment that the question would unsettle her and give him the upper hand.

It did, but for just an instant. She looked vulnerable and desperate. Then she squared her shoulders and fixed him with a steady gaze. "A father for Garrett," she said candidly. "But you don't want to raise anybody's children, remember? Do you really think we have anything more to discuss?''

He thought there was probably volumes, but he was a little unsettled himself at the moment, and he didn't know what the hell to make of her.

He held his ground. "A father for Garrett," he pointed out, "would result in a husband for you. Have you thought about that? Or is there some fancy accounting here I'm unaware of?''

Her shoulders slumped visibly. Garrett began to fuss, and she put him up to her good shoulder. "I said I longed for it. I didn't say I thought I could have it. Please, Nate—''

"All right.'' He went to the door. She followed and stood aside as he opened it. He turned to look down at her. "I'm leaving. But the minute I have you figured out, I'm coming back.''

She smiled grimly, thinking that should take some time. She didn't understand herself. "Goodbye, Nate," she said. "Thanks for everything.''

He took hold of her shoulders suddenly, apparently changing his mind about leaving. He pulled her close.

*WHAT'S GOING ON, Mother? That feels good. It reminds me of the first time I saw you. He had his arms around us then, too.*

"So, according to your double-entry bookkeeping system," he began. Karma rolled her eyes, knowing he was about to use his creative logic to try to undermine hers once again. "You were debited with dinner, so I should be credited with something."

"You can be given credit," she said smugly, "for an aggravatingly persistent nature."

He gave her a reproachful smile. "I mean credited as in an accounting sense."

"No. You see, *I* was debited with roses," she explained patiently, "and we debited *you* with my presence at dinner." She shook her head at him with concern. "You're just not getting the hang of this, are you? If I credit you, I have to take something from you. Remember? I explained this all to you yester—"

He cut her off with a nod. "I understand. I *want* you to take something from me."

Her brow furrowed. "What?"

He maintained a blandly innocent expression. "A kiss."

She looked back at him a full ten seconds, then expelled a nervous little breath. "Nate, I don't—"

"You said the world turns on it," he insisted. "A debit requires a credit. An action somewhere generates a reaction some—"

"All *right!*" She stopped him with a sharp tone of voice that was directly at odds with the trembling, melting feeling inside her. "Do you think you can keep your mouth closed that long?"

He looked dismayed, though there was amusement in his eyes. "If that's the kind of kiss you want to take. But I was rather hoping..."

She closed her eyes to summon up patience. And to help her resist the impulse to laugh. "I mean, can you be quiet that long?"

"I promise to try."

"Good. Are you ready?"

"Oh, yes."

He freed her hand, letting both of his fall to his sides. She took that as a sign that the initiative was hers.

She knew this was major trouble, but she'd be damned if she'd let him think she was afraid of this contact, as he'd suggested several days before. As Bert had suggested.

It occurred to her that, deep down, she had to prove it to herself. She had to give it everything she had.

Nate awaited her touch with a heart that had flatlined in anticipation. One more moment of waiting, and some cardiologist would have to crack his chest and massage his heart by hand. Garrett gurgled. Nate took him from her.

Karma raised her hand to the side of his head and combed her fingertips through the short hair there. He felt every pad of every finger against his scalp. Sensation rippled all the way down his spinal column. He struggled to keep his free hand still.

Her fingers explored his hair, slipped slowly down the nape of his neck, then tugged, encouraging him to lower his head.

He watched her eyes as he complied, and saw that they were focused on his mouth. The effort to remain passive became monumental.

Her lips were parted—in concentration, he guessed, rather than in passion. But he parted his on the chance that he was wrong.

He was.

The first touch of her mouth to his seemed to ignite something inside her that changed the contact from a game of one-upmanship to a deadly-serious communication.

Her lips were warm and pliant, and her tongue traced his for an instant in a cautious exploration. Then it delved inside, as though caution were the last thing on her mind.

And that was when he lost restraint.

Karma wasn't sure what was happening to her, except that for the second time ever in her recollection, she was following a path she knew to be dangerous. It was little comfort that he'd also been responsible for the first time.

She could have kept the kiss simple. She should have. But his mouth was warm and mobile and so deliciously tender that she had to know more. It was as though she found herself in some dark and velvety place that beckoned her deeper.

She felt his hand splayed between her shoulder blades, then in her hair, holding her close as his tongue toyed with hers. The earth spun out of control, and she clutched at his shoulder, the baby between her and him.

Nate's hand moved down to her back and roved over her hip, confident and possessive. She heard her own little groan against his mouth.

Garrett screeched—loudly.

*HELLO. Does anyone remember I'm here? I'm happy that you're happy, but I believe I have a hand jammed between two of Nate's ribs. Mother?*

KARMA DREW BACK and took the baby from Nate, horrified that, for an instant, her needs and not Garrett's had been uppermost in her mind.

"Oh, baby," she said apologetically, holding him up to study his puckered little face. "Are you all right? Did I hurt you?"

*JUST MY FEELINGS. Can we eat now?*

NATE WATCHED her fuss with the baby, and tried to calm his rampant libido. So. He was right. She'd convinced her brain that she wanted to be alone with her baby, but her body had other ideas. He suspected her heart did, too.

But she smiled at him with every appearance of control. "Well, there we are. Debit dinner, credit kiss. We're square. Goodbye, Nate."

He studied her—her face flushed, her hair rumpled from his hand, Garrett wriggling fussily at her shoulder—and decided that goodbye was the only solution. They were a powder keg and he was a lit match. The obvious result of their union would not be healthy for either of them.

The strange thing was that, though he knew that to be true, at some basic level where he made all serious decisions, he didn't seem to care.

He simply smiled and reached a hand to Garrett's back. "See you," he said, and walked out the door.

Garrett began screaming immediately.

*No. I want Nate to stay. Where's he going? Call him back.*

WITH A GROAN, Karma closed and locked the door, accepting that she was probably in for another sleepless night. But she'd done the right thing. She was sure of it.

"DO *YOU* THINK I did the right thing?" Karma leaned over Garrett, who had just been diapered and changed. He was inspecting a bright orange cloth toy shaped like a pumpkin. "You know, I *thought* I had, but—" she looked around surreptitiously "—I wouldn't admit this to just anyone, but I've missed him. I know you have, too."

Garrett hit her in the face with the pumpkin. She took that for an affirmative.

"But maybe I did do the right thing, because we said goodbye almost three weeks ago, and he hasn't called."

MOTHER. *Goodbye means you're going away. That's why he hasn't called. You could call him. He has that phone thing that he carries with him. What is this, anyway? Do I eat it?*

"WELL, we're doing fine, aren't we?" Karma lifted Garrett and placed him in the swing she'd put near the computer. "I'm picking up more work all the time, and I've even figured out how to do it with you around, you little noise machine, and with me having only one good hand to work with. I still haven't figured out how to work sleep into the equation, but you have to start sleeping nights sometime. *Tell* me you're going to be sleeping nights sometime."

BUT I LOVE IT *when I wake up and it's dark and lonely and I see your face over my crib.*

"WELL, look, Garrett. I want to talk to you about Friday night. See, I've been invited to Diantha's party." Karma sat at the computer and spoke to her son as she called up Davis Dentistry on the screen.

OH, *good. A party. I like those. Is this Diantha person bringing pizza like Aunt Bert does?*

"IT'S NOT THE KIND where friends come over and we all curl up on the sofa and watch you be cute. I'm going *out* to this one, and you're going to stay here with Aunt Bert. You know how much she loves babies."

*THEN LET HER stay with one. Maybe one of those dorky girls that are always at Coffee Country when we go in there. I want to go to the party.*

"I WON'T BE GONE for very long, but I probably should go, because I spend so much time with you that I feel as though I'm losing all my social skills. Not that I was ever very good at them, anyway. And not that you're not stimulating company, but I need adults, you know. People who will talk to me. And this is a Halloween party. That's why we have a jack-o'-lantern on the kitchen table, and smiling paper ghosts taped to the windows. Next year I'll take you trick-or-treating. But this year you have to stay home."

*OH. So all this effort I'm making to carry on a conversation isn't appreciated. Well, that's fine. Go to your party. I'll stay home with Aunt Bert and tell her all about my day and see if she isn't fascinated. Don't think twice about me. I'll just mind my own business in this thing that bounces me around while that obnoxious music plays over and over.*

KARMA WATCHED GARRETT happily occupied in the swing, and felt as though she were finally getting somewhere as a mother and as an accountant. Experience lent her a certain facility with him that was providing her comfort and excitement and reinforcing her conviction that having a baby had been a good idea.

She simply skipped over in her mind the idea of the baby having a father. It was too confusing and upsetting to contemplate, and she felt as though she'd reclaimed control of her life and her situation.

The baby was thriving, and the business was getting healthier every day. She was reestablishing organization, and she took satisfaction in that sense of having everything in her life in its proper place.

She smiled at Garrett. "I was so smart to have you," she said. "And I was smart to say goodbye to Nate Foster."

*DON'T TRY TO CHARM ME. I'm not speaking to you.*

"ALL RIGHT. I want to know how you got your figure back in five short weeks. In that flapper dress, you look about a size three! You even look wonderful with your arm in a cast!"

A dancehall girl wearing theatrical makeup, a dime-size beauty mark on her cheek and a smile that looked vaguely familiar forced a cup of punch into Karma's hand and backed her into a corner. "What are you using? A fat-free diet? The 'Buns of Steel' video? A shake for breakfast and lunch and a sensible meal for dinner?"

Karma peered at the painted face. "Nancy?"

"Yes. Why? Have the six pounds I've gained made it impossible to tell?"

"Will you *stop* with the six pounds!" A tall blond Southern belle appeared at Nancy's shoulder. She swatted her arm with her folded fan. "No one is aware of it but you. You look wonderful." She shook her head at Nancy, then turned her attention to Karma. "Hi. Remember me? Jo Arceneau, from Coffee Country and Serena Borders's Lamaze class?"

"Yes, of course." Karma smiled. "Congratulations on your daughter. Life with a baby is certainly a revelation, isn't it?"

Jo laughed. "Really. Who'd have guessed we could get by with so little sleep, and so little confidence in what we're doing."

"I was clever enough to marry a man who already had two children of his own," Nancy said with a teasingly superior air. "His experience was invaluable."

Jo didn't seem to see the advantage. "But for the past five weeks, you've been coping with a new baby *and* two small boys. That can't have been fun."

Nancy smiled, her eyes filled with warmth. "It's been wonderful."

Jo frowned at Karma. "She's entirely too cheerful. Do you have any bad news with which we could douse her good humor? Diantha! Great party!"

A bejeweled Gypsy, gray hair wound into a bun into which she'd placed tiny flowers, hurried by in a flurry of colorful skirts. "Hi, everyone!" Diantha said. "Eat lots, and don't worry—the stars promise svelte bodies for all."

Jo elbowed Nancy. "Hear that?"

As Diantha bustled away, a vampire appeared in their midst with the swirl of a black silk cape. It fluttered about Jo as he wrapped an arm around her.

She smiled up at him, then at her companions. "You all know the count. Ryan, remember Karma Endicott from our Lamaze class?"

"Of course." He smiled and offered his free hand. "How's the baby?"

"Growing," she said vaguely, studying his face. "You have no fangs, Count."

"He keeps them in a glass on the bedside table," Jo said with a laugh.

He raised his cape to cover her mouth. "It's ethnic," he said with an exaggeratedly cultured accent. "My family's from southern Transylvania. There's a strong Bulgarian influence. No fangs."

Jo pulled his hand down. "Just a lot of 'bull.'" She laughed heartily at her own joke, then looked around the silent group. "Bull—get it? *Bul*garia. Just a lot of bull."

Ryan Jeffries grabbed the arm of a passing pirate and pulled him into their midst. "Hey, Blackbeard. Do you have a plank Jo could walk?"

Karma recognized Jave Nicholas under the woolly beard and mustache. His coat was made of a colorful brocade, and he carried a plumed hat. He managed somehow to look handsomely piratical, despite the phony accessories.

"What's her offense?" he asked.

"Bad jokes," Nancy replied.

"I regret," he said, "that my plank remains in the harbor with my ship."

Nancy put a hand to her hip in a gesture of displeasure. "Well, what a silly place to keep it."

"I do, however," he said, giving Nancy a quelling glance, "know a gentleman who *can* see that she suffers for her misdeeds." He looked around the crowded room, apparently spotted his quarry, and beckoned. "Over here, Officer!"

A policeman appeared in full blue uniform, leather belt creaking at his waist. "Trouble, matey?" he asked.

Karma's heart lurched as the man's bright blue eyes met hers. They didn't register surprise, though she was sure *hers* did.

"Matey?" Jave repeated, apparently taking issue with the name. "I'm the scourge of the seas. The terror of the Barbary Coast."

Nate nodded. "Sorry. Is there a problem, Mr. Scourge, sir?"

Jave fluffed the lace at his sleeves. "That's better. This young woman—" he indicated Jo "—has offended her companions with bad jokes."

"My," Nate said, unhooking the handcuffs from his belt. "Comedic crime. That's a felony. Come along, young lady."

He reached out so suddenly, so smoothly, that Karma didn't see trouble coming. But the next moment, there was a handcuff around her wrist.

"But, it's Jo who..."

"I'm sure the bad joke," he said in explanation to the foursome that watched him prepare to take away what they considered the wrong perpetrator, "was due to *this* woman's bad influence. We must fight crime at its source."

"Ah..." Karma tried to protest, but the music and laughter were very loud, and she was being led away by the second half of the handcuffs, which was now closed around Nate's wrist.

# Chapter Seven

"You have the right to remain silent," Nate advised Karma as he pulled her out onto Diantha's front porch and closed the door behind them. He led her to a cushioned wicker love seat, then saw that it was occupied by a life-size scarecrow holding a pumpkin.

He changed direction and headed for the railing that ran the length of the porch. He leaned a hip on it where the porch column connected, and braced a foot on the railing. That allowed him to pull Karma right up against him.

She found his sudden nearness almost paralyzing. In the weak porch light, his blue eyes, now on a level with hers, looked dark and intense, despite the amusement she saw there, and his white-toothed smile seemed wolfishly dangerous. His fresh-scented cologne mingled with the salty, autumnal fragrance of the night. Her heart raced. Her pulse thumped. Everything else inside her waited.

"You have the right to remain silent," he repeated softly, his free arm snaking around her waist. "But I wouldn't recommend it."

"Why not?" she asked in a whisper.

"Because I want the whole truth, and nothing but the truth."

"About what?"

His arm tightened, and she felt every soft curve of her body in contact with every muscled plane of his.

"About whether or not you missed me."

Impulse told her to melt against him and tell him the truth. She'd thought about him often. Relived their dinner over and over. Dreamed of him holding Garrett, holding her. Missed him terribly.

But common sense reminded her that, apart from those inexplicable feelings, she was coping fine without him.

"I thought about you," she admitted, trying to wedge a little space between them. Feeling his muscled warmth against her was making it difficult to think. But he didn't loosen his grip, and she quickly discovered that wriggling was a mistake. They were far too close to move *anything* without serious consequences. "I don't imagine you missed me, with Emmie, Hadley, Alexa, Maris and Barb to keep you company these past three weeks."

He shook his head, his eyes roving her features with frowning concentration. "I haven't seen them. You look lovely, but you look tired. Not sleeping?"

"How come you haven't seen them?" she asked. She tugged on her right arm, which he had cuffed to his left. "Nobody who has a baby gets any sleep. And I've been working a lot. Business is picking up."

He lifted his wrist to accommodate her movements. "I'm glad about your business, but don't ruin your health. I haven't seen my ladies because I was on vacation. What *are* you doing with that arm?"

If she raised her arm, his hand lay against her breast. If she lowered it, her hand lay against the inside of his thigh. She couldn't help fidgeting.

"Well . . . it's just awkward," she said. "One arm in a cast, and the other in a handcuff. Can't you unlock us?"

"No," he replied, clearly without giving the matter any consideration. "But maybe I can make you more comfortable." He turned her around so that her back was to him, and pulled her against his body. His cuffed arm circled her waist. "Better?" he asked, his breath a soft tickle against her ear.

"Sort of," she replied breathlessly. His legs cradled her body, and she felt both deliciously comfortable and as though she were about to fall off an emotional cliff. "So you finally went to Canada?"

"Yes, I did."

"And you had a great time?"

"No, I didn't."

"You didn't?" She turned her head in surprise. She stopped just short of turning her body, remembering that she'd probably dump them both off the railing. "I thought you wanted solitude in the wilderness, you and nature and a panful of trout."

"That was before I met you," he said, planting a kiss just behind her ear. "That was when I was a happy bachelor looking for adventure."

His words and his actions were elevating her blood pressure. "Aren't you...anymore?"

"I don't know," he replied honestly. "I'm confused." He nipped the lobe of her ear. "And it's all your fault. Yours and Garrett's. I went away finally because you were driving me crazy. I thought the solitude would allow me to clear my mind and just *be* for a couple of weeks. But..."

He sighed. His breath ran along the cord of her neck and made her shiver.

"Cold?" he asked, holding her closer, wrapping his other arm around her, too.

"I'm fine," she said softly, her voice strained. "But what?"

"Well . . . you know what's wrong with solitude?"

"What?"

"It encourages you to think. And all I could think of was you. So I spent a weekend at a campsite, where there were other people, but that was worse."

"Why?"

"It was filled with families. Men with women, couples with babies, children with grandparents, all kinds of cross-generational groups having a wonderful time together."

"And that's bad?"

"If you're trying to convince yourself that that isn't what you want, it is."

"So, you came home."

"No." He leaned forward and put his cheek to hers. "I stayed and observed—jealously."

Because of their position, she was forced to lean back against him or topple them both forward. "Why jealously?"

"Because," he said moodily, thoughtfully, "I never had that. Well, I guess I did while my mother was alive, when I was small enough to forget the details of what it was like to live in a family, but not too small to retain the longing to have it again. I went to military school at seven, then to college, then to medical school, then into residency at a Portland hospital. My memories consist primarily of meals at a cafeteria table, nights in a dormitory, and people who moved in and out of my life but never stayed. I remember a father who was simply an acquaintance."

Karma turned her head to look into his eyes. She saw the sadness of his last statement there. She kissed his cheek. There was nothing sexual in the gesture, though only moments earlier the air had been charged with sexuality. She offered pure and simple comfort. That was why he loved chaos, she thought. It filled the emptiness.

"I'm sorry," she said. "That's what you get for getting involved with my labor. You should have gone to Canada the day your vacation started."

He pulled her back so that they remained cheek to cheek, and he laughed. "As I recall, you had a death grip on me. Anyway..." His tone had changed. He'd put memories aside. "I discovered that I missed you a hell of a lot. And Garrett, too. And if you don't agree to spend some time with me, I'll have to lock you up and throw the key away."

She frowned at his logic. "If you locked me up, you wouldn't be able to see me anyway."

He nipped at her ear. "You're so innocent. I'd lock you up at *my* place, and throw away the key."

"Oh, of course."

"I have an A-frame at the edge of Eaton's Woods. Tom Nicholas..." He stopped abruptly and raised a questioning eyebrow. "You know Tom?"

She nodded. "I do his taxes, and I run into him once in a while at Coffee Country."

Nate went on. "He's a good carpenter. Just put a deck on for me. My house is rustic and warm, and generally stays pretty tidy, because I don't get to spend that much time there. I think you'd like it."

"It sounds wonderful," she admitted. "But much as I might enjoy being locked up there, it wouldn't be very good for my business. I think I'll just invite you to dinner once in a while instead."

He tipped her chin back and kissed her throat. "I love a cooperative prisoner."

"Hey, do you two want—" Ryan stepped out onto the porch. The breeze caught his cape and swirled it around him. He peered into the weak light. "Aren't I supposed to be doing that? Nibbling on necks is *my* prerogative."

"Ryan!" Jo caught his arm and tried to pull him back inside. "I don't think they'd have come out onto the porch if they wanted you gawking at them."

"What's happening?" Jave's bearded face peered out behind Jo's.

"Where?" Nancy squeezed between him and Jo.

Nate let his head fall back against the column with a thunk. "Life in a small town. You can't even take your girl onto the porch without everyone coming out to watch."

"Your girl?" Nancy asked, then added, with delight in her voice, "Really?" She turned to Jo. "Isn't that nice?"

"It's great," Jo agreed, trying to push everyone back inside. But they resisted. "So wouldn't it be nice if we gave them a little privacy?"

"No," Jave said. "We're about to have a quick meeting about the hospital's Christmas party, and we need Nate. He's the one who can fix everything."

"Jeez," Nate grumbled. "Is it that time again?"

"What time?" Jo asked Nancy.

Nancy deferred to Jave with a wave of her hand.

"The hospital throws a big party," he explained, "for all the underprivileged children in the county. We collect used toys for weeks, and repair and paint them so that every child gets a present." He smiled blandly at the group collected on the porch. "I'm chairman this year, so I'm enlisting all of you to help. So be prepared. From now until Christmas, your homes are going to become repositories for other people's junk, which you will have to rejuvenate into works of art." Jave grinned at Nate. "Much as I hate to credit Dr. Foster with any talent at all, he's the one who can always get the most decrepit toy to work. So I'm afraid you'll have to continue this rendezvous after the meeting. Duty calls."

"Does it not strike you as strange," Nate asked, steadying Karma on her feet as he lowered his own foot from the railing, "that we're having a meeting about a Christmas party while dressed for Halloween?"

Ryan shrugged. "It might, if this group had any standard for normalcy. But it includes you and Jave. Need I say more?"

"You're lucky it does, Ryan," Jave said, opening the front door and ushering everyone inside. "Because you're going to *need* a doctor. Everyone into Diantha's office."

"OKAY." Jave was seated behind Diantha's desk, where their hostess had left soft drinks and nibbles before hurrying back to her other guests. He studied the list he'd made on a yellow pad during the meeting. "Nancy's in charge of decorations, Jo is taking care of goodies with help from Diantha, I'm going to do press releases about the project and contact service groups, Ryan will arrange to have the bank used as a downtown collection site, and of course we'll use the hospital, too. Nate will repair toys that don't work, and we'll all pitch in to paint them and spruce up whatever's donated." He looked from face to face. "We're all agreed?"

"Agreed," they said in unison.

Jave grinned wryly. "Tom will be helping, of course, but most of you witnessed his row with Amy earlier this evening, so neither of them is available at the moment."

The group exchanged sympathetic glances.

"You didn't assign Karma anything," Nancy noted. "I'm sure she wants to help."

Jave turned to Karma.

"I do," she said. "I'll make a cash contribution."

Nate and Karma sat together in a battered love seat. He'd removed the handcuffs.

She almost regretted the fact.

"You don't really think you're going to get off that easy, do you?" Nate asked.

"I have to," she insisted. "The end of the year is a very busy time for me."

He frowned at her. "But it's going to be Garrett's first Christmas. You have to get in the spirit of this do. You can't do that by making a *cash contribution.*" He repeated her words with obvious displeasure.

"Oh, come on," Karma said. "Christmas 'spirit' is that warm, fuzzy euphoria generated by the merchant community to make the consumer spend. Christmas should be a time for spiritual reflection and renewal."

"And in that spirit," Nate said, "you're going to give *money?*"

Karma waited for someone in the group to support her position. But they appeared to be watching the byplay with interest.

"I'm *busy,*" she pleaded reasonably. "I don't have *time* for grand holiday preparations. And I doubt seriously that Garrett will notice."

"Of course he will," Jo insisted. "He's a Libra. Chelsea's natal chart could apply to him or to Malia. They're eccentric children. They love fuss and are very aware of color and fragrance and sound. Karma." She fixed her with a serious stare. "You have to *make* time for Christmas."

"You do." Nancy supported Jo's position. "Pete and Eddy are already starting to talk about it. And it's not commercialization to them. It's... love and magic."

"And it's not just for children," Jave said. "I have a wonderful time at Christmas. My mother cooks and bakes things she's been making since *I* was a kid, we loosen up, fill the house with gaudy stuff, shop for all the things we've convinced the kids Santa might not be able to find, just so we can see their ecstasy on Christmas morning."

Nancy went to stand behind him and wrap her arms around him. He crossed his hands over hers. "You don't want to deprive yourself of that."

"I have to get my business going," Karma said feebly.

"Find a way to compromise," Ryan suggested, wrapping an arm around Jo and holding her closer. "Jo and I will sit for you a couple of nights so you can take some time to decorate or go shopping."

She smiled, determined to apply her tried-and-true practices, even though she now had a baby in her life.

"I appreciate that, thank you. But I have the next few months planned, and, at the moment, the best I can do for your project is a cash contribution."

Jave nodded in concession. "Okay, we'll take it. Ryan's going to set up an account at the bank for other donors who'd like to do the same."

"Other *Scrooges*," Nate whispered in her ear as the meeting broke up. "I'm not giving up on you, Karma Endicott. Your attitude is reprehensible. Come on. I'll work on you while we're dancing."

Diantha's living and dining rooms adjoined, and she'd pushed all the furnishings to the edges of the room to accommodate the couples swaying to the music from a CD player.

"Good grief," Karma complained as he drew her into the middle of the crowd and wrapped both arms around her. "I'm not something you can 'work on,' like a broken bone. I suppose all that Christmas stuff is all right if you have time for it. I do believe what it's all about, I just don't see why everyone has to crowd the season with sentimentality to feel as though they've celebrated it."

"So, you don't send cards?" he asked, pulling her closer to him as a flamboyant older gentleman dipped his lady with a wide flourish.

She shook her head. "I include a greeting and a wish for a prosperous New Year with my December statements."

He rolled his eyes heavenward.

She did the same. "I suppose you send flocked cards covered with animals in earmuffs singing Christmas carols."

"No." He sounded offended. "I always look for a magi motif. I like the notion that they wanted to know what was happening, and set off to investigate, willing to take as long and go as far as necessary." He grinned. "Not unlike the mission I've assigned myself of getting *you* into the Christmas spirit."

"Nate," she said patiently, "can't you just accept me as I am?"

He shook his head. "Not that part of you. I helped bring Garrett into this world. I'm not going to abandon him to a mother who doesn't have time for Christmas."

The party was still going strong when Karma and Nate left, shortly after eleven.

"You don't have to leave," Karma told Nate. "I drove here."

"I'll follow you home," he insisted.

"I had a wonderful time," Karma told Diantha, "but I promised my friend who's baby-sitting that I'd be home by eleven-thirty. She has to go to work in the morning."

Diantha hugged her, her Gypsy jewelry clicking musically. "I'm so glad you could come. Now you've got to try to get out more. You Capricorns have to learn to take life a little less seriously."

Nate pulled up behind Karma in her driveway and got out of his car to walk her to the door. She looked back at his red Jaguar, which was illuminated by a streetlight.

"Wow," she said. "So, that's the famous car that kept you from going on vacation, even after I loosened my death grip on you."

He'd almost forgotten the story about his car being in for repairs. "Right," he said. "Good as new now."

"You want to see Garrett?" she asked. "You won't believe how much he's grown."

"Yes. Please." He followed her to the door. It was opened wide by a dark-haired young woman in jeans and a sweatshirt who looked at him with open suspicion.

"Nate, this is the famous Roberta Dawson," Karma said, tossing her coat and purse at a chair. "Bert, meet Dr. Nathan Foster, who performed *your* coaching duties when I delivered Garrett."

"Really." She offered her hand.

Nate shook it, getting the distinct impression that she didn't like him.

"I know Hadley Brooks," she said. "And Barb Wagner. *And* Alexa Winfield. Is that your entire lineup?"

"Bert!" Karma stopped in her tracks on her way to the bedroom to check on Garrett. "Wha—?"

"It's all right," Nate said, interrupting. "Go check on Garrett. I can take care of myself. As a matter of fact, Miss Dawson, I've also spent some time with Emily Drake and Maris Fuller. If you consider friends a *lineup*." He repeated her word with distaste.

"I just thought you should know that someone was counting. So Karma's number six." She picked up her purse and a paperback novel from the coffee table. "I suppose even God rested on the seventh day."

"Actually, they're all number one," he said quietly. "I value my friends. And I see you value yours."

She looked him over a moment, obviously confused by that last remark. "Karma has a life plan," she said, pointing the book at him. "It's a stupid plan that involves devoting her entire life to her child and her work, and leaving nothing for herself, but I'd hate to see it disturbed for her by someone who has no intention of replacing it with something better."

Karma came back into the room with Garrett in her arms. He looked wide-awake.

Nate reached for him, and Garrett allowed himself to be handed off without complaint. He studied Nate with wide-eyed interest, his hands waving, his legs, in the blanket, kicking.

"Hi, guy!" Nate said, lifting him high, then bringing him down close to his face. "He must have doubled his weight!"

*WELL, she keeps feeding me. Every time I ask for something, she puts that bottle in my mouth. How've you been?*

KARMA CAME to stand beside Nate, leaning her face close to his shoulder so that she, too, could smile up at the baby. "He's over ten pounds now. Aren't you, chubs?"

*THAT'S WHAT the doctor said. But I think he had his thumb on the scale.*

GARRETT SMILED WIDELY, deliberately.

"Look at that!" Nate exclaimed.

Karma nodded. "He's been doing that for a couple of days. Tell me you've ever seen a cuter baby."

Nate brought him down again and settled him in his arm. "Well, Jave and Ryan might take issue with that, but then, you know, they've got girls. It takes a *guy* to really know how to turn on the charm."

"Isn't that the truth?" Bert said with a significant glance at him. She slung her purse over her shoulder and headed for the front door. "I'll call you, Karma. Lovely to meet you, Dr. Foster."

"Miss Dawson," Nate called, trailing behind Karma as she followed Bert to the door.

Bert stopped and turned to him, an eyebrow raised in an unspoken question.

"You have nothing to worry about," he said.

"Why?" Karma looked from one to the other. "What is she worried about?"

"Your plan," Nate replied, catching the baby's fingers between his lips.

"My plan?" Karma frowned at Bert.

Bert fixed Nate with a threatening stare. "See that I don't," she said, blew the baby a kiss, and walked out the door.

Nate handed Karma the baby.

"I don't get it," she said.

"She thinks," he explained, reaching into his pocket for his keys, "that I intend to lure you out of your organized outline for life, then desert you for another member of my harem, leaving you wounded and vulnerable."

Karma laughed lightly. "I do *her* taxes because she keeps all her records in a Darby's Dresses box, and she worries about *me* being able to control my future?"

"I imagine she's just being a good friend."

"Did you explain to her that that was all you were doing with the other five ladies?"

The question sounded ingenuous, and there was no sign of teasing in her eyes. But he was beginning to know her better than to trust her innocent expression.

"I don't think she'd have believed it—just as you don't. So I'll say good-night. You said something about inviting me to dinner?"

"I have to work through the weekend. How about Monday night?"

"Perfect. I don't go back to work until Wednesday."

"Still the night shift?"

"I prefer it. Or I used to."

Karma didn't want to touch that. "Seven o'clock. With any luck, I'll have Garrett down by then. He slept six hours the other night, and when I woke up, I thought he'd gone into a coma, or been kidnapped, or something. I couldn't believe it."

*GEE, Mother. I thought you'd be pleased.*

HE LAUGHED and patted the baby's back. "Good night. See you Monday." He stopped at the door, turned and found her right behind him. God, she was beautiful, he thought, letting his eyes wander up the plume in her flapper headband. It made him smile. "Let your mind think about Christmas, okay? Come on. Jave's going to need all of our support, and money's just not going to cut it."

"He seemed to think it would do," she pointed out.

Nate shook his head. "He was just being nice." Then, because he couldn't resist the impulse, he leaned down and kissed her lightly on the lips. "Good night. Sweet dreams."

Garrett started crying when the door closed behind him.

"Garrett, come on," Karma pleaded, heading for the kitchen. "I could use a quiet night tonight, okay?"

*I GAVE YOU ONE the other night, and you thought I was sick! Why does Nate always have to leave? Why can't he stay here like he did that other time? I slept on his chest. I really liked that. And in the morning we danced around the kitchen while he cooked. You don't dance. I mean, you feel nice and soft in the morning and you smell really good, but you never dance. Where does he go, anyway?*

# Chapter Eight

"What is all that?"

Karma held the door open for Nate, who carried a very large open box. It appeared to be heavy, and things stuck out of it that Karma couldn't identify. Until Nate set the box down and placed several of the strangely curved things on the floor.

"Train tracks," Nate explained. "Ryan just dropped this off. Apparently something's wrong with the caboose."

Karma laughed. "I know a few people to whom that diagnosis would apply. Would you mind keeping an eye on Garrett while I put the finishing touches on dinner?"

"'Course not. Where is he?"

Karma brought the carrier out of the kitchen. "If you spread the blanket on the floor, he's happy to lie on his stomach and watch you."

"Okay, bro." Nate did as Karma suggested, then constructed the tracks around him. "We're going to check out this thing and see what's wrong with it, so some little boy can find it under the tree on Christmas morning. So *you* can be part of the hospital's holiday project, even if your mother doesn't want to be."

"I heard that," Karma said from the other side of the bar that separated the kitchen from the living room. In an alcove in the corner, a round table was set for two. "You can't turn him against me. He loves me as I am."

*SURE I DO, but you don't want to help with Christmas? Come on, Mom. I have to. I mean, He knows who I am. We knew each other even before I got to know you. He'll expect me at His birthday party.*

KARMA CHECKED the game hens and considered them browned to perfection. The dressing and the wild rice were fragrant and ready, and the vegetables were perfect—crisp but not crunchy. She removed biscuits from the oven and placed them in a pale green linen napkin in a basket and put them on the table.

"I'll make up our plates in the kitchen, if you don't mind," she called to him. "The table's a little small to set everything on."

"Great," he replied over the sound of a small, ailing motor revving. "I'm so used to eating cafeteria-style, that having a plate I don't have to fill will be a nice change."

Karma gave him extra-large helpings of everything. She'd always thought her childhood had challenged a child's coping skills, but at least it hadn't been lonely. Her parents had been eccentric and embarrassing, but they'd been *there*.

"Wine with dinner, or coffee?"

"What kind of wine?"

"A bottle of white zin I got for my birthday last year."

There was a moment's silence. She peered around the bar to where he lay on his stomach on the floor, examining the underside of the tiny caboose. He looked up at her.

"Don't you want to save it for a special occasion?" he asked.

She grinned. "Isn't this an occasion? My son gets to see his first electric train, a caboose gets a new life, you get a plate you don't have to fill, and I get to cook."

He looked surprised. "You *like* to cook?"

"Yes. Why?"

He shrugged a shoulder. "Well, it doesn't seem like an organized undertaking. I mean, cooking's sometimes unpredictable, isn't it?"

She dismissed that notion with a wave of her hand and disappeared again behind the bar. "I guess it is for those 'a pinch of this, beat it till it's done' kind of cooks. I follow recipes religiously. I *make* it organized."

"Of course," he said.

Karma poured the wine and placed their plates on the table. "You two ready?" she asked.

Nate appeared at the table, Garrett clutching the front of his shirt in a tight little fist. She pried it open and took Garrett, placing him in the carrier, on a third chair that she wedged between the wall and the table.

*WHAT ARE WE HAVING? I want some. I can gum it. Or are you just going to presume, as usual, that because I can't hold a fork, I don't want any?*

NATE KNEW he would hereafter consider sometime during that dinner as the moment he began to fall in love. It would take time to *be* in love, he knew; for him, the sharing of deep emotion was a slow and gradual process. But everything was changing.

This—whatever it was—with Karma was no longer a game, a diversion that might or might not become something more. It was. He'd been snared.

And it wasn't the food, although it was delicious. It was her face across the table, the long discussion about movies, music, Heron Point gossip, childhood stories, personal prejudices.

They agreed on some things and disagreed on others, but sharing them was funny and sad and intimate—and he couldn't remember ever being so comfortable and so on edge at the same time.

"I can't believe," she said with a laugh, "that you had a Flintstones sweatshirt, too. They let you wear that in military school?"

"I wore it to bed—" he grinned "—where I read *Tropic of Cancer* under the covers."

Karma studied him, her chin on her fist. "Now there's a picture. A boy in a Flintstones sweatshirt reading Henry Miller."

He inclined his head modestly. "I did my best to defy labels. I'll bet you did, too."

She frowned, thinking. "I was always *trying* to be conventional, because my parents weren't. I guess it's the old thing of wanting to be whatever it is you aren't. Except that I really wanted out of that bus." She looked around her at the somewhat confining dimensions of her little house. "One day I'll have a two-story house with a big yard, but for now, this is so much better than those days. I..."

She stopped herself, shaking her head, as though changing her mind about what she'd been about to say. She began to stack dishes.

Nate caught her hand and held it to the table. "What?" he asked gently.

She shrugged, embarrassed. "I'm sure you don't want to hear my personal discoveries. I mean, you didn't come here to—"

"I came here," he told her, "to figure out why I can't get you out of my mind. Please. Say it."

For a moment, Karma didn't know whether she was more unsettled by his admission or by what she was finally able to admit to herself. She drew a breath. She knew she could trust him with what she felt.

She shrugged a shoulder, her hand still caught in his. "It's not such a big thing, but...it was hard, you know, to love my parents, yet hate the way they lived. Inside, they were truly all love for each other, and mankind, and the earth. But we lived on top of one another, in conditions that made it difficult for *me* to feel those things. I was always angry—needing space, needing privacy." She sighed. "Just needing something else. Sometimes..." She hesitated and swallowed, then admitted with a rasp in her voice, "I regret that. I wish I'd been kinder, less demanding. I think they were generous with what they had to give. I just sometimes felt that their respect for the globe could be applied on a smaller scale to our family."

Nate pushed her wineglass toward her. "I know. Every time I went home from school, I'd behave like a monster, trying to make my father react. He was always kind, never raised his voice, and I was desperate for some sort of genuine response. But I think he truly didn't know what to do with me, figured he was supposed to love me, and that that meant taking whatever I threw his way. By the time I figured that out, he'd passed away and it was too late for both of us."

Karma turned her hand in his and squeezed it. "I'm sorry. I know it leaves a hole where all your happy childhood memories should be. I guess it's human nature to remember only what we've been deprived of. But I'm sure it'll make you a wonderful father when you can come to accept having children in your life. You'll know what they need, because you understand what you needed and didn't get."

She tried to pull free of his hand to get dessert, but he tightened his grip on her. He used it to pull her toward him and draw her into his lap.

She knew she should put up some resistance, but she couldn't think of one good reason why. She could think of no one she'd rather be with at this moment—or any time in the future. There were several unresolved issues between them, but she loved it when he kissed her, lived on memories of him when they were apart, and was perfectly willing to sacrifice common sense to have him kiss her again.

That alone, she thought, was big trouble. But some things in life were simply worth the risk.

The night he'd taken her to dinner, he'd allowed her the initiative in the kiss, but this time was different. This time, the moment he had her in his arms, he took complete control of the encounter.

He cradled her tenderly, tipping her sideways into his arm, tucking her legs up against him and holding her with an arm wrapped around her thighs.

She looped her arms around his neck, thinking absently that she could sit that way forever, in his protective, possessive embrace.

He opened his mouth over hers, and she tightened her grip on him, desire flaring between them like a flame given air. His tongue delved deeply, and she teased it, warred with it, then planted kisses along his jaw and at his ear as his lips roved along her throat to the open collar of her shirt.

He raised his head to claim her mouth again, and she met it eagerly, returning kiss for kiss. Her hands moved over his shoulders, feeling strong muscle and rigid bone under the wool of his sweater.

She felt his hand wander up the back of her thigh, into her skirt, and made herself push away and gasp for breath.

He sat her up, resting his forehead against her shoulder while he, too, drew a deep, steadying breath.

"Mud...pie," she said in a ragged whisper.

He raised his head to frown at her. "What?"

She pointed a finger toward the refrigerator. "Mud pie. For dessert. In the refrigerator."

He grinned dryly, holding on to her hand as she pushed herself to her feet. "Maybe I should get in the refrigerator."

"You're supposed to be fixing a train," she reminded him, kissing his knuckles, then pulling her hand free. "I'll get dessert."

"Right."

He had the train running in fifteen minutes. Karma, sitting beside Nate on the floor, watched the HO-gauge train circle the track. It hummed as it neatly made all the curves. Garrett, sound asleep in the carrier on the floor beside them, was unaware of Nate's success.

"Good for you," Karma said. "You deserve another piece of mud pie."

"Oh, no." Nate shook his head adamantly and leaned back on an elbow. "It was wonderful, but I'm stuffed. I'm not sure I'll marry you, after all."

He was teasing; Karma knew that. But she had to concentrate not to betray a reaction. A good thing, she decided, since she didn't know what it would be, anyway.

"Really." She leaned on her hand, tucking her legs sideways. "I didn't know you were considering it."

"Well, I've always kept a good distance from the marriageable female," he said gravely, "but I had a change of heart when I tasted your cooking."

"Thank you, I think."

"But then—" he waggled his index finger at her suspiciously "—I realized it could be a control tool."

She grinned. "You mean the power to withhold dessert?"

"No. I mean, if you made a man fat enough, he'd become too sluggardly to argue with you. He'd relax into a comfortable stupor. Like the one I'm feeling right now."

Karma let her eyes wander over his athletic leanness and found the notion laughable.

"You mean if I said something quarrelsome, you'd let it pass?"

"Probably."

She leaned over him and whispered near his ear, "The contemporary celebration of Christmas is a plot of the downtown merchants."

She was shocked the next moment, when she lay on her back on the carpet and he knelt astride her, pinning her good hand above her head.

"Ah!" she cried, laughing and struggling at the same time. "You said you wouldn't..."

He firmed his grip on her. "I'm not arguing, am I?"

"Well, not verbally, but..."

"I don't believe you were specific about that. And for a lady who likes to spell out the details..."

"Well, if you're going to *get* specific, none of this applies anyway, because for one thing, you're not my husband, and for another, you're not fat. So, what do you say to that?"

"I say I'd like to hear you take it back."

"What?"

"The Christmas crack."

"Never."

"Then I'm afraid I have to take appropriate action."

Karma felt excitement running along her nerve endings like a jolt of electricity. He was so near, so deliciously dangerous, but the only threat he seemed to pose was pleasure.

"And what would that be?" she asked challengingly.

He thought a moment. "I think this requires a two-part retribution. First, you owe me a kiss for taking rude advantage of my honest admission."

She rolled her eyes. "You were accusing *me* of having ulterior motives for being a good cook." She barely suppressed a smile. "But, very well—if you're going to whine, you may have your kiss."

"Thank you." Still pinning her hand, he leaned down to claim it. It was tender, but long and slow. When he finally raised his head, she felt intoxicated with his masculinity.

"Part two," he said, changing his grip to clasp her hands and pull her to her feet, "is an eye for an eye—so to speak."

"What?"

He reached into the box that had held the pieces of train track and retrieved a rag doll that was missing an eye and a foot, and was wearing an apron with a dark stain. He handed it to her.

"Neither of the other ladies in our group can sew. Can you?"

She hugged it to her instinctively. "My goodness. She looks like she's been through a lot."

He smiled. "Ryan said she was donated by a little girl who had loved her, and wanted to give her to another child to enjoy. The little girl's mother apologized for the state it was in, and told him privately that he could toss it away after they left. But we decided there's probably a lot of love attached to it, and that some other little girl will feel it. What do you think?"

She looked at the doll, then at him, her eyes large and limpid. Her mouth took on a suspicious twist. "I think you're an insidious manipulator."

He smiled innocently. "Thanks. I like you, too. I'll help you clean—"

The beep of his cellular phone interrupted him. He reached into the cardboard box for it, frowning at Karma. "My answering service is supposed to pick up everything tonight but hospital calls. Excuse me. Hello? Hi, Joanie. What—?"

He glanced at Karma with an expression she couldn't quite define, but chose to interpret as guilt.

"Hi, Hadley," he said with mild surprise.

Or was it feigned surprise? Karma wondered. I am not feeling jealousy, she told herself firmly as she went into the kitchen to clean up. So he carries his cellular phone with him so his girls know where to find him. So what? So he kisses me as though I provided him with something vital to his survival. He hasn't promised me anything he hasn't promised them. I'm not jealous.

And what does it matter, anyway? I'm attracted to his charm and his sexuality, neither of which is a quality that will change my mind about men. I don't want one. I don't want him. I'm just reacting to loneliness and a starving libido.

"A simple fracture?" she heard him ask. "Yes. Well, sixty-three isn't that old, Hadley, and she's a strong lady. Who's setting it? No, no need to worry. He's very good. Hadley, calm down. You're not going to be any good to her or to yourself if..." He sighed. "Yes. Sure. I'll meet you in the waiting room."

Karma turned away from the sink, wiping her hands on a towel, when he came into the kitchen, flipping the phone closed.

"I'm sorry," he said. "Hadley just took her mother into emergency with a broken leg. Seems she had pretty poor

form in the bowling lanes. Fell down and broke her fe-
mur.''

''And Hadley needs you.'' Karma walked around him to
the guest closet, where she'd hung his jacket.

She tried to help him into it, so that she could stay behind him and avoid his eyes, but he took the jacket from
her and lifted her chin with his forefinger. ''I'm just being
a friend. Her mother's a neat lady.''

Karma already felt guilty that she resented his defec-
tion. She didn't want him to compound it by being understanding.

''You aren't required to explain,'' she said, then added,
in a tone that negated her noble words, ''If I still had a
mother and she'd broken her leg, I'm sure you'd 'be a
friend' and come and comfort me.''

''Karma.'' His tone was scolding.

''Nathan,'' she said in the same tone. ''Go. I understand that it will probably comfort Hadley's mother to see
you. But even though you can be comfortable seeing six
different women, you have to understand that there is not
a cell of polygamous tendency in me.''

He smiled. Jealousy. That was a step in the right direction.

He reached out to take her in his arms. She sidestepped
him. ''No. No special privileges for you, until there are
special privileges for me.''

''Karma...'' he said again.

''Nathan,'' she repeated, ''you kiss me, then you run to
her. Of course, you probably kiss her, too.''

''I'm running,'' he said, his manner mildly impatient,
''to her mother. I explained that I—''

''I know. That you love us all as friends. But you kiss me
like a lover...'' she was so surprised that she'd said the
thought aloud that she paused for a moment, swallowed,

then went on "... and I think you're going to have to organize your priorities if this is going to go on."

Now he was annoyed. He didn't like having his motives
questioned, particularly by a woman who was seldom clear
about her own.

"Is that so?" he asked. "And what are your priorities?
Business expansion, bigger house, and a baby—precious as
he is—that you got from a sperm bank. You don't even
have time for Christmas!"

Infuriated, Karma yanked the door open. "Goodbye,
Nate," she said stiffly.

"Goodbye, Karma" was his cool reply. "Please don't
throw away the train when you're *organizing* things. I'll
come back for it."

"Don't bother," she said. "I'll mail it to you!" And she
slammed the door after him.

HE DID NOT COME BACK for the train. It had been almost a
week.

Karma vacillated between hating herself for her selfish-
ness one moment and being convinced she'd been right to
upbraid him the next. She wondered how Hadley's mother
had come through. And just how long Nate had stayed
around to comfort Hadley. He might still be doing it, for
all she knew.

Work kept her very busy, and it was now habit to lay
Garrett on a blanket on the overstuffed chair beside her
while she was on the computer. He arched, turned, twisted
and kicked until he finally exhausted himself and went to
sleep. He seemed to learn something new every day.

*I CAN'T WAIT until I can use the computer. I like the pie
charts and the graphs. How's Nate? Did he come over? Did
I sleep through it?*

KARMA GAINED two new clients, Garrett slept through the night once again, but kept her up three nights running, just, she was sure, so that she wouldn't grow overconfident.

And she repaired the rag doll. She gave it two new black button eyes, and replaced both legs with a muslin fabric that matched the arms. Feeling artistic, she added a striped fabric at the bottom for socks, made a pair of Mary Janes out of felt and topped the skirt with a lace apron. And while she was at it she replaced the red yarn hair with a curly yarn that made her look as though she'd just had a perm.

When she was finished with it, she placed it near her computer and found that it made her smile. She wondered if she were going crazy, or if she *did* feel the love in it? She hoped it would affect its new "mother" just that way.

But Nate hadn't come to retrieve it, or the train. She considered calling him, then rejected the idea. She could imagine him receiving a call from her on his cellular phone while he was with Hadley or Barb, and found the idea distasteful. So she packaged up the train and did what she'd told him she'd do. She took it to the post office and mailed it to him one blustery mid-November day. She held on to the doll, telling herself she wanted to add a bow to the hair.

She went from the post office to Coffee Country for a change of scenery.

She found Devon behind the counter, and ordered a cappuccino. Nancy and a young blond woman sat at a table in the corner, poring over items spread out before them. Beside them, in a playpen lined with blankets, lay a beautiful baby.

"Karma, hi!" Nancy beckoned to her to join them. "Will you look at Garrett?" She stretched her arms up for him as Karma drew near. "Hi, handsome!" She kissed his cheek. "Have I got a couple of girls for you!"

"Is this Malia?" Karma asked, remembering vaguely that the day she delivered, Nate had mentioned that Nancy's baby had thick dark hair. She lay on her tummy, "swimming" with busy arms and legs. She wore pink corduroys and a long-sleeved cotton shirt with pink bunnies on it. In her spiky dark hair was a pink bandeau.

Karma took an empty chair, suddenly cheered by Nancy's company. Though she noticed quickly that she and her companion seemed far from cheerful themselves.

"Do you know Amy Brown?" Nancy asked, indicating the young woman seated across from her in a red sweater with tiny white hearts on it and a ruffle trimming the neck and arms.

"Ah . . . no." Karma smiled at her. The first thing that caught her attention was how unflattering the fussy sweater was on her sturdy, angular frame. The second was that her warm smile distracted one from noticing anything else.

"She's the PR director at the hospital. Remember that special series of articles on the birthing rooms at Riverview?"

"Yes. They're what made me decide to have my baby here instead of in Portland. Not that I had much to say about it, when he arrived three weeks early."

Amy nodded appreciatively. "That's *precisely* what we were trying to do with the birthing rooms. I'm happy to meet you."

"We'd like your opinion," Nancy said. "On these Christmas decorations." Then she looked at her severely. "And I don't want to hear any of that bilge you were handing out at the Halloween party about not having time for Christmas. Can I put Garrett in with Malia?"

"You can try," she said. "He hasn't met other babies yet."

*I DON'T KNOW ABOUT THIS. I know I've seen her before, but we've never actually touched. I know she's a girl. I believe they're inferior, right? I mean, is that supposed to be hair? Aren't there any other guys? Mother!*

"I'M RIGHT HERE, sweetie." Karma waved at Garrett, who lay on his stomach, looking suspiciously at Malia. "It's all right. Ask her for a date. I think she likes you. Now." Karma turned her attention to the snowflakes, stars and trumpeting angels spread out on the table.

Devon brought her cappuccino in a glass cup. It wore a tall head of foamed milk.

"What do you think?" Nancy asked. Karma heard forced cheer in her voice. "Pete and Eddy and I made the snowflakes and the stars. Amy made the angels.

"Actually, Tom cut the stars out with his jigsaw," Nancy said. "And the boys and I painted them." The last few words were spoken weakly as Nancy and Amy exchanged a grim glance.

"What is it?" Karma asked candidly. "I can see something's wrong." Then it occurred to her, as she glanced at Devon, behind the counter. "Where's Jo?"

Nancy put a napkin to her nose, her mouth trembling. "Gone," she said.

Karma turned to Amy. "Gone where?"

Amy sighed. "To Connecticut. For good."

"What? You mean she and Ryan have—?"

Amy shook her head. "She went alone."

"Wait." Karma tried to pull together what she knew about Jo Arceneau. "But isn't the baby Ryan's? I mean, I know she acted as surrogate for her sister and Ryan, but she can't take Chelsea to—''

''She didn't,'' Nancy said, sniffing. ''She left her with Ryan.''

''But...she loves her.'' Karma felt a clutch in her stomach at the thought of Jo without her baby. The night of the Halloween party, everyone had laughed at her portfolio of photographs.

Nancy nodded, fresh tears springing up. ''That's why Ryan sent Chelsea to Connecticut with Diantha. Did you notice the health food store was closed?''

Karma was having difficulty keeping up with events. ''But *Ryan* loves Chelsea.''

Nancy sniffed again. ''He loves both of them, so he wants them to be together.''

''I don't understand,'' Karma admitted. ''Why did she leave?''

Nancy shrugged. ''Doubts, confusion. You know how love is. And then, there's poor Amy here, who's thinking about moving to New York after the New Year because my brother-in-law is being such a jerk.''

Karma turned sympathetically to Amy. ''I'm sorry,'' she said. ''I can relate, though. Men are a menace to our mental health.''

It was ironic, she thought, that she'd come here looking for distraction from her problems and an infusion of good cheer.

GARRETT: *A menace? Us?*
Malia: *Yes. You make us crazy.*
Garrett: *I thought you came that way. What's this? I want it.*
Malia: *Mom! He's got my pacifier!*

"You two get along," Nancy said to the babies. Then she turned to her companions. "Okay. We're going to put all that aside and do what we have to do here, because those poor children need a Christmas party, whether or not we're in good spirits." She picked up a snowflake and handed it to Karma. "These are made from foam sheets. The fairgrounds where we're having the party is huge, though, and it'll take hundreds of them to really look festive."

Karma held it up. The lightness of the material made it spin and look very much like an oversize version of the real thing. "I think it's wonderful."

"Good. I thought we could hang those from the rafters. The stars can go on the walls in a random pattern...." She placed two on the wall beside the booth and leaned back to look at them. "They should look pretty under the light. And the angels..." She reached for one to hand it to Karma.

Karma noted that it had been drawn with style and artistically painted. Glitter had been sprinkled on the gown that trailed behind it. It appeared to be about a foot and a half long.

"I think we'll put some over the stage," Nancy said. "And where Santa will be sitting." She smiled winningly at Amy. "That means you'll have to make about a dozen."

Amy nodded. "What do you think about making the gowns different colors?"

Nancy nodded. "Good. And the glitter will look great overhead." She frowned, then smiled determinedly. "Jo and Diantha were going to make cookies and other goodies, and as an act of faith, we're going to pretend that's going to happen. Oh, and another piece of good news. You know April, the candy striper at the hospital?"

"Yes," Amy said. Karma nodded, remembering her, too. "Well, she and her mom have volunteered their services to watch our babies the day of the party."

There was a squeal from the playpen.

*MALIA: I'm staying with my brothers. They love to have me around.*
*Garrett: No one's leaving me behind. They're talking about cookies. And didn't somebody mention Santa Claus?*

NANCY FOLDED HER ARMS and looked at Karma. "We need some little things for teenage girls and mothers. I think we've got older boys and fathers covered, because the ladies of Saint James's Church have been knitting hats and scarves all year long. Isn't that great?"

Amy and Karma nodded dutifully.

"But we need some little gifts for girls and women. I know you're busy, but can you think of anything you can do that we can help with that would be appropriate?"

Karma saw it in her mind's eye the moment Nancy began to describe what was needed. And she remembered with sudden clarity the ingredients required and the wonderful fragrance produced.

"I can make a cinnamon bear ornament," she heard herself say, "that's pretty simple, looks cute and smells heavenly." She stopped, unable to believe she'd volunteered that information.

"*You* can make them?" Nancy asked.

No. She didn't have the time. She had a business to run, and a new baby, and she didn't believe in all this...

"Sure." That was her voice again. "Jo..." The mention of her name cast a brief pall over their enthusiasm. Karma tried again. "Jo carries cinnamon. I can get it right here. Sure," she said again to convince herself. "I'll provide the ladies' gifts."

Nancy looked around surreptitiously. "What if it puts you in the..." She lowered her voice. Karma and Amy leaned closer to hear. "...in the *Christmas spirit?*"

Karma swatted her arm. "Very funny. I'm perfectly capable of making ornaments without catching the bug."

Amy patted her shoulder consolingly. "I hate to tell you this, but the way you volunteered those bears, you've already got it."

Karma sat back and looked at her companions accusingly. "If I'm infected, I want you to know I hold you both responsible."

Nancy scooped her stars and snowflakes into a tote bag. "How's Nate doing? Is he feeling any better?"

Karma blinked. "What do you mean?"

"He got food poisoning." Nancy seemed surprised that she didn't know. "I'm sorry, I thought you guys were seeing each other."

"Well..." she said with a wry twist to her smile, "I'm never quite sure how that's going. How sick is he?"

Amy snickered commiseratingly. "I know just what you mean." Then she frowned seriously. "He's been off work for three days. Got something bad at a birthday lunch for Joanie."

"Jave and Tom have been checking on him," Nancy said, "but neither of them has that much time. That first night, he was really bad, Tom wanted to stay with him, but I guess he's a terrible patient. He wouldn't let him. I think he even threw something at him."

Consumed with guilt for having thought the worst about him, Karma bought two pounds of cinnamon, scooped

Garrett out of the playpen and headed for the supermarket.

There she bought applesauce, the other ingredient in the cinnamon bears, a stewing chicken and a package of noodles, Jell-O, the ingredients for custard, and several other things she thought Nate might like. Then she called the answering service that picked up her calls when she was out and told them she'd be away for the rest of the afternoon.

She strapped Garrett into his car seat, then turned the Volvo in the direction of Eaton's Woods.

## Chapter Nine

Karma had never seen a more beautiful setting for a home. Nate's A-frame sat in a clearing on the very edge of Eaton's Woods. Fir trees and mountain ash clustered around the rustic structure, creating a carpet of dry combs of golden leaves and clusters of red berries that crunched under her tires as she pulled up behind Nate's Jaguar.

Several steps led up to a front porch, where a rough twig sofa and chairs were grouped around a low table. Window boxes were filled with ornamental flowering cabbage.

"Okay, Garrett," she said, lifting him out of the back of the car and into the carrier. "We're going to visit Nate and see if he needs anything."

*ALL RIGHT! I'll bet he's missed me.*

THE AIR was chilly and damp, the sky overcast with heavy dark clouds. She tucked the baby's blue quilt in tightly and made her way up the steps with the carrier, then went back for the bag of groceries.

She rapped lightly and waited. There was no answer. She peered through loosely woven curtains and saw a stone fireplace, heavy furniture in a rich green—but no movement of any kind.

He had to be home, if his car was here. But if he was ill, he might be sleeping. Or he might simply be too ill to get to his feet.

Concern growing inside her at that possibility, she tried the door. It was locked. She left the groceries, but picked up the carrier and walked around to check the back.

The new deck he'd told her about ran the entire length of the back of the house. She climbed the stairs at the side and discovered a picnic table with a collection of pumpkins on it.

Karma tried the latch on the French doors and was surprised but pleased when it gave. She pulled the door open, stopping when the left side squeaked mournfully. She turned sideways and slipped inside, afraid of waking Nate.

She couldn't help the *ooh* of envy that escaped her when she found herself in a kind of sitting room decorated in shades of green and beige. One wall was brick, one was all books, and the others were decorated with old logging photographs and memorabilia.

She tiptoed through the room toward a doorway, wondering if it would lead her to Nate's bedroom. She stopped on the threshold and peered around it.

*WATCH OUT, Mother!*

"ALL RIGHT, freeze!" a raspy male voice shouted, right beside her.

She turned, her heart leaping into her throat at the sight of a putter swinging directly toward her head.

She screamed and ducked and closed her eyes. But nothing struck her.

"Karma?" that same voice asked in frail surprise.

She opened her eyes to see Nate in ratty gray sweat bottoms, still holding the putter in midswing. He lowered it with a thunk, as though holding it required great effort. She saw beads of perspiration standing out on his forehead. His face was pale under several days' growth of beard. She noticed, however, that his broad shoulders and muscular chest seemed unaffected by his illness. He looked terrible, but somehow the sight of him was wonderful. She didn't bother to analyze that.

She smiled. "Are you finished? May I play through?"

Nate wondered if he was hallucinating. He felt like hell, and he could barely lift his eyelids, much less the putter he'd taken up against what he thought was an intruder. The effort must have caved in what was left of his ability to reason.

But he thought he saw Karma standing there—looking fresh and scrumptious in gray slacks and a fuzzy pink high-necked sweater. Her hair was caught at the side of her head in a straight, gleaming ponytail.

Weak from lack of food and sleep, he frowned at the image, wondering if it was real. Had he heard her voice?

Then she touched his cheek, her hand soft and cool, and what little reserve of strength he'd mustered to protect his home deserted him. He leaned a shoulder against the wall and felt himself begin to slide down it.

"No, don't do that!" she cried. She quickly placed something on the floor, then slipped an arm between him and the wall. "Nate, don't fall! If you do, I'll never get you up again. I've only got one good arm, remember?"

Her face was inches from his. He tried to focus on her, but he couldn't steady the picture. "Go away," he said. "I'm fine."

"Yeah." She held on to him with remarkable strength. "You look fine. Okay, are you listening to me?"

"Can't help it," he said, leaning limply against her. "You're shouting in my ear."

"Sorry," she said. "I'm panicky. I don't want you to fall on the floor. But if you take three steps sideways, you can fall onto the bed. Can you do that?"

"Three...steps?" he asked in disbelief. "I don't think so."

"Sure you can," she insisted. "Here. You're still holding the putter. Just lean on it, and on me. And we'll take three steps. Just three. Come on. You can do it."

He felt her wedge her shoulder under his arm, pull his arm around her shoulders. He tried to resist but, for the moment, at least, she was stronger than he was.

"Come on, Nate. One..." She stepped away from the wall, taking him with her. The room reeled. He leaned heavily on the putter and lurched forward.

"Two, three!" she said as they landed together on the bed.

He felt the soft mattress take his weight, and the relief was so enormous for a moment that he couldn't bear the thought of moving.

"Well, that was a little faster than I'd planned," she said with a laugh, "but whatever works." She pushed against him.

He felt her arm under him, her body fitted to his side, her leg hitched over him. He wanted nothing to disturb that intimacy, but she seemed very determined. She pushed at his shoulder and pulled her arm out from under him. He regretted that.

But the next moment, her arm was under his and she was coaxing him backward, up to the pillows. He pushed himself along with the little reserve of strength he had left and landed lifelessly in the cradle of her body. He smiled to himself. That was nice. But again she managed to get free.

Then he felt her hand around his ankle, lifting his leg onto the bed. She did the same with the other, then pulled the blankets up over him.

Now that he didn't have to spare the energy to remain upright, he was able to focus. That ponytail dangled forward toward his face as she leaned over him. Her large brown eyes were soft with concern, and her smile was tender.

"Can you keep anything down?" she asked.

He managed to hook an arm around her and hold her to him. The ponytail fell onto his face. She laughed against his cheek, then pushed herself away from him by wedging her cast between them.

"Let me rephrase. Can you hold *food* down?"

"Don't know," he said. "Haven't tried for days."

"Okay." She sounded suddenly brisk. "We'll try you out on fruit gelatin. If that works, you can have soup tonight."

"Tonight?" he asked. She was smoothing his blankets, tucking them in. "You're coming back?"

She patted his head. "Not exactly. Rest. I'll have the gelatin ready in a few minutes."

NATE AWOKE to the sounds of a baby crying. It was night, and here on the edge of the woods there was very little light from town. Blackness surrounded him, but he tried to sit up, tried to make sense of the sound of a baby crying in his house in the middle of the night.

Then he remembered. Karma had been here. He was aware that he felt a little better, just a little stronger. He'd had Jell-O. Then he'd had chicken noodle soup. It had been delicious after several days of nothing.

The crying stopped, and he heard a soft, crooning voice. Karma? Was she still here?

That question was answered for him a moment later when his bedroom door creaked open and he felt her presence in the room. The scent of magnolias came to him first, then the scent of baby powder as she leaned over him and placed a hand on his forehead. It was warm, and it moved to his cheek.

He caught it there and placed his own hand against it. "Why are you still here?" he whispered.

"I'm just being a friend," she whispered back.

He remembered the words from their disagreement the night he'd left her to go to Hadley's mother. He squeezed her hand punitively. "This is beyond the call of friendship. *I* didn't stay the night with Hadley."

"Maybe you're not as good a friend as I am."

Nate felt something wriggle against his body. He put a hand out and felt Garrett's foot dangling from Karma's arms. "Garrett," he said softly. "How are ya, buddy?"

*FINE. I like it here. Are you ever going to get out of there and play with me? We're making stuff in the kitchen. It smells great, but it's not to eat. Want to come and see? It's the middle of the night, and she doesn't even mind that I'm up!*

"HE'S FINE. If you don't mind..." her voice took on a suddenly casual tone "... we're going to hang around tonight and see how you are in the morning."

"What time is it, anyway?"

"Just after eleven."

He tried to focus on her in the darkness. He saw the light color of the baby's blanket, the porcelain of her face, the gleam of her eyes. "What about your work?"

"I went home for my laptop," she replied. "I'm working on it when Garrett's asleep. When he's awake and deigns to allow me time, I'm making Christmas ornaments. Nancy and Amy have coerced me into helping out for the party. The ornaments are best made in a kitchen, and yours is bigger than mine, so it's easier to do them here. Do you mind?"

"Of course not. But…I hate to disrupt your life. I mean, I'm not in danger of death, or anything."

She made a very disdainful, very feminine sound. "And you call yourself a doctor. You aren't strong enough to get up and get food, and until you feed that six-feet-something of stubborn pride, you're not going to get better."

She tried to pull away but he kept a grip on her hand. "And where did you get your M.D.?"

"I have common sense," she said. He wondered if she knew she was rubbing her thumb across his knuckles. "I don't need a degree. Go back to sleep. Toast and soft-boiled eggs for breakfast."

"Can't wait," he said. But he brought the palm of her hand to his lips and kissed it. "Thank you," he said.

"You're welcome," she replied. Her voice was barely audible. "Good night." She pulled against him again, and this time he thought it safer for both of them to let her go.

"Night, sport."

*NIGHT, Nate.*


PLACIDO DOMINGO'S VOICE boomed from the radio, though Karma had it turned down very low. It was

4:00 a.m. She'd settled Garrett in the travelall she'd brought back with the laptop. It opened into a bed and fit on the sofa in the shadowy living room.

But she had raging insomnia and was into cinnamon bear production big-time. Two dozen of the ornaments sat on a cookie sheet to dry, redolent of the cinnamon and applesauce that were their basic components. The bears were made of eight little balls formed in the flat of the hand, a bigger one for the stomach, four smaller ones for arms and legs, and two smaller still for ears. A small loop of wire made them ready to hang.

The eyes were made with the indentation of a pen or pencil tip. When the bears were dry, they would be dressed with a thin ribbon tied into a bow.

Seeing the little army of bears, Karma was reminded sharply of the many dozens her mother had made every Christmas. She recalled how much she'd loved helping with them as a child, how wonderful the cinnamon had made the bus smell, how much fun it had been to park the bus in a friend's driveway over the holidays and to remain in the same spot for several weeks.

She'd loved that the most. There'd been playgrounds, backyard swing sets, basketball hoops, dime stores and candy shops. Her allowance had been minimal, but it had been so much fun to look at all the toys and other niceties the bus lacked that she didn't mind being unable to spend.

Until she'd become a teenager. Then she'd hated everything about the life—the constant moving, the day-to-day uncertainty, the curious picture her parents made, her mother in her long, bright dress, her father in his beard and coveralls.

It wouldn't have been so bad, she'd always thought, if they were shy and reticent people. But they'd been loud and cheerful, eager to talk to anyone, always full of funny stories and outrageously sunny philosophy. She'd wanted to die.

Then, thanks to a caring teacher, she'd gone away to college and discovered a wonderful new world of comfort and order and stability. Though exuberant in her new lifestyle, she'd discovered that she missed her parents' cheer in this more sober environment. But they'd have been miserable in a conventional setting, and she would never go back to life on the road. And the accident had taken them.

She smiled as she thought of them, then felt a salty tear on her lip. She swiped at her eyes and uttered a little laugh, then dabbed at her mouth with a paper towel.

Twenty-four perfectly formed little bears looked at her from the cookie sheet, reminding her that she'd gotten more from her childhood than she sometimes thought. And that there had once been a time when she'd enjoyed the warmth of Christmas.

One perfectly formed little baby reminded her that the future was bright with promise, if she took the best of what she remembered and coupled it with the best of what she'd learned. Then she would put all of it into protecting and caring for the son who would be her reach into infinity.

Karma set the bears aside to dry, tidied the kitchen, then covered the rest of the dough and put it in the refrigerator. Garrett slept on.

Karma looked out the window and found that the autumn sky was still dark at 5:00 a.m. She curled up on the sofa with her coat over her shoulders, and decided to nap for a couple of hours, until Nate was ready for breakfast.

She closed her eyes and found herself wondering what life would be like confined with Nate on a bus. The palm of her hand tickled, and she remembered the touch of his lips, there in the darkness of his bedroom. She closed her hand tightly and fell asleep.

"ARE YOU AWAKE?"

Nate heard the voice and surfaced from sleep long enough to assign it an owner. It wasn't Karma. He lost interest and slipped back into the downy comfort of his pillow.

"Nate." The whisper was accompanied by a jab in his shoulder.

He grumbled a complaint.

Then he smelled coffee. The aroma was strong and rich and he could feel the heat coming from it. For the first time in days, it didn't make his stomach roil. He felt himself salivate for it.

He opened an eye and saw Tom Nicholas kneeling beside his bed, passing an open paper cup of coffee under his nose.

"Is that for me?" he asked. His voice sounded thick, and not quite conscious.

Tom held up a bag. "And there's a cranberry scone to go with it. Are you awake?"

Nate wanted to push himself up, but he wasn't sure he had the necessary reserves of strength. So he took a minute to simply consider it. "I'm trying to be."

Tom put the coffee and bag on the bedside table and went to the doorway and peered out. Then he came back and said under his breath, "You know, I don't want to alarm you, but there's a beautiful brunette asleep on your sofa. And she has a baby. Are you listening to me?"

Nate nodded into his pillow. "Beautiful brunette. Sofa. Baby."

"What's Karma Endicott doing there?"

"You said she was sleeping."

"Okay, that's it."

Nate heard the crunch of paper as Tom grabbed the bag and cup and prepared to leave.

"I'm out of here. Next time you need someone to nurse you through the plague, call my brother."

"Okay. Okay." Nate pushed himself to a sitting position and winced against the daylight. "I'm up. I didn't call you, you came despite all my protests, and it was bad chicken salad, not the plague . . . though it did feel fatal."

"Whatever you say. What about Karma and the baby on the sofa? Is this your wild past come home to roost?"

Nate opened his eyes a little wider. So he hadn't dreamed last night. She'd been here. "That's my nurse," he said, pushing himself shakily to his feet.

Tom reached out to steady him when the last few inches became difficult. "Where are the square white shoes and the Stalinesque manner?"

Nate grinned and turned in the direction of the bathroom.

"Well, I only brought two coffees," Tom said. "Maybe I should put on a pot."

"Help yourself. I need a shower. Don't wake her."

"Afraid she'll prefer me to you?"

Nate gave him a not-a-chance look. "Please. She's a very discerning woman."

KARMA *did* seem to be enjoying Tom's company, Nate noticed twenty minutes later, when he walked into the kitchen, freshly showered and wearing jeans and a red-and-gray plaid flannel shirt. She was placing scones and cups of coffee on a tray, and he was giving Garrett his bottle. Dark jealousy rampaged through Nate's chest. He drew a steadying breath. He knew the emotion was unwarranted, but it was virulent all the same.

"Hi!" Karma noticed him with obvious pleasure and came toward him to take his arm in her good one and help him toward a stool. He gave Tom a superior look over his shoulder. "Are you sure you should be up?" she asked.

"I'm sure," he said. "And I think I can handle coffee and a scone."

She looked at him doubtfully. "I don't know. You just started eating real food yesterday."

He was touched by her concern, and confounded by the knowledge that she'd stayed all night and slept on the sofa. And he felt all kinds of other things he wasn't strong enough to do anything about this morning. But this afternoon might be another story.

"As I recall," he argued, letting his eyes betray what he was thinking, "we decided during the night that you have the common sense, but I have the medical degree."

Her cheeks grew pink and her eyes grew languid. He felt his pulse pick up and knew it had nothing to do with a relapse.

Her eyes held his and told him in no uncertain terms that her thoughts were following his. Then she seemed to remember Tom's presence and turned her attention back to the tray.

Nate went to take Garrett from Tom. "Hi, big guy. What's new with you? Gained another pound this week, didn't you?"

*I DON'T SEE HOW. All I get's milk, and you guys get all the good things. Like what's that triangle thing with the little red stuff in it? Can I have a bite? With butter. Nobody ever gives me butter.*

"YOU'RE going to be on people food in no time," he said, teasing Garrett's lips with the nipple of the bottle. "But for now, this is your cocktail, buddy."

Tom took the tray from Karma, and they gathered around the farm-style table in the middle of the room.

"I'll take him so you can enjoy your scone," Karma said, trying to do just that.

Nate pushed her hand away. "I'm fine. He probably needs a little guy company. It's too bad he has to be exposed to the likes of Tom at such a tender age, but life is hard."

Tom shook his head at Karma. "That's the thanks I get for helping him through the fever crisis."

Nate rolled his eyes. "There was no fever crisis. You turned my electric blanket up too high and almost roasted me." Nate passed Karma the butter. "Never let a carpenter nurse you. They tend to repair things with nails and glue."

Tom made a face at him. "I'm good enough to cut out stars for the Christmas party."

"I saw them," Karma said, passing the butter on to Tom. "I was at Coffee Country yesterday, and Nancy and Amy were firming up their plans for decorations." She frowned suddenly at Nate. "Did you hear that Jo moved to Connecticut?"

Before Nate could comment, Tom said cheerfully, "No, she's back. Just this morning. Nancy told me."

Karma raised her good arm in the air. "All right! Nancy believed she'd come home."

Tom grinned. "She should write romances, instead of murder mysteries."

"Anyway," Karma said, wondering if there was something she could do about Amy's floundering romance, "your stars are beautiful, Tom. Have you seen Nancy's snowflakes?"

He nodded. "Was there this morning. She and the boys are still cutting them out."

Karma glanced conspiratorially under her lashes at Nate. "Have you seen Amy's angels?" she asked Tom.

It took him a moment to answer. "Ah... just the prototype."

She nodded enthusiastically. "It's beautifully done. I didn't think she was looking very well, though."

Tom's gaze sharpened on her. "Why not?"

Nate pretended interest in his coffee.

Karma shrugged a shoulder and broke off a tip of her scone. "She looks... I don't know. Wistful. Even heartbroken. She was talking about moving to New York to be with her sister."

Tom looked stricken for a moment, but then he took a sip of coffee and sat back in his chair. "Might be good for her. I'm not sure she's enjoying her work at the hospital."

"I think she likes it fine," Nate said. "I think something else is bothering her."

Tom met his steady gaze head-on. Nate didn't flinch. The implication that Tom himself was Amy's problem was plainly visible on his face. Tom finally excused himself and grabbed his jacket off the back of his chair.

"It was a pleasure meeting you, Karma," he said politely. Then he turned to Nate with a far less congenial expression. "And you—I hope you *do* have a fever crisis."

Nate smiled amiably. "I'll see you to the door."

Tom marched to his truck, which was parked behind Karma's Volvo. Nate followed intrepidly.

"My life," Tom said, stopping at the driver's-side door to growl at his friend, "is not your business."

"I beg your pardon," Nate replied, "but it is. You're going to blow off this relationship, because it's easier to hurt than to get better."

Tom spread his hands in a gesture of utter frustration. "How in the hell would you know?"

"I do," Nate said calmly. "And if you were just ruining your life, I'd think, 'Hey. There are enough of us around who love you to do our best to see you through.' But you're ruining hers, too. And she doesn't have the kind of understanding support you have."

"At least," Tom said quietly, angrily, "I'm not afraid of babies."

Tom accepted that barb with equanimity. "You'll notice there's one in my kitchen right now. I'm trying to learn to deal with *my* fears. You should do the same." He slapped Tom on the shoulder. "Thanks for the coffee and scones."

Tom shrugged him off. "Go to hell."

Nate waved and headed back to the house. "See you there."

He found Karma standing just inside the doorway, the baby asleep in her arms. She'd obviously been eavesdropping. She smiled wryly. "You think maybe we were too subtle?"

He wrapped an arm around her and drew her inside. "He'll come to his senses. I have faith in his intelligence. But what I really want to know is, *is* there a subtle message in the fact that you heard I was ill, hurried to my aid, tucked me up in bed, fed me, and stayed the night to watch over me?"

He led her toward the kitchen as he spoke. He took the baby from her and shushed him when he stirred. He placed him in the carrier, then drew Karma into his arms.

*Aw, come on. I spend so much time in this thing, it's growing onto my backside. Could we go somewhere? Do something? I like it when we walk around. Or when we're all in the car.*

"YOU KNOW," Nate said, his eyes looking deeply into her eyes, "a man could think you were being more than a friend."

"I was." She wrapped her good arm around his neck and met his gaze boldly, letting him see the truth as she knew it. "I was being a friend and a nurse," she added teasingly.

"A nurse who stayed the night."

"On the sofa."

He held her tighter, his eyes smoldering. "Well, let's do that the right way tonight. Or, why wait till tonight?"

Nate swept her up in his arms before she could protest.

"Put me down," Karma said, laughing. "You've just been out of bed an hour after four days of... Ah!"

He reeled, with an attack of dizziness, she guessed, and strode forward to drop her in a sitting position on the counter. He leaned his upper body against hers weakly as he laughed in self-deprecation.

"Maybe we should wait until tomorrow night," he said, then raised his head to add weakly, hopefully, "Unless you're the type of woman who likes to be in charge?"

She kissed his forehead. "Oh, I do. But I have work to do, and you have to rest. I imagine they'll expect you back at the hospital soon."

With a surge of energy that surprised her, he wrapped his hands around her thighs and pulled them around his hips until there was no space between their bodies, until they shared a single heartbeat.

She sobered, shaken by the power of her desire for him and his for her. Caution seemed insignificant in the face of it.

"It's about to happen, you know," he said, his turbulent blue eyes on a level with her wide brown gaze. "We're about to become lovers."

"We have to know more..." Her voice was a frail whisper as she felt every one of his fingertips against her thighs, even through the fabric of her slacks. Sensation rippled up every vertebra.

"I adore you," he said softly, his lips a millimeter from hers. "What else is there to know?"

She couldn't think, couldn't reason. She dropped her forehead against his shoulder and simply held him.

They leaned into each other for a few moments. Then Nate's voice, filled with soft amusement, said suddenly, "Why, Karma Endicott."

She lifted her head. "What?"

He pointed to the tray of cinnamon bears drying in the corner of his counter. "What are those?"

"Ornaments," she replied. "I told you about them last night, remember?"

They studied each other quietly for a moment, each indulging a personal memory of those few minutes in the darkness.

He grinned. Her heart thumped in response.

"For the party?" he asked.

She nodded. "Nancy said—"

He interrupted her, his smile indulgent. "Karma. You've caught the Christmas spirit."

"No, I haven't," she answered quickly. "I was bullied into this."

"Karma." His scolding tone suggested she was lying. "They look as though they were made with care and attention."

"I do *everything* with care and attention," she said. "That has nothing..."

"Mmm..." he said, focusing on her lips. "I like the sound of that."

He took a gentle fistful of her hair, pulled her closer, and kissed her soundly. She clung to his shoulder with her good arm, feeling her temperature rise, her heartbeat quicken to the point of explosion, her limbs turn to jelly.

Nate knew he was losing all reason. He wanted this woman with a desperation that made him forget that he hadn't wanted a wife, that he hadn't wanted children.

All he knew with any certainty was that he wanted *her.* Her ardent lips along his jaw, her small hand exploring his back, her knees tightening around him in what he hoped was a physical reaction to what her mind was imagining— all drove him to the brink of frustrated madness.

Then, almost simultaneously, two jarring sounds forced him to free her. The phone rang, and the baby cried.

With a groan of reluctant acceptance, Nate lifted Karma off the counter and set her on her feet. He went to the telephone.

MOTHER, *where are you? Why does this always happen? I rest my eyes for a few minutes and everyone disappears! Are we going out? Can I have one of those little brown things that smell so good? Where's Nate? I want Nate.*

KARMA picked up her son and held him against her, grateful that he'd awakened and forced her back to reality. One more moment of Nate's persuasion, and she'd have forgotten that a few things remained unresolved between them.

He hung up the phone and turned to her, a wry quirk to his smile.

"Hadley?" she asked. "Barb?"

"Joanie," he replied.

She stopped and frowned. "Is that a new one?" With the hand that held Garrett, she pointed to her purse, on the back of a kitchen chair. "Would you put that on my shoulder?"

He obliged her, then pinched her chin. "No. She's an ER nurse. Flu's going around the hospital, and there's no one to cover for me tonight, so I guess I'm back on duty."

Karma felt both disappointed and grateful for the reprieve. She wanted to be with him more than she wanted anything. But the squalling bundle in her arms reminded her that she had more than her own needs to consider.

She sighed and smiled thinly. "You really need a few more days' rest."

He took her face in his hands and leaned down to kiss her gently. "I'll be fine. Let me take Garrett while you get your jacket. Hey, buddy. What's all the fuss about?"

*ARE YOU COMING WITH US? Did you eat all those triangle things? I'm sleepy. We were up working most of the night, you know, and something's not right with my mother, I can feel it. She's nervous, or worried, or something. Please come with us. She smiles more when you're around.*

"CAN I LEAVE THE BEARS to dry a few days?" Karma asked. "I'm afraid they'll get jostled in the back of the car."

"Of course," he said. "That means you'll have to come back for them."

She looked around her at the cozy, rustic environment and nodded. "This is a wonderful house. Coming back would be no hardship."

He was happy to hear that. He followed her to the car with Garrett in a football hold in one arm and the carrier dangling from his other hand. Garrett complained loudly when he placed him in the car seat.

*I WANT YOU to come with us!*

"COME ON, buddy," Nate coaxed futilely, checking straps and buckles. "Be good for your mom. She's had a long night."

*I WAS THERE part of the time, too, you know. I want you to come with us!*

KARMA SIGHED in resignation as Nate closed the car door for her. She opened her window. "He has a fit every time you and I part company. I hope you realize this means I'm in for another day of not being able to concentrate on the computer, and another sleepless night."

He leaned into the open window to kiss her lingeringly. "You can make more bears," he said softly, then kissed her again. "And we'll have to think about a solution that'll make us all happy."

She raised an eyebrow doubtfully. "Is there one?"

"Christmas," he said, "is the season of miracles."

"It won't even be Thanksgiving," she pointed out, "for another week."

He looked at her sternly. "I will not believe you're hopeless. I will turn you into a believer."

She kissed him. "I believe in you. Is that enough?"

He was touched out of all proportion by the simple dec-
laration. "It's a damned good start," he said, then backed
away, while he still could. He ducked down to wave. "I'll
probably be working long hours, but I'll call when I can."

Karma blew him a kiss and backed out of the driveway,
Garrett screaming in the back seat.

*NOBODY KISSED ME! I wanted him to come with us! How
come I always have to sit back here all alone? I can't move
in this thing. I like it better on the floor, where I can get
some action going.*

*Are you listening to me? I wanted him to come with us!*

KARMA found Garrett's screaming, purple face in the rear-
view mirror and smiled at him. "I know, sweetie. I'm going to miss him, too. I know you think he belongs to us
because he's been around from the moment you arrived,
but he isn't really ours. And you have to understand that.
I'd like it to be different—and it might. But it might not.
You have to be ready for that. Okay?"

*OF COURSE NOT! I want him!*

# Chapter Ten

"Karma. Hi, it's me."

"Nate, hi!" Karma needed no more identification than the sound of his voice on the telephone. Her lack of concentration over the past few days was only partly due to Garrett's continuous screaming. Loneliness was also responsible. She thought about Nate continuously.

"Did you get my message?" he asked.

She had. He'd called to tell her he was working back-to-back shifts, and that he missed her. When she called back, he'd had a patient and been unable to come to the phone.

"Yes," she replied, wondering if she should tell him she hadn't erased it, that she'd played it over and over just to hear his voice. "How are you feeling?"

"I'm completely recovered," he said. "I had a forty-year-old man going into cardiac arrest just as I was walking in the door that first night back. And things haven't slowed down since. How's Garrett?"

She groaned. "I imagine Attila the Hun was probably a better baby than he's been the past few days. I can't seem to make him happy."

*ARE YOU TALKING TO HIM? Tell him to come home! I want him now!*

"CAN YOU hear him screaming?" she asked. "The little darling's decided he hates me. Nancy has volunteered to take him for me for a few hours this afternoon so I can get some shopping done without driving everyone else out of the store. I don't suppose you'll be having a coffee break about that time?"

Nate would rather have been able to say yes to that question than win the lottery. But just the knowledge that she'd asked it helped blunt the disappointment.

"I'd kill to be able to say yes," he said wearily, "but that would only contribute to my work load. We've got a rent-a-doc from Portland, and he's great, but I hate to leave him alone."

There was an instant's silence. "A rent-a-doc?"

He laughed. "We use a staffing agency in Portland that provides us with doctors when we're shorthanded. They have a more formal name, but that's what we call them. It's sort of like a temp service, only they're medical people."

"What a world," she said, marveling that such a thing existed. "Well, I guess I'll just have to think about you when I stop at Coffee Country, and pretend you're sitting across the table."

She heard a smile in his voice. "And I'll think of you when I snitch the waiting room's coffee. Did Nancy tell you about Thanksgiving?"

"No."

"We're invited for dinner. I managed to get the afternoon off, but I have to go in at midnight. I'll pick you up at two, but we'll have to use your car. Mine doesn't have room for Garrett's car seat."

She felt a stir of excitement. She'd envisioned a lonely meal of turkey roll and Rice-a-Roni, with Nate working and Bert going to her parents' in Seattle.

"That would be fine, but are you sure Garrett and I are invited?"

"Yes, she was very specific. She said bring your lady-love." There was a velvet pause. "That's you."

A little shiver ran the length of her body. "How dare you tell me that," she scolded weakly, "over the telephone!"

"I'll reiterate," he promised, his voice rich and quiet, "when I pick you up Thursday. Wear that suit you wore the night I took you to dinner."

His name was shouted with loud urgency somewhere in the background.

"Gotta go," he said. "Kiss Garrett for me. I'll take care of you myself on Thursday."

Karma hung up the phone, putting a hand to her palpitating heart. Then she picked up her screaming son and rocked him from side to side.

She kissed his cheek. "That's from Nate, baby," she said, so thrilled by the phone call that she almost didn't notice that Garrett remained unappeased.

*WELL, how come he couldn't deliver it himself? Where is he, anyway? I want him here! And isn't it time for milk?*

"WHAT IN THE HELL did you say to Tom?" Jave asked Nate. He stood behind him at the candy machine in the hospital's deserted cafeteria. It was 2:00 a.m., and Jave had been called in to replace one of his technicians, who'd gone home ill.

Nate took a chocolate bar out of the chute and stepped aside. "I told him he'd rather be in pain than get over what happened," he replied, his brow furrowed. "Brutal, I know, but I'm getting desperate. I told him he could ruin his life, but he had no right to ruin Amy's."

Jave put two quarters into the machine and pulled the lever for salsa-flavored corn chips. "Did you tell him I asked you to spy on him?"

"No." They walked side by side to a round table in a corner. "He figured it out for himself."

Jave ripped the bag open as he fell into a chair. "Thanks a lot. You were supposed to learn everything so shrewdly that he didn't suspect, so that if it worked I could be the hero. Now, I'm the villain. See if I engage your services again."

Nate leaned his head back against the wall. He was so tired he felt as though his bones were made of paper. He bit off a third of the candy bar and chewed.

"Well," he said after he swallowed, "I'd let you dismiss me, but I care too much. What are we going to do about him?"

Jave popped a red chip into his mouth and shook his head. "He's that close to coming around." He held his thumb and index finger an inch apart. "But it's more than putting the pain behind him, it's consigning his friend and the fire department to the past. And he can't do it until he can absolve himself of the blame."

"Everything's so damned complicated," Nate grumbled moodily. "Even things that shouldn't be."

Jave grinned. "Like love?"

Nate closed his eyes and sighed. "I haven't even slept with Karma, and I love her so much it makes me crazy."

Jave laughed softly. "Been there. Done that."

Nate opened his eyes, but it required effort. "And you and Nancy are happy now?"

"Deliriously."

"No lie?"

"No lie. I understand Karma's making Christmas ornaments for the party. Nancy thought they were wonderful."

"Yeah. Cinnamon bears. They're all over my kitchen. I'm in trouble, Jave."

Jave pretended surprise. "I thought you hadn't slept together yet."

Nate tossed his empty candy wrapper at him. "Not that kind of trouble. I think about her all the time. I love her baby."

"Uh-oh."

"I know. I'd make a nervous-Nellie father."

"Cheer up. Maybe she won't have you."

Nate smiled wearily. "You always know the right thing to say."

"Dr. Foster to the ER, stat!" an urgent voice called on the intercom. Nate remained still for one second, gathering his forces. "I'm going to have my name changed," he threatened. Then he stood, slapped Jave on the shoulder and loped for the door.

"How about Dr. Nervous Nellie?" Jave called after him.

KARMA DIDN'T HAVE TIME to say hello. She opened her front door at two o'clock Thursday afternoon and was swept up into a pair of arms so eager she barely identified their owner before they crushed her to him.

But she now knew Nate, she thought, with a power that went beyond the five senses. There was a connection between them that didn't require sight or sound or touch. She could be blindfolded now, she thought, and know him the moment he drew near.

But she was very glad she wasn't deprived of her standard senses when she held on fiercely to his strong shoulders, when she smelled his herbal cologne, tasted his eager mouth, saw the love in his eyes, and heard him say in deadly earnest, "I love you, Karma. I *love* you. And, God, I've missed you."

Karma leaned against him and let the love words bathe her in their warmth. They made up for the loneliness of the past week—even for the loneliness of a lifetime.

She felt suddenly as though the sun had been turned on directly over her head.

"I love you, too," she said, hugging him tighter. "Do we really have all afternoon and evening?"

Pride, satisfaction, awe—all roiled in Nate's chest like some wonderful storm. She loved him. Well. He'd wanted to hear that admission more than anything, but there'd been moments when he doubted it could ever happen. He was humbled by the fact of it, and gave himself a moment to savor it.

"We do," he said finally, setting her on her feet and closing the door behind him. He laced his fingers in hers again and swept them downward so that they were body to body. Then he stood back in surprise and held up the two hands he held. The left one no longer sported a cast.

"All right!" he said, running his fingertips gently into her sleeve. "When did this happen? How does it feel?"

"Yesterday," she replied. "And it feels wonderful. Good as new. And it certainly simplifies my life."

He kissed her hand, then wrapped her arm around his neck. "Want to forget the dinner and stay home?" he asked with a waggle of his eyebrows. "See what else you can do with it?"

She nuzzled his cheek. "We can't. I'm bringing the pies. Besides..." She raised her head to smile into his eyes. "It's Thanksgiving. And we have so much to be thankful for."

The look in her eyes was a caress. Nate felt it everywhere.

She took his hand and pulled him into the kitchen, where Garrett, in his carrier on the kitchen table, shrieked angrily.

"I wanted to show you what I've been working on," she shouted above the baby's cries, "but I think you'd better pay attention to him first."

Nate lifted Garrett out of the blankets and held him over his head. The baby stopped screaming, but looked far from pleased. His large dark eyes threatened a new eruption of displeasure.

"What's happening, dude?" Nate asked, playing him like a trombone. "We're going to dinner. You're wearing a spiffy new outfit, and your mom and I are in love. What could possibly be wrong?"

*WHERE HAVE YOU BEEN? I've been calling you for days! This suit is dorky! Would you go out with something that has snaps on the legs and a sailor collar? Where's my bow tie? Mother has no sense of style, where I'm concerned, and those girls are going to be there. I bet they'll have a lot to say about my suit.*

*You and Mother are what?*

NATE PULLED HIM to his shoulder and patted his back. "It's okay," he said. "Just relax. Everything's going to be fine." He stopped in surprise at the sight of the small kitchen, cluttered with Christmas decorations in various stages of preparation. "Whoa! Did you and your mom do all this?"

He pointed to a group of flat Christmas shapes that looked as though they'd been made of candle wax.

"What are those?" he asked, then sniffed the air. He smelled clover.

"They're made of beeswax," she said, "in a candy mold." She pointed to the half-dozen bare wreaths that hung on cabinet knobs. "Those are made from the grapevines behind Jave's house. Nancy let me cut them the other day, when she watched Garrett.''

He studied the circular and elliptical shapes. ''How did you make them malleable?''

''You soak them in warm water in the bathtub. Amy's going to decorate them for the fairground doors. Oh. And before I forget to return this to you...'' She took the rag doll from her computer desk and handed it to him. ''Here she is. All well again. And you thought *you* were the one with the medical degree.''

She gave him a teasingly superior look as she made to walk past him to the guest closet.

He caught her arm and pulled her to him, Garrett crushed between them.

*ALL RIGHT. This is more like it. Now, see? If you stuck around, we could do this all the time.*

''YOU'D BETTER PACK some things for the baby,'' Nate said as he nuzzled Karma's ear. Then he straightened to look into her eyes. His bore a message that she understood clearly. ''Because I'm taking you home with me after the party.''

She framed his face in her hands and kissed him. ''Yes,'' she said.

NANCY'S DOOR was opened by an older woman wearing a white sweatshirt with a giant sunflower on it. She had wiry gray hair and a serious expression.

''Yes?'' she asked gravely.

''Hi, Aggie,'' Nate said warmly. He stood behind Karma, with Garrett in his arms. ''Happy Thanksgiving.''

She looked from him to Karma. ''You're here for dinner?''

"Yes."

"Show me your passes."

Karma saw the humor in the woman's wink at Nate and held up the pie in her left hand. "Pumpkin custard," she said, then held up the other. "Apple. We decided against mince."

The woman smiled broadly. "Good decision. Welcome. You must be Karma. I'm Aggie, Jave and Tom's mother. Since I'm the only mother-in-law here, I feel called upon to be difficult. The good cheer at this party is so thick, I thought some balance was required. Come in, come in."

The two boys who'd been with Nancy when she stopped in Karma's room at the hospital took their coats.

"You know Eddy and Pete?" Nate asked Karma.

She nodded. "Garrett and I met them right after he was born."

"Wow!" Pete said of Garrett. "Look at how big he's gotten. Malia isn't that big."

"Chelsea is, though," Eddy said. "She's a real porker. It's so weird that all three babies were born on the same day, in the same place."

"They all wanted to try the hospital's new birthing rooms," Jave said. In a white sweater and slim jeans, he strode toward them, carrying two glasses of wine. "Welcome. Come on. We're all in the kitchen. Nancy and Jo are cooking together." He winced, then added under his breath, "Mom insists she won't set foot in the kitchen, because this is Nancy's show, so we may have to send out for pizza. I just want you to be forewarned."

Karma handed him the pies. "It's just wonderful to be here. Thank you for inviting me."

Jave smiled at her before turning in the direction of the kitchen. "I'm glad you were free. I understand you've caught the Christmas spirit. I saw one of your bears."

"No, I haven't," Karma said. "What I caught was some bullying from Nancy. That's all."

"Really." He didn't seem convinced. "Hey, guys," he called to the occupants of the kitchen. "Look who's here."

Jo and Nancy stood over an open oven in which a very white turkey sat in a roasting pan. Ryan Jeffries and Tom Nicholas sat at the table, peeling potatoes.

Everyone looked up with cheerful greetings. Tom booed at Nate, then pointed to the chair beside him with a fractional smile. "Park it. You can do the green beans. And you're not going to get out of it by holding a baby."

"Here." Aggie appeared beside Nate. "Give him to me." She pointed to the edge of the room, where a playpen held Malia and Chelsea. "Let's see what kind of a ladies' man he is."

*MALIA: Hi. Did you mug a sailor for that suit?*
*Garrett: Don't start with me. Where'd you buy your hair?*
*Chelsea: Hey! What's the matter with you two? Our parents are having a party. Try to get along.*
*Malia: Yeah? Well, watch your binky. He's a thief!*

KARMA WENT to join Jo and Nancy. She gave Jo a heartfelt hug.

"Shouldn't the bird be browning by now?" Nancy asked worriedly. She wore a jeweled black sweater over white stirrup pants, and over them—as an apron, Karma guessed—was a pale green hospital coat.

Jo shrugged an elegant shoulder in a blue silk blouse. A barbecue apron protected a long, matching skirt. She fairly glowed. "Well...white meat is supposed to be healthier, isn't it?"

Nancy looked up at her with a frown. "White meat *inside,* not outside."

"Did you put butter on it?" Karma asked. "Have you been basting?"

"The butter keeps falling off," Nancy said, "and burns in the bottom of the pan."

Karma bit back a smile. "Do you have cheesecloth?" she asked.

Nancy turned to Jave, who was placing a colander of green beans in front of Nate. "Honey, do we—?"

"Bottom drawer, right side," Aggie called before Nancy could finish the question. She'd positioned a rocking chair near the playpen, and she had one eye on the babies and one on the television.

The boys had taken their places with the men and were making faces as they peeled carrots and turnips.

"A small pan to melt butter in?" Karma asked.

"Right." Nancy handed Karma a small saucepan and a cube of butter, then wrapped a colorful cobbler apron around her. She grinned at Jo. "I love a take-charge woman, don't you? Even if she doesn't have the Christmas spirit."

"Don't hassle me." Karma laughed. "It's too early for the Christmas spirit."

Jo shook her head. "Mine starts when the first leaf falls and doesn't quit till the middle of January." Then she frowned worriedly as Karma cut off a length of cheesecloth and placed it in the pan with the butter. "Oh, God. She's going to cook cheesecloth."

Nancy looked over Karma's shoulder. "Maybe she's making cheese*cake?*"

Karma blinked worriedly at one woman, then the other. "It frightens me that you two are feeding children."

Jo shook her head. "Ryan cooks at our house. And the baby's still taking milk."

"Aggie cooks for us," Nancy admitted. "But I insisted she wouldn't have to lift a finger today."

Karma pushed her sleeves up. "Well, we're all lucky you invited me. We're going to cover this anemic bird and hope it isn't too late." She carried the pan, along with the cheesecloth soaked in melted butter, to the open oven door. She lifted the cheesecloth with a fork and opened it out over the turkey, then poured the butter left in the bottom of the pan over the top of the cloth.

"That'll give it some juice to work on, and pretty soon we'll have something to baste with. Tinfoil?"

Nancy handed it to her. She fitted it over the bird, pushed the rack in with a hotpad and closed the door. "Do you have a baster?"

"Second utensil drawer to the right," Aggie called.

Nancy found it. "Baste every half hour. Can I do anything else?"

Jo eyed her respectfully. "Can you make gravy?"

"Sure."

"Without a *can* of gravy?" Nancy asked.

"Yes. We'll have to wait for juice from the bird. Did you save the giblets?"

"Now how did *you* rate a woman who can cook?" Ryan asked Nate as he plopped a peeled potato into the pan of water that stood on the table between him and Tom.

"Who cares?" Jave said. "It looks like dinner is saved."

Nate looked up at the counter, where Karma was moving comfortably, laughingly, between Nancy and Jo, and felt a curious warmth inside him that he identified as domestic happiness. God. It was happening. He'd been so sure he'd be the only holdout in his circle of friends. An here he was, in the midst of their married and child-rearing circle and feeling very much as though he belonged.

Karma turned away from the counter to look toward the playpen, then caught his eye when she turned back. She winked at him. He winked back. He was lost.

*GARRETT: That's my mother. The one that's cooking.*

*Malia: Mine's wearing Daddy's hospital coat. And that's him in the white sweater.*

*Chelsea: Mine's the one peeling potatoes with Malia's uncle. Where's yours?*

*Garrett: The one in the black turtleneck.*

*Malia: He's not your father. He has to live with you to be your father. The one in the black turtleneck lives in the woods. Daddy and I took him soup and stuff when he was sick. And Mom and I went to your mother's house, and it's not the same place. He's not your daddy. You don't have one.*

*Garrett: He is, too. He was there the day I got here. He comes over all the time.*

*Chelsea: To be your daddy, he has to stay over. Everybody knows that.*

*Malia: Yeah. And I still think that's a silly suit.*

A SCREECH erupted from the playpen, followed immediately by a long, mournful wail.

Aggie lifted Garrett out of the playpen and tried to rock him, but he continued to scream.

"Oh, that's temper," she said with a laugh. "What did you girls say to him?"

Karma, chopping giblets, put the knife aside and began to dry her hands.

But Nate stood. "I'll get him," he said. "You keep the food going." He took Garrett from Aggie and held him to his shoulder. The baby settled there with quieter, calmer sobs.

*DID YOU HEAR THAT? They said you're not mine! How come? Why not? If they have a dad, why don't I? They're probably wrong, aren't they? Aren't you my dad?*

"WHAT'S THE MATTER, buddy? Didn't lunch agree with you?" Nate walked into the dining room, pacing with Garrett as he patted his back and tried to quiet him. He'd always been a tearful baby, but he sounded particularly unhappy now.

"It's all right, you know," he said, walking to the window with him and holding him so that he could look out. "Can you see that? Trees that are red and gold. Cozy neighborhood houses with chimneys smoking and turkeys cooking. This is the life. You've got it made. You get to sleep curled up to your mom."

*BUT I DON'T HAVE A DAD!*

"AND YOU KNOW WHAT? Tonight, you're going to have to start sharing her with me. She's not going to belong just to you anymore. She's going to be mine, too. And I'm going to be hers."

*THEN . . . does that make you* mine?

"THIS IS kind of a big move for me," Nate went on, easing Garrett into a sitting position on his arm. "I didn't think I'd ever be able to get serious about a woman and a baby. But your mom's very special—and so are you. So, you promise me you're not going to make me crazy with worry? Hang upside down from monkey bars, and stuff like that?"

*I DON'T KNOW. You promise me you're going to stay?*

"I CAN'T BELIEVE," Tom said, his eyes glazed with satiety, "how delicious that was. I fully expected you to poison us, Nancy."

Nancy smiled blandly at her brother-in-law. "Thank you, Tom. Actually, you have Karma to thank for the success of our Thanksgiving feast. And, of course, all of you who peeled spuds and vegetables."

"She can make gravy," Jo marveled, "without a *can.*"

Ryan patted Jo's back supportively. "It's all right, darling. You did make good coffee."

She smiled proudly. "I did, didn't I? Well, I can cut pie, too. So if you gentlemen want to settle yourselves in front of the football game with one or the other of the Christmas projects, I'll bring pie and coffee along in a few minutes."

Karma began to stack plates, and Nancy slapped her hand. "No. Your work is done. You relax while I clean up."

"*I'll* clean up," Aggie volunteered, "with Pete and Eddy's help, while you feed the baby."

Both boys groaned.

"Santa's watching, guys," Tom reminded.

"Then maybe you should help them," Jave suggested, "because you have a lot to do to get off the naughty and onto the nice list. In fact, in only a month's time, I doubt that you could—"

"Who asked you?" Tom demanded. "Did anyone ask you? Come on, guys. We'll show your father how this is done with style and efficiency."

"Ha!" Nate carried the platter, with its almost bare turkey carcass, to the kitchen counter. "For efficiency to result, you would have to be absent."

Ryan followed with two empty bowls. "Or at least tied to a chair."

Tom glared at them, then put an arm around each of his nephews. "The moral here, guys, is that you can't help being stuck with your brother, but you should exercise great care in picking your friends."

Nate and Ryan stayed to help, taking every opportunity to harass Tom. Aggie loaded dishes into the dishwasher with experienced speed, then filled the sink with sudsy water for the roaster and the outsize pots and pans.

"Those should soak for a little while," she said, shooing men and boys out of the kitchen. "Thank you for your help. Go have your pie and watch the game."

"You'll notice that your *good* son," Tom said exaggeratedly, indicating Jave's absence, "didn't stay to help."

Aggie patted his cheek. "I know, but he made the dressing and brought the extra chairs in from the garage while you were on the computer with the boys, playing Zork."

Eddy smiled up at him sympathetically. "I guess you should pick your mother carefully, too, huh, Unc?"

Tom sighed. "That's a little more difficult to do."

Pete shook his head. "It wasn't for us. We picked Nancy."

Nancy appeared just in time to hear the pleasure with which her stepson spoke the words. She wrapped her arms around him and hugged him. "Thank you. That was the best thing anybody ever did for me. Did anyone save me a piece of pie?"

"No pie," Jo said severely, passing her by with a dessert plate in each hand, "until you pick a Christmas project and settle down in front of the television. We don't want you tracking crumbs all over the place."

Nancy frowned at her. "Jo, this is my house."

"I know, but I promised to clean up afterward, and I'd rather not be faced with a mess. Pumpkin or apple? You can help me cut out snowflakes."

Jave and Ryan and the boys settled on a tarp on the carpet with stars cut out of pine and a can of yellow paint.

Jo and Nancy lay on the floor, a board between them, a stack of foam sheets, and two snowflake patterns. Malia lay on a blanket on the floor beside her mother, fast asleep.

Aggie sat in the rocking chair, with Chelsea in one arm and Garrett in the other.

*CHELSEA: I love this time when they need to rest, so they rock us to have an excuse.*
*Garrett: Yeah. Cool.*

NATE, faced with a coffee table covered with stars and a jar of glitter, looked around for support from Karma. But she was nowhere in sight. He went into the kitchen and found Tom leaning pensively in a corner of the counter. "Have you seen Karma?" he asked.

Tom looked almost surprised to see him there, as though he'd been far away in thought. "Huh? Ah, yeah. She went outside."

"Outside?" Nate repeated in surprise. It was cold, and threatening rain. "Why?"

Tom focused on him. "Who can explain why women do what they do? You do what you think they want, but you aren't doing it right, or your motives aren't right. Go figure."

Nate was torn for a moment between wondering where Karma had gone and wanting to be available to his friend's suddenly communicative mood. Sure Karma was in no danger, he leaned a hip on the counter beside Tom.

"We're talking about Amy?" he asked carefully.

Tom nodded. "She thinks a part of me is closed off to her."

Nate reached to the coffeepot beside them and poured two cups. He was going to need caffeine for this.

"Is it?" he asked, handing Tom a cup.

Tom sighed deeply and looked down into the dark brew. "I don't know. I guess it's true. I guess part of me is closed off even from *me.*"

"Why? Because you think you're so bad?"

Tom looked up at him. His eyes, Nate saw, were haunted. "I left a friend alone, and he died."

Nate knew the whole story. "You left him," he said quietly, "because you thought you heard someone calling for help."

"We didn't find anybody. The building was surrounded by police and firemen. No one could have gotten out unnoticed."

"I imagine a building on fire is full of strange and eerie sounds."

"But I left him, for something that wasn't there."

"Tom," Nate said gently, reasonably, "you and your friend were victims of an accident. You lived and he didn't. It's nobody's fault, it was just the way it happened. If you don't accept that and move on, you'll survive, but you'll be as dead as Davey."

Tom closed his eyes and rubbed his forehead. "My mind knows that. It just can't make it settle inside, you know?" He ran a hand over his chest, as though something hurt there. "Nancy thinks I should go see Davey's parents." He opened his eyes again and smiled faintly. "They were great. I spent a few weekends with them when Davey and I went hunting."

"Why don't you? Maybe it'll help."

"Maybe." He sighed and took a long pull on his coffee cup.

"And maybe if you explain to Amy how you feel, *she* won't feel closed off."

"I've told her some of it," he said, then downed the rest of the coffee in a gulp. "But I wouldn't let her see my leg."

Nate frowned. "She asked to?"

"No." Tom put the cup on the counter with great care. "We were...making love, and I wanted the lights out. She agreed, but then she wanted to...touch my leg, and I wouldn't let her."

"Tom—"

"I know. I have it all figured out. I hate myself inside, so I hate myself outside. Besides which, the leg's ugly."

Nate put an arm around his shoulders. "Sometimes, Tom, you are such a lunatic that it amazes me you look so normal. I guarantee you she will not find it ugly, but you've already got that figured out. You have to come to that peace with yourself. So, for God's sake, do it. You're making Nate and me crazy with worry."

There was a sudden crash from outside, and a high-pitched scream. Nate recognized the sound instantly. Karma!

He ran out the back door, Tom following, and found Karma sitting astride the lower branches of a mountain ash in the middle of Jave's neat, square lawn. She held tightly to an upper branch.

On the grass was a collapsed ladder and a large basket, out of which spilled a big clump of moss.

"What are you doing?" Nate demanded, righting the ladder. Tom held it steady while Nate climbed halfway up. "You don't strike me as the tree-climbing type."

Karma frowned down at him. "I'm not tree climbing," she explained, "I'm moss collecting. And the pursuit happens to involve climbing trees."

"See?" Tom offered to Nate from below. "With that kind of reasoning, who can ever figure out what women are doing?"

Nate was too concerned to be amused. He held his hand out to her. "We'll split hairs when you get down from there. Come on."

Karma took his hand and reached gingerly for the second step from the top with one of her simple black flats. His hand lent her sufficient balance and confidence to let go of the branch and step out with her other foot.

Bent almost double, she grabbed the top of the ladder in both hands and paused a moment to steady herself.

Nate leaped to the grass and waited until she was within reach, then swung her to the ground. He confronted her immediately. "What in the hell did you think you were doing? Where did you get the ladder?"

"Jave lent it to me." She held out the hem of the old gray sweater that covered her elegant suit. "Along with his sweater."

Nate turned to Tom. "Jave lent it to her," he said, in a tone that suggested he'd lent her a nuclear device.

Tom nodded with appropriate disgust. "The man's a swine."

Karma was surprised and a little amused by Nate's obvious annoyance. She was also touched and maybe even thrilled. He'd been afraid for her. No one had ever worried about her in that way.

She reached down for the clump of moss she'd collected and held it up to him. "Technically, I think it's a lichen, but we call it moss."

Tom folded the ladder with a grin at Nate. "I'll just leave you to your botany lesson. If it turns to biology, call me."

Nate studied Karma impatiently. She forced herself to withhold a smile. "This is moss," she explained gravely, "that I intend to use to decorate flowerpots for table centerpieces for the party. In big cities, you can buy it in flower or craft shops. The only place to get it in Heron Point is from a tree."

He considered her. Though his expression didn't change, she thought she could see his irritation thinning.

"So you climb a tree," he said impatiently, "in that beautiful outfit, with no one around to help you, with an arm that's been out of a cast all of twenty-four hours..."

"No," she replied. "I climbed the *ladder*. I only got into the tree when the ladder fell." She put a hand back to a tear she'd felt when she snagged the seat of her slacks on a burl. "I think I did ruin the outfit, though."

Nate pulled her to him and investigated the tear with a gentle pass of his hand over her left hip. The breath clogged in her throat.

"Well, that's too bad," he said, freeing her only far enough that he could look down into her face. "I really liked this suit on you."

"But I ruined it in the interest of the Christmas party." She smiled winningly. "That should absolve me of guilt."

He studied her, but granted her no absolution. "So, now you're making Christmas centerpieces?" he asked.

"Yes," she replied.

"So... then... you've caught the Christmas spirit."

"Well, I wouldn't say that. I just got a little caught up in Nancy and Jo's enthu—"

"Admit that you've caught the Christmas spirit," he warned, "or I'm going to kiss you."

"I haven't," she insisted. "But Jave needs all this stuff prepared, and Nancy and Jo can't possibly—"

He followed through on his threat with satisfying thoroughness. He kissed her long and hard, and she felt limp when he'd finished.

He shook his head over her. "You're going to be a lot of work, Karma Endicott."

She dropped hers against his shoulder. "But you're going to love every minute of it, Nathan Foster," she promised.

## Chapter Eleven

Goodbyes were noisy, filled with hugs and handshakes and plans for the next get-together to assess the status of the gifts and decorations, the first weekend in December.

Nate honked as they drove away, Garrett sound asleep in the back.

The night was dark, the streets deserted except for an occasional taxi or police car. Light blazed from the windows of homes snugly closed against the outside world. It was a family night.

Karma felt her heartbeat accelerate. Nate had promised to take her home with him tonight. Did he still intend to, or had he thought it over and changed his mind, remembering that there were other women in his life, less demanding than she was?

But he turned toward the road to the woods. Her senses responded, so heightened that she swore she could feel the movement of her blood in her veins.

By the time he pulled into the driveway, she could feel every separate cell functioning, every breath drawn in and expelled. Life was suddenly drama. She was about to make love with Nate.

For the first time in her recollection, time was something to savor and explore. It seemed to pass in slow motion as she watched Nate reach into the back seat for Garrett. She'd come to love the sight of her baby against his shoulder, the way he could hold him protectively with one long hand, and still use the other dexterously to lock and close the car door, then reach out for her and pull her into his arm.

Karma wrapped her arm around Nate's back, placed the other hand on her son, and felt the unity of their alliance, three separate parts of one cohesive whole. It brought tears to her throat and to her eyes.

"What?" Nate asked worriedly.

She hugged him fiercely. "It just feels so wonderful. The three of us. Does it feel wonderful to you?"

He kissed her upturned mouth. "That's too small a word for what I feel." Then he handed her his keys. "Give me the diaper bag and the carrier, and you open the door."

The house was dark and cold and smelled deliciously of its woodsy surroundings.

"Careful where you step," he warned. "There's a rocking horse with a bad runner somewhere in the middle of the—"

There was a thump and a little cry as Karma collided with it.

"Room," he finished apologetically as he flipped on the light. "Sorry."

"My fault. I got cocky," she said. "I thought I knew my way to the kitchen in the dark. My goodness! Where did all this come from?"

Karma looked around her at the array of toys spread out on every flat surface. On the floor were large items—the rocking horse on its side, a tricycle with a flat tire and a broken basket, a child's table-and-chair set badly in need of repainting.

"Donations are coming from everywhere. Tom's supposed to pick up the table and chairs and the rocking horse when he has time. The other things Jave and Ryan and I are going to work on."

On the sofa, the chairs, the coffee table, was a vast and motley collection of cars, trucks, dolls, tea sets, books, puzzles, games, and large boxes with odds and ends in them.

Nate was moving through the house, urging her to follow.

When he didn't head for the bedroom, as she expected, she thought he was going to the kitchen. But he passed the kitchen and started up the circular stairway. She hadn't investigated the second level when she spent the night nursing him.

"What's up here?" she asked, trailing several steps behind him.

He stopped to wait for her to catch up. "My bedroom," he said.

"I thought it was down there." She pointed over the railing to the room where she'd found him when he was ill.

He shook his head. "That's a guest room. I slept there for a few days because I felt like hell and it was easier than coming up here. Come on."

The loft bedroom and bath took up the entire second level. Tom had finished the walls and floors with planking he'd rescued from a scuttled dinner-cruise boat in Portland.

Old maps had been easy to find, and he'd bought a painting of a square-rigger at a hospital-auxiliary art auction. Aggie, interested in the project, had found a ship's lamp and a writing desk at Sam's Secondhand Barn.

The colorful quilt on the bed had been his grandmother's, and he had a sampler above the bed that *her* mother had done. All Things Bloom With Love, it read.

A stone fireplace like the one downstairs took up most of the opposite wall.

Karma stopped in the middle of the room and looked around, her eyes rapt, a soft smile forming on her mouth.

"What a beautiful room," she finally whispered. Then she turned to him, a curiously amused suspicion in her eyes. "Did Alexa help you? Isn't she the decorator?"

He placed the sleeping baby carefully in the middle of the bed, then went to wrap her tightly in his arms. "No. Tom and Aggie helped me. Forget my ladies, okay? There's only room for you in my life now. You fill my dreams, my thoughts, my plans."

Karma sighed against him. "You're everything I ever wanted."

Nate found that incredible, but refused to question his good fortune. He pulled her gently away from him. "You find a comfortable place for the baby while I build a fire."

He took her coat and hung it with his jacket in the closet.

Karma settled Garrett in his carrier and placed it on an overstuffed chair a safe distance from the fireplace. He'd had a big day, and he slept deeply, contentedly.

She went to kneel beside Nate as he patiently fed kindling to the frail beginnings of a fire.

There was something primitive about the action, something so different from her orderly world that she felt disoriented, vaguely out of step with life as she knew it.

She was trembling inside. She had to share a truth with him that she hoped wouldn't change anything, but she had to admit that it could. She opened her mouth to form the words. The single syllable "I..." came out just before courage stalled somewhere in her chest.

Nate looked over his shoulder at her as he leaned two logs against each other over the burning kindling. "Yes?" he said.

She opened her mouth to try again, but he had to turn his attention back to the fire as one of the logs caught. He added more kindling and leaned a third log against the other two.

In a moment, the fire was burning merrily, and he pulled an iron screen decorated with the pattern of a sailing ship across the hearth. He turned to her, a forearm balanced on his upraised knee, his smile warm and interested. "Now, what did you say?"

She stared at him, lips parted, knowing she owed him the truth, in all fairness, but knowing also how desperately unhappy she would be if it changed anything—if it changed tonight.

He looked into her eyes, and his interested smile turned into a look of gentle concern. He grinned suddenly. "Are you nervous?" He put a hand to the side of her face and stroked his thumb gently over her cheekbone. "It's okay. So am I."

She leaned forward to kiss his cheek, falling more deeply in love with him because of that admission. It made it easier to be honest. She leaned back to look him in the eye.

"I'm more than nervous. I'm ... a virgin." She hitched a shoulder in sudden embarrassment. "Sort of."

Nate stared at her in astonishment for a moment, then dropped his raised knee and sat back on his heels.

"A what?" he asked.

She nodded, as though to assure him that he hadn't misunderstood her. "A virgin," she repeated. Then, with a nervous wave of her hand, she tacked on, "Well, you know—technically."

He narrowed one eye. "Technically?"

Karma nodded, her cheeks pink. "Well, I've had a baby, but I explained all that. The sperm bank and everything. It was a surgical procedure. Other than that..." She raised that shoulder again. "Technically... this is my first time."

Nate had calmness down to a science. And he was grateful, because this was the last thing he'd expected her to say. A virgin? Karma, whose baby he'd helped deliver, was a virgin? The woman he'd been dreaming all day of making love to all night... was a virgin?

He felt awe, amazement, the pressure of responsibility.

Karma saw the turbulence in his eyes and felt her own particular panic. "I only mention it," she said, swallowing, "because I... will probably be..." She made an openhanded, helpless gesture. "You know... less skilled than you probably... expected."

He scolded her with a look. "All I expected," he said quietly, "was a woman as eager to be with me as I am to be with her."

She wanted to wrap her arms around him, but she kept their knee-to-knee distance, still uncertain of his reaction.

"I *am* eager to be with you," she said, her voice thick with longing. "No man has ever been as important to me as you are. I'd saved up all my love, and when I didn't think I'd find anybody, I went to the sperm bank for Garrett. But now..." Tears welled up in her eyes, and she rose on her knees to frame his face in her hands. "Now I wish I'd waited a year so that he was yours."

"Oh, Karma," he groaned, kneeling, too, to take her in his arms. Every concern he felt fled, because love was guiding him—the love she offered, and the love he returned. "I was there when he drew his first breath. And I'll be here from now on. That's what fatherhood's about— take it from someone who knows."

She wrapped her arms around him and held. "Thank you." She kissed his throat, his chin, his mouth, then looked into his eyes and tried to explain their curious circumstances. "I usually resist doing anything I'm not good at. I study the subject, analyze the data, consider my approach from all angles." She smiled ruefully. "You can't really do that with sex and treat it with the reverence it deserves."

He couldn't help but smile. Not simply because he knew something she didn't—a fact that delighted him on some basic level—but also because she was trusting him to take her where she'd never been. Because she loved him.

All the love and tenderness he felt for her tripled.

He tipped her face up and kissed her. "Stay right here," he said. "I'll bring a blanket and pillows."

He went to a closet across the room and returned with a down comforter that he spread on the floor, a little distance from the fire. She moved aside to help him, then caught the pillows one by one as he tossed them from the bed.

Before joining her, he went to the chair where she'd placed Garrett in his carrier and peered down at him.

"Sound asleep," he reported as he came to kneel with her in the middle of the thick comforter.

She opened her arms to him, wanting to hold him, wanting to be held, to relish the wonder of this choice.

"Are you warm enough?" he asked, running his broad hand up and down her spine. "Maybe we should wait a little while and give the fire time to—"

She smiled up at him. "I don't want to wait another moment. Lead on, and I'll do my best to follow."

Nate felt sure he could drown in the look of love in her eyes and never even make an effort to surface again. But he had things to teach her.

"All right." He held her away from him, just enough to allow him access to the top button of her shirt. "First of all, we're both wearing entirely too many clothes."

He unfastened just a few buttons, and the silky, oversize garment fell off her to puddle at her knees on the blanket.

Her ivory skin glowed in the firelight, her small breasts, in a scrap of vanilla lace, distracting Nate in his task of undressing her.

He unfastened the simple hook at the front of her bra and slipped it off her shoulders. Then he cradled her in his arms and tipped her backward so that she lay on the blanket. He kissed each pert little globe and enjoyed her ragged sigh of pleasure.

He dipped his fingertips inside the waistband of her silky slacks and pulled them down. A strip of lace that matched the bra came with them.

She was slender and delicately built, a small waist flaring only slightly to gently rounded hips and long, graceful legs.

Nate tossed the clothes aside and braced his hands on the blanket on either side of her waist to grin at her. "It's too bad you ruined that outfit, but you look magnificent without it."

She smiled shyly and reached up to unbutton his shirt. "*Magnificent* is probably a little strong. I know that it applies to you, though," she said, her task finally completed.

He smiled and frowned simultaneously. "You've never seen me . . . naked. Have you?"

"Not exactly," she admitted, liking the vaguely worried look on his face. "I've seen you bare chested. Remember when you were sick and tried to bean me with the putter?"

"Oh, yeah." He knelt up to pull the shirt off, then yanked a snowy white T-shirt over his head. He leaned over her again to kiss her. "I'm afraid I don't remember what I was wearing—or not wearing. You were very lucky I was weak, or you might have found yourself somewhere in the park, or on the roof of Columbia Chocolates, downtown."

She smiled. "Not too terrible a fate." She put her hands to his chest and sat up, continuing to push him backward as she rose onto her knees and forced him to lie back. She knelt astride him and unbuckled his belt.

As an afterthought, she turned to look behind her, and noticed that he still wore his shoes. "Uh-oh," she said. "I think I've broken the pattern of graceful disrobing."

"Not a problem," he said, toeing off the shoes. "Loafers. You're a fine student. Gifted, even. Do continue."

Nate watched the top of her glossy dark head as she concentrated on unfastening his belt and the zipper of his pants. He could die a happy man now, he thought, with the memory of Karma eager to undress him.

Then he felt her fingertips against the flesh at his hipbone as she reached inside his slacks to pull them down. Air caught in his lungs. His brain was starved for oxygen, he was sure, but it didn't matter. It seemed no longer connected to his body, anyway.

Though he was a man used to making rapid-fire decisions and following them with quick, decisive action, he couldn't form one coherent thought.

He braced up on his elbows as Karma pulled the fabric down his legs and off, then watched her eyes peruse his body with smiling interest before she came back up to sit beside his waist and drape her upper body over his.

She ran a fingertip over his bottom lip, her expression suddenly serious. "And you're as beautiful *inside*, as well, aren't you?" she asked on a whisper. "How did I get so lucky?"

"Karma." His voice caressed her name, even as he turned onto his side and pulled her beside him. He held her to him and swept a hand along every silken hill and hollow of her.

Her small hands explored every inch of him, her innocence an erotic counterpoint to her bold touch. She smoothed a path along his back one moment, then stroked his hip the next, pitching him to the brink of madness.

She nestled against him with a sigh of pleasure, of rightness. He wrapped his body around hers, thinking that already he couldn't remember what it had been like when she wasn't in his arms.

Karma felt as though her entire world had been distilled into the warmth of Nate's arms. And the tightness of his embrace seemed to enlarge her world, rather than diminish it.

It gave life a density she'd never understood before.

Nate stroked the length of her thigh, then up again, this time along the sensitive inside. She bent her knee to accommodate him, and turned her face into his throat when he dipped a finger gently inside her.

It was an intimacy she'd never accorded anyone before, and it was a revelation to her how right she'd been to be so discriminating. As he found that pearl of sensitivity and caressed it, it was as if a light went on inside her. Feelings seemed to acquire substance. Pleasure was in the texture of his touch. Love had a face.

And she saw it above hers, burnished by the firelight, as her body, even her soul, seemed to be caught in some exotic, languid orbit she was powerless to resist. Then it seemed to tighten, and the world began to spin, drawing her deeply toward the heart of its mysteries.

Then it fragmented with the sudden explosion of pleasure as wave after wave of sensation rolled over her. She looped her arms around Nate's neck and held on, whispering his name.

Nate felt her pleasure as if it were his own. Given the recent birth of her baby, and her admission of virginity, he was willing to be satisfied with that.

But she was touching him, urging him to move atop her. "Karma..."

She took a firm hold of his shoulders. Her dark eyes were determined in the undulating light. "That was absolutely..." She smiled. "Well, there is no word. But I don't want just pleasure. I want *you.*"

That decimated every argument he could present—except one.

"It'll probably be uncomfortable for you," he warned.

She nodded. "*Wanting* you is uncomfortable." Then she lifted herself against him and kissed him forcefully. "Please?"

Nate entered her carefully, and when she made no complaint, he thrust more deeply, absorbing her small gasp against his shoulder.

"I'm fine," she assured him when he raised himself off her. She wrapped her arms around his neck and pulled him resolutely down to her. "I'm fine. Make love to me."

Her eagerness for him, and the wonderful rightness of being enclosed by her body, filled him with a profound tenderness, as well as a passion that he had under control—just.

He began to move inside her, alert for the smallest sign or sound of discomfort. But she looked up at him with lazy eyes, her dark hair like an inky cloud on the blanket. She smiled lovingly at him, and then her brow furrowed and she arched her back, uttering an indeterminate little sound.

Then he felt her body shudder around his, and his control disintegrated. They trembled together in the dancing light.

Karma continued to cling to him when they'd collapsed together and he'd pulled the other half of the blanket over them. She could think of nothing to say that could begin to express what she felt.

She'd known making love with him would change her world, but she hadn't realized it would change *her.*

All the angles in life seemed to have softened, and all the careful compartments in which she'd kept emotions and dreams had disappeared. Orderliness had been replaced by a chaotic tangle that held surprises that startled her, and muddled many of the truths she'd long believed in.

Amid the delicious pleasure, a little bud of fear began to grow inside her.

"I wish you'd say something," Nate encouraged worriedly, stroking her hair spread out on his shoulder.

She kissed his collarbone, wondering if *he* felt changed.

"I feel different," she admitted breathlessly. "I want to mix the colors in my closet, take the dividers out of my desk drawers, maybe even tear a page out of my phone book and throw it away."

He laughed. "I'd take that slowly. You might implode."

"I know. It's a little scary." She needed desperately to analyze it, to understand it. "I guess I feel..." She didn't know what she felt. She couldn't think clearly, and that alone was alarming.

On one level, making love with Nate made everything warm and wonderful. On another, it had shaken her grip on life as she knew it, as she'd worked so hard to build it. *That* was terrifying.

Nate brushed the hair from her face, his eyes dark with concern. "What is it?" he asked.

It was ironic, she thought, that the very man responsible for this feeling of being lost, adrift, was all she could hold on to as she struggled to right her world.

"Nothing," she whispered, resting her head in the hollow of his shoulder.

"Everything's going to be all right," he whispered, pulling the blanket up around her and stroking her hair. "I promise."

She hoped he was right.

# Chapter Twelve

"I thought you were so tired, you *had* to have breakfast in bed!" Karma, whipping eggs and milk for omelets, shouted teasingly toward the noise in the living room.

In the four days since Thanksgiving, they'd fallen into the habit of making love when Nate came home in the morning, and following that with breakfast.

She knew she was courting danger with this relationship, but she'd convinced herself she could indulge it, as long as she promised nothing, surrendered nothing.

And being in his arms at night, and across the table from him when he came home from the hospital in the morning, filled her with such physical satisfaction that it was easy to dismiss the threat to her professional peace of mind.

"Just because you worked all night," she went on, "and made love to me twice, you think you should be waited on? Well, one of the times doesn't count. We did that under water, and that reduces physical exer— Aaah!"

Karma screamed at the unexpected sight of Tom Nicholas standing in the kitchen doorway, a large cardboard box in his arms, a baseball cap on backward.

He appeared as shocked as she did. Not that that was any surprise. How often did one find a woman wearing a long apron over a T-shirt and flannel boxer shorts. He looked around himself, as though wondering if he was in the wrong house. Seeing that he wasn't, he stammered apologetically.

"Karma, I'm sorry! I'm...ah... Where's Nate? I was supposed to drop this off and pick up some...some wooden...toys."

Karma held a hand to her thumping heart. "It's okay. I just didn't hear you come in. Ah—Nate just got home a little bit ago." She smiled and turned back to her task, embarrassed that he'd overheard her teasing remark. "You'll find him—"

"Right here." Nate appeared in the doorway beside Tom. He had Garrett against his shoulder and a wry smile on his lips. "Morning. Broke in to steal my valuables?"

Tom put the box down and glowered at him. "I came to give you these, and pick up the other stuff. Sorry. I thought you wouldn't be home yet, so I let myself in. I didn't know...you and Karma... I mean, only four days ago you were grumbling at her for climbing trees. You know, you could tell me these things."

Nate snickered. "Like you're so free with *your* life's details."

Tom ignored that and asked, with genuine awe, "Underwater?"

Nate ignored *him* and glanced across the kitchen at Karma. "Did he scare you to death?"

She waved a tea towel dismissively. "Not enough that I can't fix him an omelet, too. Cheese and sausage."

"Thanks," Tom said, smiling at her and shaking his head. "I'm meeting Ryan and Jo at nine. Promised to help them move."

"Oh, that's right." Nate ran a hand over his face. "I'll sleep for a few hours, then come and help you guys finish up this afternoon."

"Good deal. I'll just take the rocking horse and the table and chairs and be on my way." He began to move away, then stopped. "Oh. Nancy asked me to tell you that we're all going to the tree farm next weekend to pick up the tree for the party. I'm borrowing a flatbed from Heron Point Hardware. We're meeting at Coffee Country Sunday at eight, and Aggie's watching the babies. That okay, Karma?"

"Sounds great."

Nate helped Tom by carrying two small chairs back-to-back in one hand. Tom leaped into the back of his truck and took them from him. He asked once again with a grin, "Underwater?"

Nate rolled his eyes. "Bathtub, blockhead."

"Oooh..."

Nate turned serious. "You're doing all right with that leg."

Tom indicated the cold but sunny weather. "Feels pretty good when it isn't raining."

"Anybody looked at it for you lately?" Nate asked.

Tom turned to respond, obviously presuming it had been a professional question. Then Nate saw him realize that it had been personal and referred to his refusal to let Amy touch it. He expected Tom to react defensively.

To his surprise, Tom leaped out of the truck, chucked Garrett under the chin and pointed to the house. "With a pair of legs like that waiting in your kitchen, I can't imagine why you're worried about mine. See ya."

*HEY. Where you going with that horse?*

NATE CARRIED GARRETT back into the kitchen, and leaned over Karma to kiss her neck while she poured sausage and cheese onto the egg mixture in the pan. It smelled heavenly, and so did she.

*CAN I HAVE SOME OF THAT? Maybe a little of that orange stuff you guys have every morning. I'm getting a little tired of the milk.*

NATE LOOKED DOWN at Garrett, who gave him a wide smile. He held the baby up so that Karma could see him. "I think he likes it here. He was smiling. Come on, buddy. Do it again. Smile." He tickled his chin.

*OKAY, there's your smile. But for that I expect some of that stuff in the pan.*

KARMA SMILED over his delight. "Who wouldn't love this house? Who wouldn't love you?" She kissed his chin, then made a face. "Is this night shift a forever thing?"

He shrugged. "I've always preferred it. I had nothing else to do, and most of the other staff have families." His eyes rested on her, the look in them suddenly significant. He caught the back of her neck and pulled her to him. "Why? Do you miss me at night?"

"Horribly. But that's life, I guess. I'll just have to suffer."

He reached around her to turn off the heat under the pan. He braced an arm against the counter to hold her there, and stilled her protests about breakfast with a kiss.

"Actually," he said when he raised his head, "you *don't* have to suffer."

She brightened. "I don't? You mean you can change shifts?"

He inclined his head, the gesture noncommittal. "I'm trying, but it'll probably take a while. Jackie Palmrose, the

ER doctor on day shift, may be moving. In which case the day-shift slot would be open. Her husband is considering taking a job in Portland after the first of the year. But it's nothing definite yet."

She frowned, confused. "Then . . . why don't I have to suffer?"

"Well, there's a treatment for your condition," he explained, watching her eyes.

She studied him suspiciously. "What?"

"A kind of patch," he said, reaching into his pocket. "You know—like the insulin patch for diabetics, and the patch to combat seasickness that you wear on your skin to dis—"

She nodded. "Yes, I know. But how does that—?"

He put Garrett into her right arm, and took her left hand. "Now, this has to be worn on the third finger," he said, slipping on the simple half-carat marquise-cut diamond. "And my love will be with you, even when I'm not."

He heard her gasp, saw her eyes widen and soften with love as she looked from the ring to him. Then, to his complete surprise, fear rose out of her expression and, right beside it, a misery he couldn't begin to understand.

She lowered her eyes, her mouth working unsteadily. She rubbed an index finger over the brilliant surface of the diamond, then pulled the ring off.

She handed it back to him, her eyes brimming with tears.

*MOTHER! What are you doing?*

"I CAN'T," she whispered. "I want to, but I can't."

He was astonished. He'd thought marriage was what she'd wanted all along. He felt an odd disorientation.

"Why not?" he demanded.

She tried to push against his chest, but he stood firm, still blocking her with a hand on the counter.

"Nate, please—"

"You're not going anywhere," he said with dark resolve, "until I understand this. I thought we loved each other."

She looked into his eyes, her own bleak and confused. "We do. I *love* you."

"But you don't want to marry me."

"I do," she said, "but I can't."

This was going in circles, getting nowhere. "Why," he asked, his voice rising, "can't you?"

She gestured around the kitchen, which was strewn with Christmas projects, toward the living room, where toys had been collecting for weeks, and tried to speak, but didn't seem able to.

He had to interpret that himself. "You mean the mess? You can't marry me because the house is messy?"

She shook her head quickly. "No," she said, her voice strained. "Because this is how you make me feel *inside.*"

He stared at her, desperately hoping to understand what she was telling him. "I make you feel . . . messy?"

Her voice was tight with tears. "You make me feel chaotic, out of control, stacked up—like I haven't a clue where I'm going, or what's going to happen next. And I can't sort anything out."

He took a step back from her. "That isn't me, Karma. That's *life.* You've just been watching it all these years. Now you're living it."

"Maybe," she conceded, "but it doesn't change the fact that I feel that way." The confusion she felt was exaggerated by his nearness, and she took advantage of the step he'd taken backward to slip around him. "And what kind of a wife would I be, when I don't know where I'm going?"

He turned impatiently and folded his arms. "I thought that was clear. Expand your business. Live for Garrett."

She gave him an accusing glare as she paced around the table, still wearing the apron over a pair of his boxers. Garrett, in her arms, looked mystified. "My point exactly," she said. "That was always so clear in my mind. Now it's not. I can't remember what I want."

That was the first positive thing he'd heard her say. It was flimsy, but he was convinced it was positive.

"Maybe," he suggested, watching her come around the table toward him, "that's because what you want is changing."

She stopped two yards from him, her chin at a stubborn angle.

"I have worked long and hard," she said, "to get my life on track. Having Garrett early disorganized everything, but I was just getting a grip on things again. I don't want to lose that."

He frowned at her, shaking his head. "Karma, I want for you what you want for you."

She gave him a disbelieving look. "Oh, right. This morning I told you I was getting serious about renting office space, and what did you do?"

He remembered clearly. It had been wonderful. "I kissed you and began . . ."

She put a hand out in a "stop" gesture. "*I* remember what you did. I'm just trying to make another point. You distract me from what I've always wanted. You make me forget how important it is to plan, to get your priorities in order, to remember your long-range goals."

"That's because," he pointed out gently, "you always forget to live the moment. And don't try to tell me you didn't enjoy this morning as much as I did."

"I wouldn't." Karma resented the suggestion that she might. "I *told* you I love you. I just need more time to get my work done. More focus on...on..." She couldn't even concentrate sharply enough on what she wanted to tell him it was.

"I'm sorry," she said finally. "Maybe Garrett and I should go home."

*NATE! Did you hear that?*

HE CAME toward her consideringly, hands loosely on his hips, the long, lean body she now knew intimately moving with easy grace. "Do you want to go?"

The last thing she wanted to do was leave, but she'd thrown commitment back in his face. What could either of them do after that?

"No," she admitted. "I love you. I just need...less playtime and more worktime."

"All right." He stopped just inches from her, his eyes dark and grave. "We'll try that. It should prove which one of us has the better angle on how to run a relationship."

He took the baby from her. Garrett went without complaint.

"Garrett and I will finish fixing breakfast," he said.

"I can—"

He drew away when she tried to take Garrett back. "Just consider that sitting room in the back your office. I'll make a point of watching Garrett more often when I'm home, and I won't touch you unless you ask."

That didn't sound healthy to her. "Nate, I..."

He pushed her gently out of the kitchen. "Go on. I promised to help move Jo and Ryan this afternoon, so you'd better make use of the time."

"But you won't get any sleep before you go back to work tonight."

He smiled at her as he tossed away the omelet and prepared to start over. "Then we won't have to worry about my feeling amorous, will we?"

THEY LIVED like a pair of amiable friends. Karma hated it, but she refused to admit that Nate had a point.

He watched Garrett mornings so that she could work, then slept afternoons, while she concentrated on the Christmas projects, if the baby's mood allowed. They ate dinner in fraternal politeness, then Nate went to work. She thought about him much of the night.

He never seemed inclined to make time for them, and she, perversely, refused to complain.

All around them, the Christmas season blossomed. The house was filled with toys. Those in the living room had been repaired and painted, those in the spare bedroom awaited the caring hands of whoever had time to work on them.

Jave and his boys and Ryan came over once a week to collect a boxful to take home and work on, then returned the repaired ones and filled the box again. Karma marveled at their generosity and their good humor.

Tom repaired everything wooden, and had made a dozen trucks out of pine, with wheels and steering wheels that turned. Jave and Nate and Ryan had inspected them in Tom's absence and praised the carpentry and the care that had gone into them. Then they had worried over his situation with Amy.

Karma went to the toy shop downtown to pick up presents for Garrett, Chelsea, and all of Jave and Nancy's children. Fir swags of greenery and small white lights were draped on every Heron Point storefront, every light pole, and across every intersection.

Store windows were filled with sparkling decorations and sumptuous gifts, the bakery showed off gingerbread houses and pressed cookies in Christmas motifs, and shoppers and excited children were already clogging the sidewalks. Rain fell instead of snow, but it was Oregon, and everyone expected it and had long ago learned to live with it.

Umbrellas bloomed like poinsettias all around town.

If Karma called a client, she was treated to the sound of Christmas carols when she was put on hold.

She remembered that, last year, it had annoyed her. This year, she rather enjoyed it, though she and Nate were like ships in the night. She so missed the warm camaraderie they'd enjoyed before he proposed.

But Garrett seemed pleased with his surroundings and the time he spent with Nate. He ate well, slept for longer periods, smiled continually, and grew.

It rained buckets on their Christmas-tree safari Sunday. Karma stopped in her tracks when she saw Amy in the group collected at Coffee Country for breakfast. The shop was closed for regular business.

"Amy!" she gasped.

She'd worked with her and Jo on decorations several afternoons at Nancy's and thought she had the dearest heart, the sweetest smile, but the worst fashion sense, of any woman she'd ever met.

But today, her tall, well-proportioned figure was dressed in snug jeans into which she'd tucked a white turtleneck covered by a red-and-blue plaid flannel shirt.

Her hair, which had always been long and lank, had been trimmed to just below her ears and hung in a glossy bell shape, parted on the side and slipping seductively over one eye.

She wore light makeup and a confidence Karma had never seen in her before.

Nate, who'd been talking to Tom as they walked in together, slammed into Karma's back. He moved away quickly, as though the contact had hurt him.

Karma's glance scolded him for making so much of it.

He responded with a blink of bland innocence. Then he noticed Amy. "Jeez. Amy? Is that you?" He pretended to peer closer.

She laughed and nodded. "Thank you. That's very flattering," she said. "I'm glad you all approve of the new me." She smiled at the group, who applauded and whistled. "I decided I couldn't go to New York a frump, so I went to Portland for a makeover. Hi, Tom."

The tension in the air was palpable, as everyone awaited the meeting of these two who simply could not get their relationship together. Karma hoped Nate hadn't made it obvious to everyone that they weren't the only ones having difficulty.

Amy smiled charmingly at Tom, and behaved as though he were Jave, or Nate, or Ryan—just another of her male friends.

Karma wondered if Nate had given her lessons.

"You can have my seat," Amy said to Tom. "I've got a few things to do at the hospital, so I'll meet you all at the tree farm."

Tom hadn't said a word since he'd walked in the door, and he continued to watch her, speechless, as she walked out to her car.

The men looked confused. The women exchanged knowing looks. Tom seemed to have gone into a coma. Jave pushed him into a chair and handed him a cup of coffee.

IT LOOKED, Karma thought, as though the tree were being selected by ducks and derelicts. The tree farm provided a few hooded yellow slickers that were distributed to the women. The men, dressed to haul the tree, wore their oldest clothes. They moved through the evenly planted forest shouting eagerly to one another when a possibility was spotted.

They gathered for a consultation, then dispersed again, looking for one that was taller, fatter, more even.

Karma finally found the perfect tree alone on a slope in the middle of a field. "Look!" she breathed to Jo, almost as though she were afraid it would move away if she spoke too loudly. "I wonder if we could have that one?"

It was a noble fir about twelve feet high, beautifully proportioned and majestic in its solitude.

Jo beckoned Nancy and Amy, who were debating the qualities of a smaller, less spectacular tree at the edge of the lot.

"Oh, that's *it!*" Nancy said.

"Oh, definitely," Amy agreed. "But can we have it? It isn't in with the cultivated ones."

Jo put her little fingers to her lips and whistled shrilly. The men, dispersed throughout the forest, turned to look. "Come on!" she shouted. "We found it!"

Everyone gathered around it, like a group of eccentric druids. The men seemed to consider Tom the final authority.

He walked around it, the shoulders of his lined denim jacket drenched through, rain dripping from his hair into his eyes.

Karma noticed Amy's study of his spiked eyelashes, then her quick glance away when he nodded and turned to the group. "Looks perfect to me. Call Mr. Widdoes."

Mr. Widdoes was the tree farmer, who made a point of sitting back before his fire while shoppers selected their tree. He was happy to trek out with his saw when the tree was chosen, but the buyer had to haul it away.

Nate called him on his cellular phone and explained the location of the tree they'd selected.

"We can have it," Nate reported as he closed the phone and lowered the antenna. "He'll come and cut if for us, but we have to haul it down the hill."

Tom nodded. "I brought tarps and rope. Somebody want to come with me and help me bring them up here?"

"I vote we send the women," Jave said.

Ryan agreed. "I second that. All those in favor?"

Three male hands went up.

As the other women began to protest, Karma folded her arms. "You gentlemen seem to be missing the fact that you're outnumbered, and therefore outvoted."

Ryan frowned. "We're four to four. The best you can hope for is a tie."

She shook her head. "Tom has to go to unlock the toolbox on the flatbed, so he's not a vote. All those in favor of the *men* going to get the tarps and rope, say aye."

Four female hands went up.

"Pardon me, but *you*," Nate said to Karma, "have missed something important here. Tom can simply hand one of you the key."

Amy stepped away from the knot of women and confronted Tom, her expression faintly smiling. "Really?" she asked. "I'll bet I could talk him out of it."

Tom was both shocked by her willingness to tease him, considering their circumstances, and apparently con-

cerned, judging by the way he studied her face, about just
what form of persuasion she intended to use.

He folded his arms, prepared to stand firm. "I'll bet you
can't."

Amy dropped her hood back, stretched her arms forward to reach beyond the confinement of her vinyl sleeves,
and wrapped her arms around his neck.

While the rain came down in sheets, she kissed him with
a fervor and a determination that made Jave and Ryan look
at one another. Nate shifted his weight.

The women gaped silently.

The kiss went on.

Karma watched enviously. She missed the physical side
of her relationship with Nate with an intensity that was almost pain. But she knew what he was doing by keeping his
distance, and she refused to acknowledge that it affected
her. Life did need order. It did have to be taken seriously.
And if he seemed intent on proving that the extra time for
it could only be taken away from time in bed, then so be it.
She could hold out as long as he could.

She caught his eye across the crowd and knew he was
reading her mind. She held his gaze boldly, then looked
away when Jave moved.

He snatched the keys from Tom's lifeless fingers at
Amy's back, and grinned at his companions. "Since none
of us has brought diving gear, we'd better go for the tarp
and ropes before we all drown."

The women applauded the decision, then made themselves scarce when Tom and Amy finally pulled apart.

NATE DIRECTED Jave, Ryan and Tom as they hauled the
tree onto his back deck. It wouldn't be decorated until the
night before the party, which was scheduled for the eigh-
teenth of December. Then they joined the women inside to

celebrate their success with Karma's homemade chili, corn bread and salad.

Jo had found *It's A Wonderful Life* on television. She and Ryan and Jave and Nancy occupied either end of the sofa in cozy twosomes.

Amy sat by the fire, buffing her hair with a towel, and Tom sat on the floor with a dump truck from the bottomless pile of toys to be fixed.

"I don't get it," Nate said quietly to Karma in the kitchen. "I thought Amy and Tom resolved their problem at the tree farm. But they still don't seem to be speaking."

She sprinkled more chili powder into the pan. "Men. You miss all the subtleties. I think that kiss was intended to show him what he'd be missing if he let her go to New York." She looked up, her own expression now blandly innocent. "You're telling me you're not acquainted with the tactic?"

"Tactic?" he inquired.

She gave him a look that openly doubted his need to question. *"Tac-tic."* She enunciated the word. "As in a campaign launched to defeat an opponent. Hotpad, please."

He handed her the quilted square. "Are we opponents?"

"Thank you. That seems to be the position you've taken."

He pretended confusion. "By providing you with what you claimed was missing?"

"By withholding," she said judiciously, wrapping the pot holder around the handle of the pan, "what should never have been at issue in the first place."

"Sex."

"Lovemaking."

"But you put it at issue." He held a pottery bowl steady as she poured the chili into it. "You said it distracted you from work."

"No, I . . ."

"Nate!" Ryan called from the living room. "Leave her alone! You're holding up dinner."

Karma threatened Nate with a glance as she hefted the bowl. "To be continued at a later date."

"Why not tonight?"

"Because I have a headache."

GARRETT: *It looks beautiful, Mom. But how come we can't keep any of this neat stuff? I know you said it's for less fortunate children, but the rest of us need stuff, too, you know. Is there anything to eat?*

Malia: *Don't you ever think of anything but food?*

Garrett: *Yeah. Got your binky?*

Chelsea: *Come on, you two. It's Christmas. Santa's watching, remember?*

KARMA FOLLOWED Nancy, Jo and Amy as they looked over the fairgrounds in its holiday splendor, and simply stared, amazed by what their efforts had brought about.

Picnic tables with red-and-green paper covers filled the room, a wide aisle cleared in the middle where the children would walk up to see Santa.

Tom's wooden stars, painted yellow and adorned with glitter, were hung in a random pattern all over the walls and caught the overhead light like the Milky Way.

Snowflakes and angels hung from the ceiling on fishing line, turning and dancing on the air, their beauty genuine enough to mimic the real thing.

Every table was decorated with her moss-trimmed flowerpots filled with votive candles. They filled the room with the fragrances of bayberry, cinnamon and vanilla.

But the real wonder was the treasure trove of toys locked in the office, every one beautifully wrapped and identified by age and gender with a tag. Jave, Ryan and Tom had been up most nights for the past week in Nate's living room repairing and painting the last of the toys.

Karma had paced the floor with Garrett, who was in an insomniac phase, and poured coffee and made a final batch of cinnamon bears.

"We did it," Jo said in wonder, her eyes roving the room as she smiled. Chelsea lay fast asleep in her arms. "Did you ever think we'd finally see it all come together?"

"Yes," Nancy replied, patting Malia's back as the baby groped for the tie on her sweatshirt. "Despite our quirks, we're a remarkably efficient team."

Across the room, the men were putting the finishing touches on the tree. The doctors and nurses had provided the ornaments and lights, and one of Amy's angels had been placed at the top of the tree and touched the ceiling.

"Okay!" Nate, atop the ladder, shouted to Ryan, who'd moved toward the back door. "Kill the lights!"

The room went dark, and everyone in the room *aah*ed in unison.

The tree was a pillar of light and color in the darkness. The wooden stars picked up its light and glittered like a falling sky. The angels and snowflakes also collected its light and sparkled as they turned on invisible strings.

Amy uttered a quiet little gasp of distress. "I . . . have to go," she said, her voice frail in the darkness. "See you guys tomorrow at the party."

"Amy?" Nancy followed her as far as the door, then turned back to Jo and Karma. "Already gone. I swear, if that brother-in-law of mine doesn't come around, and soon, he's getting a fat lip for Christmas. And speaking of which, Karma..." She lowered her voice. "Is something wrong between you and Nate? You're so...polite."

Jo leaned closer to hear as Karma smiled wryly. "He proposed," Karma said.

Nancy asked in puzzlement, "And that's bad?"

Karma sighed and shifted Garrett to her other arm. "No, of course not. But we have...different approaches to life. I've worked so hard to get my business going, to make plans. But loving Nate has..." She sighed, as though the admission was hard. "It's made me think about more babies, more time at home. More Christmas parties!"

"Is that so terrible?" Jo asked.

"Love is...sort of...dissolving what I want. Or used to want."

"Is it fair to blame Nate for that?" Nancy asked.

Jo pushed her long blond mane aside and patted Chelsea's back. "I know it's not politically correct," she said, lowering her voice as the men approached them, laughing over something that earned Nate a playful shove, "to talk about women compromising anything in a relationship, but with the right man, you get back a lot for whatever you give up. Trust me."

The group dispersed quickly, Jave and Nancy leaving to pick up the boys, and Jo and Ryan hurrying off to relieve Devon at Coffee Country. All the downtown merchants were open late for Christmas shopping.

"Do you want to stop and eat on the way home, so you don't have to cook?" Nate asked as they walked out to the parking lot. He pulled keys out of his pocket. They were driving Karma's Volvo, rather than his Jaguar, because of the infant seat.

She made a sudden decision. "Let's pick something up," she said briskly, snatching the keys from him and handing him the baby. "It'll save time."

*YEAH, let's pick something up. But make it soft. My throat's starting to hurt.*

"FOR WHAT?" he asked as she unlocked the passenger-side door.

She held his gaze for a moment, then walked around to the driver's side. "You'll see," she said across the roof of the car.

Nate was grateful he had steady nerves, because there was something dangerous about Karma tonight that he'd never seen before. It was as though she were driven by some demon even she didn't understand.

She was considerably beyond the speed limit when they reached Burgers, Burgers and turned into the drive-through lane with competence but a shrill squeal of tires. They rocked to a stop at the menu. She ordered without consulting him.

Nate looked over his shoulder to check on Garrett and found him smiling.

*COOL! Are we trying out for the Indy?*

NATE GUESSED they hit fifty in the ten yards from the menu to the window. He had no idea how fast they were going on the road home, but he watched the side mirror for signs of a flashing red light.

It was the most fun he'd had since the day he'd proposed. Their careful neutrality was coming to an end. He felt his pulse pick up as he braced for the confrontation.

It came after they ate in relative silence and she put Garrett to bed in the back office.

Nate had built a fire and was making coffee, thinking it might lubricate what was bound to be a difficult discussion.

But she took the basket of the coffeemaker out of his hands, put it aside, and pulled him by the arm into the living room.

"Fair is fair," she said cryptically. "Take your shirt off."

He heard the words, but couldn't put them together in a sensible formation. *Fair is fair—take your shirt off?*

"Pardon me?" he said.

"Never mind," she growled impatiently. "I'll do it." She unbuttoned his shirt and pulled it out of his pants. Her eyes collided briefly with his as she operated with an unnerving determination. "I'm going to make love to you. If you have any objections, speak now."

"Do we have time for this?" he asked. He knew he was pushing it, but he'd never seen her this out of control. He couldn't help going for it. "Don't you have a profit-and-loss statement to produce for—?"

The shirt unbuttoned, she pushed it off his shoulders. He pulled his arms out obligingly and let it fall.

"I'll do it after," she said, her eyes snapping at him.

He felt a fleeting scrape of her fingernails as she pulled his T-shirt up. She had to strain on tiptoe, body to body with him, to get it off. Selfishly, he did nothing to help her. He was sure all his vitals were off the chart.

She tossed the T-shirt away, then pulled off her sweater and dropped it on the pile.

He held on to his control with his fingernails.

"That's fine," he said in a carefully removed tone. "We can make it quick."

She unhooked the front closure of her bra and dropped it, then put her fingertips inside the waistband of his jeans.

He felt his stomach muscles kick against her hand.

"We're going to take it slowly," she said, leaning against him so that he felt her breasts flatten against his stomach, the impression of their berry tips creating a memory he thought he would carry forever. "And you're going to regret withholding sex to teach me that work isn't everything."

He held his hands away from her, closing his eyes as she planted kisses across his pectoral muscles. "So far," he said in a thready voice, "I'd be hard put to...regret anything."

She unbuckled his belt. "But I'm not finished yet," she said softly. "Come with me."

She tugged him toward the sofa, unzipped his jeans, then pushed him backward onto the cushions, removed his shoes and tugged the jeans and briefs off.

He had to struggle not to move as she placed a pillow under his head. She kicked off her shoes, then wriggled slowly out of her slacks and panties.

By the time she'd finished and he saw every delicious curve of her enhanced by the firelight, he was beyond control. He grabbed her wrist and pulled her down astride him.

"I was trying to show you," he said, his hands running greedily over her back and hips, "that there *has* to be time for love and play. That even successful labors mean nothing to a soul that can't have fun."

She smiled suddenly, blindingly. "You were right."

He smiled, too. "Well. I love it when you see things my way."

"But our lives do need a little more structure."

"No, they don't." He grinned wickedly. "But do make me regret my high-handed methods. I like the way it's going so far."

"You're so bad," she said, leaning over him with purposeful intent.

He wrapped his arms around her in welcome. "I work at it."

# Chapter Thirteen

"I thought this place was beautiful last night," Karma said to Nate as they did a last perusal of the room to make sure everything was going smoothly. "But it's even more beautiful swarming with children."

Parents occupied the tables, talking and laughing, and examining the gifts left at each table. But the children fairly hummed with excitement, their little bodies fidgeting on the benches as they watched the man and woman wandering up and down the aisle, strumming and singing Christmas carols.

Denise DiBenedetto and Willie Brock, Nancy's mother and stepfather, country singers who'd just finished a southwestern tour in time for the holidays, had insisted on being part of the festivities. They'd even painted stars and cut out snowflakes.

"This project is always very satisfying," Nate said, pointing toward the clock drawing very close to twelve noon. "But it was even more so this year..." He put an arm around her shoulders and pulled her close to kiss her temple. "Because I got to do it with you."

She smiled at him, drunk with the love she felt for him. Last night hadn't solved everything, but at least they'd agreed to disagree peacefully. "You're just self-satisfied because you made me a believer in Christmas."

He kissed her again. "That, too. Did you call April and her mom?"

Karma nodded. April and her mother were watching "the three fussketeers," as the babies were now known among the group. "She said Garrett slept this morning and was a little cranky, but he went back to sleep after she fed him. I hope that's just a cold."

"That's what it looks like," Nate said. "And he's just had his checkup. Any pediatrician's office is a hotbed of germs, no matter how much they sterilize. Come on. We'd better get ready."

Nate pulled her toward the curtain behind the big chair, borrowed from the mayor, where Santa would sit to distribute gifts.

Their group had laughed over their bigamous Santa, who would require two Mrs. Santas to help him—Aggie in a long red dress and apron for the line of girls, and Diantha in a long flowered skirt and blouse and wire-rimmed spectacles for the line of boys. The sexist arrangement was the best they could come up with to help in the sorting and arrangement of presents.

"But the first kid who bad-mouths my outfit," Aggie threatened, "gets nothing for Christmas."

The role of Santa had been assumed by Jo's father, Matt Arceneau, who'd come from Connecticut to spend Christmas with Jo and Ryan. He'd needed a lot of padding to fulfill the physical requirements of the role, but he came equipped with a twinkle in his eye and the kind disposition of a man who gave to children. Karma had not been surprised to learn that he taught American history in a Connecticut high school.

When Riverview Hospital's chief of staff went to the microphone to announce that Santa was ready to distribute toys, pandemonium broke loose.

It took hours to see that every child had the right toy. Karma and Nancy lined up gifts by age on the girls' side, and Nate and Jave did the same on the boys'.

Karma had kept her eye on the square package, wrapped in red and silver Santas, that contained the rag doll that she would always think of as the beginning of her life change. She'd peered through the curtain to see it given to a sturdily built little towhead in a clean but well-worn denim pinafore over a white blouse. She'd had scuffed brown shoes and an eager look in her eye. Karma hoped she wouldn't be disappointed.

By the time each child had a toy, the noise level, even in the huge room, was deafening. But, considering the noise was mostly composed of laughter and cries of delight, no one minded. Parents and those children not completely consumed with their toys went through a buffet table laden with Jo's and Diantha's cookies, and coffee and punch.

Karma used Nate's cellular phone to call April's mother, but found the line busy. Desperate for caffeine after those grueling few hours, she worked her way through the crowd to the table where Jo and Ryan held forth behind tons of cookies and a mountain-high stack of paper plates.

Jo slipped her a cup, pointing behind her to a little boy lovingly clutching one of Tom's wooden trucks in one arm and a Santa cookie in the other. The frosting was all over the child's face.

"I think we're a success," Jo said.

"Have you seen Amy?" Karma asked, groaning with pleasure as the coffee hit her taste buds, then started a warm path to her stomach.

Jo passed a plate to a little girl in braids and indicated the door with her chin. "She's had to schmooze with the press all afternoon. They've taken scores of pictures. I'll bet next year we get lots more help on this thing."

"And where's Tom?"

Jo pursed her lips and shrugged her shoulders. "Never showed up."

Karma stepped aside as a pair of giggling girls rushed past her. "What?"

Jo shrugged. "I don't know the details. I guess he left town for a few days."

"At Christmas? On the day of the party?"

"He called Nancy and said he'd be home for our party Christmas Eve. About that, would you mind bringing pies again? Same kinds?"

"Sure." As the line at the food table grew longer, Karma moved away, with no purpose in particular except to savor what was left of their event.

She couldn't help a small twinge of sadness in the midst of all the excitement. There'd been such fun for her in working with Jo and Nancy and Amy, who'd become her friends, and with Jave and Ryan and Tom, for whom she'd developed a fondness almost as dear.

Because of Nate and Garrett, she'd experienced the love and spirit of Christmas as she never had before.

Karma wandered up the side aisle, content that the afternoon was an unqualified success, and that all the hours spent tracing, cutting, pasting, gluing, painting, mixing and baking had been transformed into the happiness of several hundred little children.

Then, out of the corner of her eye, Karma caught a flash of blond hair and turned to see the little girl in the denim pinafore sitting cross-legged in the middle of a table pushed against the wall to clear a path to the back door. In her arms, in a death grip, was the rag doll. Karma felt tears burn her throat and her eyes. The rag doll would be loved.

The little girl looked up and saw her and turned the doll to face her. "Look," she said. "I got a baby!"

Karma went to sit on the edge of her table. "Well, she's very pretty. Have you given her a name?"

"My mother says Noelle would be nice, because that means Christmas." She hugged the doll to her again. "But I'm going to call her Kathy."

Karma smiled, hoping this bright little girl would find her way out of difficulty and to happiness and success.

"He isn't real, you know," the little girl said, pointing toward Santa, who was now wandering down the aisle, talking to children and parents. "That's just a man inside."

Karma felt compelled to challenge her worldly knowledge. "If he isn't Santa, where did he get so many presents?"

"People fix them up for us." She seemed delighted by the idea. "There's no Santas, just people."

"I see. Well, do you mind that your baby isn't new?"

The little girl looked surprised at the question. "No," she replied with all apparent honesty. "I'm not new, either. I'm five."

Karma hugged her; she couldn't help herself. Then she looked up to see Nate coming toward her.

"Hi," she said, pulling him toward the table. "This is Kathy..." She pointed to the doll in the little girl's arms and saw understanding in Nate's eyes as he glanced at her. "And this is her new mother."

"Hello," Nate said to the little girl. "I'm happy to meet you. And that's a very pretty baby Santa gave you."

Karma glanced at him quickly with a shake of her head, but she was too late to save him.

"Santa isn't real," the little girl said seriously. "He just pretends. People give him the stuff to give to us."

Nate raised an eyebrow in surprise. "Are you sure?"

She nodded. "Yeah. Mom said. The hospital people do this. It's not like a trick or anything, they do it to be nice, and the little babies like Santa, so I guess he's okay. But he isn't real. Only the hospital people are real. There's my mom."

She pointed to a young woman in jeans and a fleece jacket trying to hold on to one little boy pulling against her while buttoning a second one into a raincoat.

"I have to go," she said.

Nate lifted her to the floor. She smiled back at them before running to her mother. "Merry Christmas," she said.

Nate took Karma's face in his hands and brushed her tears away with his thumbs. "I'd say your rag baby is in very competent hands."

EVERYONE went for pizza after cleanup, but Karma begged off, concerned about Garrett.

"Why don't you go with them?" she asked Nate. "I'm sure Jave would bring you home."

He began to shake his head even before she'd finished. "As though I'd enjoy it without you. Come on. We'll get Garrett and have sandwiches when we get home."

Karma hugged him. "Thank you. What a day! I can't wait to get home."

Nate smiled as he negotiated the dark country road that led to April's family's farmhouse. Karma was anxious to go home—to his home, to the rustic retreat that he'd built as a bachelor palace and which *she'd* filled with cinnamon bears, drying moss, an accounting business and a baby.

Not precisely what he'd planned for himself, but he couldn't imagine being happier than he was at this moment. Unless he was married to her.

"You heard that Tom left town?" she asked.

He nodded, turning his brights on. "My guess is that he's gone to see the Porters. Jave thinks so, too. He told Nancy he'd be back by Christmas Eve."

A week and three days. Karma felt a rush of excitement—followed by that little niggling of fear that she guessed was the curse of every God-fearing cynic. Happiness always made you look over your shoulder and wonder what rain cloud might be following you.

Karma smiled against it, thinking she felt strong enough to take on anything. She didn't expect the challenge to be accepted so soon.

She knew something was wrong the moment a wide-eyed April let her into the quietly lit house. The sound of a baby's cries came from somewhere inside the house, but there was a labored sound to it, a curious rasp that raised gooseflesh on Karma's scalp.

She ran through the house in the direction of the sound, past Malia and Chelsea, asleep on a blanket on the sofa, Nate and April behind her. She found April's mother in the small bathroom, holding Garrett partially upright in her hands. She'd turned on the hot water in the shower as a kind of vaporizer.

"Thank God you're here," the woman said. Her face was pale, and her eyes were wide with worry.

Karma tried to take him from her, but Nate pushed her hands aside and took him, laying him on the flat of one arm, Garrett's head resting in his hand. He held the baby's jaw down and peered inside. Garrett whimpered pitifully. He sounded to Karma as though he were breathing his last.

"I was about to call an ambulance," April's mother said. "I don't think this is just a cold. He was doing fine this morning, but when he woke up this afternoon, he seemed suddenly worse. And there's that whistle in his breath. Then he's gotten much worse this evening. I called the fairgrounds, but you'd already left. I'm sorry."

Karma fought the impulse to rip the baby from Nate's arms and hold him to her. "What is it?" she demanded. "What's wrong?"

He shook his head. "I'm not sure. But it's no cold. Something's blocking his airway. Here, hold on to him and keep his head up." He went into the other room to call an ambulance.

"I think it's epiglottitis," he said to the dispatcher. "There's a stridor in his breath and the epiglottis is swollen."

The dispatcher sounded distressed herself. "Dr. Foster, our teams are both out. One's at a traffic accident at the other end of the county, and one's on a broken-hip call at the nursing home."

Nate swore, punched the phone off, and hurried back into the bathroom to take Karma by the arm. "Come on," he said. "We're going to the hospital."

Nate felt perspiration break out on his body as they ran to the car. He helped Karma in with Garrett, then ran around and started the car even before he closed his door. His hands weren't shaking; they never shook. But everything else inside him was the consistency of pudding.

*Keep it together,* he told himself firmly. *You've got to keep it together.*

Karma felt suddenly as though *she* couldn't breathe, as though *she* had a fever. Every labored little breath seemed to rip her own throat. She found herself breathing deeply, as though that could make Garrett do the same.

"Nate..." she said worriedly as the motor sparked to life.

Nate raced down the dark lane while calling the hospital on his cellular phone.

"I'm coming in with a three-month-old on the brink of respiratory arrest," he said. "I suspect epiglottitis." He listened a moment, then put the phone to the steering wheel just long enough to use both hands to turn onto the road. "Yeah," he said into the phone. "His doctor's Dade. Right. Garrett Endicott."

The brakes screeched and the tires squealed as Nate negotiated another turn. Gravel spewed in all directions.

"Nate, he sounds awful!" Karma said, barely fighting off panic.

"Sit him up against your arm a little higher," he said, flooring the accelerator. "Ten minutes. We'll be there in ten minutes."

Nate heard the baby's broken gasp for breath and felt dread, like a cold finger, hit every one of his vertebrae. Garrett didn't have ten minutes.

Nine minutes. He could be there in nine minutes. Then they could intubate him, give him antibiotics...

Old memories filled the darkness surrounding the car, rose around him like threatening specters—a baby gasping, purpling, dying under his hands. Clogged tubing, a mother crying.

He raced around a car, caused another coming from the other direction to screech onto the shoulder, moved back into his lane and prayed, *Please, don't make me have to do this. Please. I don't want to do this.*

Seven minutes.

Six minutes.

Garrett tried to drag in air in one noisy rasp that stopped in the middle like a broken note. Then Karma screamed.

"Nate, he isn't breathing. I don't think he's breathing!"

*Damn it! I said I didn't want to do this!* Nate jerked the car off the road and down into the darkened parking lot of the mooring basin.

"Get in the back with him," he ordered Karma while he reached into the glove compartment for his flashlight, into his pocket for the knife on his key ring.

She didn't question him, but did as he asked. The pen in his pocket was the stick variety, and he reached over the back seat to hand her her purse.

"Do you have a pen?" he demanded, getting out of the front seat and kneeling down in the confining space in the back. There was barely room to move back here. He wouldn't be able to do this!

He steadied himself as best he could and turned the light on Garrett's face. He was turning blue.

Karma produced a pen. Another stick. He swore, panic threatening to overtake him. Then he noticed the narrow white-paper-wrapped drinking straw protruding from the pocket of a vinyl organizer on the back of the driver's seat. He thanked heaven for Karma's compulsion for tidiness.

He snatched it out, ripped the paper off and cut it to about three inches long with his knife.

Using the barrel of a pen for an airway had become such a cliché anyway, he thought absently to distract himself from what he had to do. He'd seen it on "M*A*S*H," he'd seen it on one of those live-action cop shows, he remembered vividly the illustration of it in his emergency medicine text. But he didn't want to do it!

"Now hold this on his throat," he said, handing her the light.

He felt for the cricoid notch. On an adult, it was a small indentation between two ridges of cartilage. On a child, it was a minute space just above the vocal cords that only an experienced touch could find. And he'd always resisted working on children.

He tried to block out Karma's soft weeping and his own terror and remember his anatomy. Then he found it, almost nothing more than a suggestion of space in the tiny throat.

His heartbeat thudding in his ears, he positioned the sharp blade of his pocketknife precisely where he would make the incision.

"Nate!" Karma whispered, one fist going to her mouth when she realized what he was about to do, the other hand placed protectively over her baby.

He ignored her anguish. He ignored his own. He prayed for the steadiness for which he was well-known when there wasn't a child involved—when this child wasn't involved.

He tried prayer one more time. *All right, if you're going to make me do this, you damn well better stand by me!* It occurred to him that the style was poor, but the sincerity was certainly there.

Everything inside him trembling, though his hand was steady as a rock, he made the small incision. With great care, he separated skin and tissue with his thumb and forefinger, and didn't even register Karma's sob.

He held his hand out to her. "The straw."

She put it in his hand, and he inserted it into the incision. A whoosh of breath came through it almost immediately.

"All right!" he shouted. Then he pushed at Karma as he held the straw in place. "You have to drive. Go!"

Joanie, the rent-a-doc, McNamara and Dade met them in the parking lot. Mac and Dade took Garrett right up to surgery, and Nate sat with Karma in the waiting room. She lay curled against him, alternately sobbing and praying. His mind was blank.

"Epiglottitis," Dade reported cheerfully a miraculously short time later, as he sat down on the other side of Karma. "Nate was right. Comes on almost without warning, usually the result of the flu. Can be fatal if you're a long way from a hospital—unless you happen to be riding with an emergency room doctor. Good work, Nate. Neat little cricothyrotomy. Bitch to do on babies."

Karma sat up and sniffed. "You mean he's going to be all right?"

Dade nodded. "We'll have to keep him a few days, get some antibiotics into him. Can you stay?"

"Yes, of course."

Karma felt as though she'd been reborn. Watching Garrett choke had been like death, and watching Nate make the incision in her son's throat had been like being pitched into hell. But hearing that her baby would be fine was like coming alive again on a sunny morning.

"I'll arrange for a bed for you, Karma," Dade said. "Nate, go get a drink. You look like hell."

As the doctor left, Karma wrapped her arms around Nate's neck and sobbed again, but this time she wept with happiness. "Oh, Nate. He's going to be all right. You saved him! You saved him!"

Her delirium ran so high that it was long moments before she became aware of Nate's unresponsiveness. Then she drew away apologetically, knowing he loved Garrett as much as she did, certain he was simply experiencing delayed terror now that the crisis was over. And suddenly she knew beyond a doubt that nothing short of marriage could contain her love for him.

"You saved Garrett's life," she told him, leaning forward to kiss his lips. "He's fine. He's going to be fine."

But he sat there stiffly, his eyes unfocused, his hands in his lap. He finally forced himself to meet her eyes and smile. He knew the result was thin. "Right," he said. "You go stay with him, and I'll check in with you in the morning."

And that was when the new terror hit her. That was when she felt as though she had died a second time.

"Check in with me?" she asked in a flat tone.

She saw him try to force a smile. "I meant I'll come and see you."

"Nate, I don't..." she began, prepared to confront whatever this problem was.

But he shook his head. "Tomorrow we'll talk ab—"

He tried to push off the vinyl sofa, but she held him down with a hand on his shoulder. "No. I want you to tell me what you're thinking."

That was the last thing he intended to do. He stood and pulled her with him. "Come on. We'll find out where they're putting him, and I—"

She caught his arm and pulled him to a stop as he headed for the door. "This is your nightmare realized, isn't it? This is why you didn't want to fall in love, why you didn't want to be a parent."

Nate put a hand to his eyes, feeling as though the last two hours had been two weeks long. "Do we really have to do this now?"

"Yes," she insisted brutally. "Garrett is in a hospital bed, and I want to know if he's going to have you in his life tomorrow."

There were moments when he admired her ability to lay the truth bare. This wasn't one of them.

He tried to dig deep down where the truth was and find a way to make her understand it. "I can't tell you what it felt like to cut on him," he said. His voice was low, as though he'd blown some kind of personal fuse. "That fragile flesh, that tiny space . . .'' he gasped, the memory a pain.

"Nate," she said, tears in her voice and in her eyes. "You saved his *life.*" She swallowed and cleared her throat. Her voice came out stronger, fuller. "You knew what to do, because you're a doctor. You have the advantage over so many other parents. If I were in love with another accountant," she said, her voice rising, "my son would be dead now!"

Nate shook his head. "Maybe if he were a little bigger, a little older . . ."

She laughed mirthlessly. "Nate, if he were bigger, he'd be riding his bike downhill with no hands. If he were older, he'd be driving!"

Nate refused to accept her logic. Somewhere between the beginning of the incision he'd made in Garrett's throat and the end, he'd known he couldn't deal with having a child, after all.

He shook his head, his heart like an anchor in his chest. "Karma, I love you. And I love him. But I can't do this. Maybe you were right all along. I'm not sure this will work."

Cold dread filled her being. This couldn't be. Not now that she finally understood that she *wanted* to belong to him, wanted to make him exclusively hers—legally, spiritually, in any and every way she could seal the bargain. "What?" she asked flatly.

"I got lucky tonight," he said, "but it could just as well have ended badly. Believe me, I know. Would you have still loved me then?"

She uttered a sound of angry exasperation. "Nate, I love you more than my own life, and I think you're the kindest, most caring, smartest, most wonderful man I've ever met. But I *don't* think you're God! I adore the skill in you that saved Garrett's life, but do you think I'd have blamed you if he'd died?''

He couldn't reason anymore. He didn't even want to think. He needed to fall down somewhere and sleep for a week.

"I don't know," he said. "I only know I can deal with being responsible for an adult's life, but I don't want to be responsible for a child's."

Karma thought that was pretty clear. But she wasn't going to make it easy for him. He had to say it. "So, you want out?"

He looked at her, misery in every line of his body. "Be honest," he said. "Aren't *you* afraid to invest your love in something you can lose without warning?"

Karma let herself admit that it was over. It hurt like hell, but she imagined it would for a long time. "It seems," she said, snatching her purse off the sofa, "that I've already done that." She stalked out of the room.

"Look at him," Bert cooed, leaning over the crib to hold both of Garrett's hands. He made wild noises and smiled, showing her his gums. "You'd never guess there'd been anything wrong with him. He's turning into such a cutie. And what a grip!"

*Wait till I'm ready to pitch! I feel so much better! But where's Nate? Is he coming over soon? When do we eat?*

Karma leaned beside her, amazed at her son's recuperative powers. Only three days after that horrifying ordeal, he was bright eyed and pink cheeked, and looked suddenly longer, bigger. She guessed it was her own relief that was "enlarging" him, but whatever it was, she took comfort in it. He was all she had left.

It was strange, she thought, that just three months ago, before the automobile accident that brought on labor, he'd been all she had, and she'd looked forward with excited anticipation to their lives together. She'd envisioned working with him beside her, walks on sunny days, and books to read and games to play when it rained. She'd seen long, lazy evenings when they would learn about each other and plan his future.

Now both of them knew that would never be enough. They'd have been happy together, but their lives wouldn't have had that dimension of surprise, curiously coupled with security, that Nate gave them.

There wouldn't be as much laughter. There would be no broken toys awaiting repair and cluttering the house for months before Christmas, no one striding through the house with Garrett in a football hold, no one leaving roses in her mailbox. The sob she held back burned in her chest.

"What are you going to do now?" Bert asked gently as Karma turned on the new musical mobile Bert had brought Garrett.

"The same thing I did before," Karma replied. "I've acquired a lot of new clients, and the first of the year is a very busy time for me. Mrs. Bennett's going to come over half days so I can work hard and get enough money together to rent a work space. We're going to be fine."

Colorful little fabric animals danced in a circle to the tinkling music, and Garrett's eyes grew big as he watched. He waved his arms and kicked his feet. He was changing, Karma thought, feeling both maternal excitement and personal loss. Nate wasn't here to see him.

*Wow! Those are cool! Thanks, Aunt Bert. The music's a little tinny, though. Nate plays* The Three Tenors. *Now, that's music. Why are those animals out of my reach?*

SHE LED BERT to the living room, trying to turn her thoughts in another direction.

"I really appreciate you picking us up at the hospital this morning."

Bert dismissed her gratitude with a shake of her head. "My pleasure. Ryan told me to take as long as I needed to make sure you were okay. He said to tell you Nancy and Jo will bring your dinner by tonight."

Well, she wasn't *so* alone, she told herself bracingly. She had wonderful friends. "That's great. But *I'm* not an invalid. I'll be fine. You go back to work."

Bert looked into her eyes and said gently, "Maybe Nate will have second thoughts. You know, men hate being afraid, and I'll bet that just scared the bejeebers out of him because he loves Garrett so much. He loves *you* so much. I mean, having to do that procedure on a tiny baby in the back of a car in the dark! With a pocketknife!"

Karma put a hand on Bert's arm to stop her. She felt woozy at the memory, recalled the stark terror of watching her baby turn blue and knowing that a knife at his throat was the only thing that would save him.

"Oh, I'm sorry." Bert pushed her into a chair. "I'll put a pot of coffee on before I go. You want me to call for Chinese takeout? A pizza?" She peered out at her from the kitchen, a grin on her lips. "A half gallon of rum-raisin ice cream?"

Karma frowned at her. "No one delivers ice cream."

"Yes, they do," Bert said. "I've had it done a couple of times. Once when the loan manager dumped me for the gift shop lady with the big . . . deposits." She waggled her eyebrows. "And once when my mother told me I *wasn't* adopted. What's your favorite flavor?"

"Chocolate—white-chocolate chunk."

"Good choice. I'll make the call."

NATE AWOKE to a loud rap on his front door. He didn't bother with a robe, but raced downstairs in his underwear to answer it.

He prayed that it was Karma. And he prayed that it wasn't. He hadn't resolved the baby problem in his own mind, but he was gradually dying of loneliness without her and Garrett.

The morning after the nightmare procedure on the side of the road, he'd gone to the hospital to see them. Karma had been calmly polite. Garrett had lain weakly amid tubes and blankets. It had been a grisly experience that he'd repeated two more days.

Then, yesterday, he'd borrowed Ryan's car and gone to pick them up and take them home, prepared to try to discuss the issue calmly and ask Karma to help him search for a solution. But Beachie had told him they'd already been picked up by a friend. In the three days since, he'd called several times and gotten no answer. He'd had to call Jave to reassure himself that Garrett was all right. Then Nancy had told him she'd seen Karma and she appeared to be fine—"physically, at least."

This was a busy time of year for accountants, he knew. And, of course, with a baby, Karma was always busy.

She probably didn't have time to hear him say he was sorry he'd hurt her, but he considered it kinder to admit the truth than to hurt her more deeply later.

But if that was her at the door, he didn't give a damn about later. All he wanted was to see her, to hold her—now!

It was Tom.

"Hi." The bill of his baseball cap faced front and was pulled down low over his eyes. He looked exhausted, but he readjusted his hat to get a better look at Nate's state of undress. "You always answer the door like that?"

Nate sighed. "I thought you were Karma. Come on in." He held the door open, then closed it behind him. He wasn't sure he had the capacity for someone else's suffering at the moment, but he'd give it a shot. It might distract him from his own.

"So... you guys have split up?" Tom asked, pulling out a kitchen chair and sitting down.

Nate, in the act of pouring coffee, turned to frown at him over his shoulder. "How do you know that? I thought you've been out of town."

"Got in this morning," he said. "Had breakfast with Jave."

Nate brought him a steaming cup, then opened the pink bakery box on the table. He'd picked up doughnuts on the way home from the hospital this morning, knowing there'd be no sausages and eggs waiting for him, no fragrant coffee cake hot out of the oven.

"You see the Porters?" He sat opposite Tom with his own cup and reached into the box for an apple fritter.

Tom pulled out a cream-cheese Danish. "I did. We talked for a day and a half. I guess they needed it, too."

"And they don't blame you?"

"No."

"Blockhead. I told you." Nate toasted him with his mug. He thought Tom looked as though he'd been to war and returned alive, but somehow changed. Seeing Davey Porter's parents had apparently helped him square himself with the past to some degree, but he probably felt that nothing would exonerate him completely. Still, it was a step forward. "What happens now?"

Tom chewed a bite of Danish, swallowed, and took a long, slow sip of coffee. "I'm working up my courage to go see Amy," he said reluctantly.

"She's great," Nate said encouragingly. "We all love her."

Tom nodded. "It's just hard to admit you've been a jerk."

Nate angled him a grin. "You should be used to it."

"Hey," Tom said, with a smile that made him look a little more like himself. "I'm feeling a little fragile here. Cut me some slack."

Tom finished his Danish, then carried his cup to the counter. "What happens now with you and Karma?" he asked.

Nate rubbed a hand over his burning eyes. "Nothing. I think it's over."

Tom came back to the table and frowned down at him judiciously. "I thought you were 'dealing' with your fears."

Nate scraped his chair back and stood. "So did I," he admitted grimly. "Then Garrett was choking, and I was sure the whole time I was going to lose him. I can't deal with the responsibility of having to keep him safe."

"Pardon me," Tom asked, "but did you miss the fact that because of you he's alive today?"

"No. I just know how easily it could have gone the other way."

Tom raised an eyebrow at him, then waved his own words in his face. "So, it's easier to hurt than to get better?"

Nate raised an eyebrow, too. "How the hell would you know?"

But Tom did know. He was better. Nate could see it in his face. But it also looked as though it had cost him something.

"I do," Tom said simply. Then he changed his tone as he took another Danish and started for the door. "You coming to Jo and Ryan's for Christmas Eve? Housewarming and wedding planning, I understand.''

"Good for them," Nate said, but he shook his head as he followed him. "I switched with our rent-a-doc. I'm doing his swings for a couple of days. He's got a date with Joanie Christmas Eve.''

"You're a chicken," Tom said accusingly.

Nate nodded. "But you're a weirdo.''

# Chapter Fourteen

The woman was skin and bone, and not as old as Nate had thought her to be when Baldwin and Prentice brought her in. The Dumpster she'd been sleeping in had been hit by a drunk driver, and she'd been bruised, but he could find no broken bones or sign of internal injuries.

He saw her look up at the IV that was dripping normal saline and a piggyback of Ancef into her. Then her eyes went to the red and green paper garlands strung around the room, to the Santas and snowmen on the window that separated the ER from the waiting room.

"Christmas," she said. "My folks is in Tennessee. Won't get to see them, though."

I hear you, Nate thought, moving to inspect the open ulcer above her ankle. My family's right here, but I won't get to see them, either.

"I drink too much," she added, lying quietly as he examined her. "Families and alcohol don't mix."

Nate looked into her eyes and saw the deadness that was the other side of desperation. She was beyond trying. She knew the addiction was stronger than she was.

"There's a good program through the shelter, Patty," he said. "You could be better in time to see your family for Easter."

She looked at him as though he were an innocent. "I been in programs."

"Then you'll be good at it."

Joanie joined him, giving him a look that said almost the same thing Patty's had said, just from a different perspective.

Many of the ER staff had long ago given up on the homeless, the druggies, the battered and the broken, some of whom they saw time and time again, mired in their weaknesses and the vagaries of fate.

Patty hadn't been in before, but her odor, and the circumstances in which she'd been found, suggested she'd been living at the bottom for a long time.

But he had a license to heal, and he figured that related to the inside, as well as the outside.

Her bleary brown eyes looked into his, and he felt a frail connection.

"Where is this shelter?" she asked.

"Downtown," he replied, exploring the ulcer. It was silver dollar size and bright right around the edges. There was scarring around it, suggesting a burn that had healed, but this part of the injury had gone much deeper. "It's right behind the park. Want me to call and have somebody from the shelter pick you up?" He turned to Joanie. "Rinse with normal saline. Polysporine ointment, adaptic dressing and fluffs. Wrap in Kerlix."

Patty sighed. "I don't know."

"You think about it," he said, "while Joanie fixes you up. This burn looks pretty old. Haven't you seen someone about this before?"

"Millie put some stuff on it for me."

"Millie?"

"She was with me the night of the fire."

Nate had reached for her chart, then stopped and turned, some sixth sense in him kicking on.

"We didn't even know nothin' was wrong," Patty went on. "We'd gone in to try to keep warm in the basement of the hotel. I woke up 'cause of the smoke and the noise, then the wall fell in and it was like all the fires o' hell was after us. I screamed at Millie, and screamed, and shook her till she was on her feet. That's when I got burned."

Nate listened to the words—then felt the ripple effect of their meaning like the resounding echoes of a gong only inches from his face. The Harmony Hotel fire? In a town the size of Heron Point, there weren't that many fires, and everyone remembered them. "I screamed at Millie," she'd said, "and screamed . . ."

"The Harmony Hotel fire?" he asked.

"Yeah. That one that was empty. Used to stand over by the bus station." She pointed a grimy finger in the general direction.

He wanted to be absolutely sure. "Tell me again what happened."

She frowned fearfully. "I didn't do it. Me and Millie was just—"

He shook his head quickly. "No, I know you didn't do it. It was a problem with the wiring. But tell me again about you and Millie."

She repeated the story, emphasizing again how she'd had to scream to wake Millie.

Nate stared at her, unable to believe it. Well. Life did have its little trade-offs. He'd had a loss, but he was going to score a win for his buddy.

As he looked up, April walked in with a tray of coffee. "April!" he called. "Is Dr. Nicholas still here?"

She nodded. "I just saw him in the cafeteria."

"Will you tell him I need him to meet me here in ten minutes? Room one." It was the only room with a door.

"Sure."

"Patty," he said to the woman, who still looked worried over his sudden interest in her relationship to the fire. "I want you to tell this story to a friend of mine. We're going to keep you overnight, get you feeling better, then I'll have somebody from the shelter pick you up in the morning. And I promise you a plane ticket to go see your family when you're finished with the program."

Her eyes widened. "Just . . . to tell the story?"

"Yes."

"But I didn't start it. Me and Millie was—"

"I know. Nobody thinks you did anything wrong. I just want you to tell the story one more time, okay?"

"A plane ticket to Tennessee?"

"I promise."

Her eyes lost their focus for a moment, and he saw her exploring all the possibilities a trip home might entail. She laughed nervously. "Honest?"

"Swear to God."

She smiled. It illuminated her face. "Okay."

Nate called Tom. "I need you to come down to the hospital now," he said.

There was a surprised silence on the other end of the phone. "The hos— Nate, I'm finishing a dollhouse I'm making for Malia. I can't . . ."

"Finish it for next Christmas. I need you here now."

"Nate—"

"Now! The ER. Ten minutes."

"The ER—?"

Tom arrived looking harried, his baseball cap and his hooded black sweatshirt speckled with sawdust. He looked at Jave, sitting on the edge of a small table, and at Nate, leaning a shoulder against the wall. Then he frowned at the patient on the gurney.

"Look," he said to Nate. "I know you two have come to depend on me for every little thing, but I'm a busy man.

I've come running to you this time, but from now on I'm unavailable for medical consultations."

Nate and Jave looked at each other. Jave shook his head. "I'm sorry. When my mother was carrying him, she was frightened by Henny Youngman."

Nate straightened and indicated Patty.

"Tom, this is Patty. Patty, my friend, Tom."

Tom pulled off his hat and offered his hand. "Hi, Patty."

Nate decided that was why he loved him. There wasn't a superior bone in his body.

"Patty has a story we'd like you to hear," Nate said.

Jave reached out to push a chair toward Tom. "Sit down," he said.

Tom frowned in confusion. "She have a wooden leg?" he whispered. "And you need me to—?"

Jave pointed to the chair. "Sit. And shut up."

"Right."

Nate touched Patty's arm encouragingly. "Tell him everything about the night you and Millie slept in the old building."

She looked at Nate, wide-eyed. "And you're gonna give me the plane ticket?"

"I promise."

"Okay. Was a year ago, maybe a little longer...." She joined both hands in her lap, and began to recount the story, telling Tom how she and Millie had been friends for a long time, only she died last year of pneumonia and drink. "We went in the old building to keep warm," she said, "and we was drinkin' wine, 'cause somebody at the church had given Millie five dollars."

Tom glanced in confusion at Nate but nodded politely to Patty.

"We got toasty warm and fell asleep, and we didn't know nothin' was wrong till we heard this rumblin' noise, then sirens. Then the wall fell down and fire came in like somebody was hosin' it at us."

Tom sat absolutely still, his expression frozen.

"What building was it, Patty?" Nate asked.

"The old hotel by the bus station."

A spasm crossed Tom's face.

"What happened after the wall fell?"

"Well, I started screamin' for Millie to get up, to get out, but it took me a while to wake her up."

"How did you do it?"

"I just kept screamin'."

Tom stared at her one more moment, eyes dark in utter disbelief. Then he got slowly to his feet. He was white.

"How," he asked weakly, "did you get out?"

"There was all these police outside. So we went down the basement. They're all connected under the street, you know, from the old days. We came up through the bus station's back room. It's got a broken window. That's how we always got in."

Tom closed his eyes. His mouth contorted, and he put a hand to it. Jave stood and went to put an arm around his shoulders.

"Somebody screamed." Tom choked the words out, leaning against him. "I told you somebody screamed."

"You're the only one who doubted you," Jave said, his voice shaky.

Nate, his throat tight and his eyes burning, smiled at Patty. "Good job," he said. "We'll admit you for tonight, and tomorrow I'll bring your airline tickets to the shelter." Having them in her possession, he hoped, would see her through detox.

Nate stood to go for a wheelchair, but then the back of his lab coat was caught in a fist and he was yanked to a stop. Tom pulled him into his arm, and the three of them stood in the tiny office, arms entangled, laughing, crying.

"How did you find out?" Tom asked, his eyes still glazed with disbelief.

Nate shrugged. He explained what had brought Patty to the ER. "She had a burn scar, I asked about it, she told me, and I knew she was your screamer from that night."

Tom pulled him into his arms, almost paralyzing him. "Thank you."

"Hey. You harass me," Nate said in a strangled voice, "I move sun and moon for you. It's a fifty-fifty friendship."

There was a brisk knock on the door, and then it burst open and Amy Brown stood there, pale and wide-eyed in a pink sweater and pants, her new hairstyle slightly disheveled. "What is it?" she demanded. "I heard that Tom was rushed here...." She looked from one man to the other, then saw Tom, obviously fit, and sagged visibly with relief. "Well, you look all right," she finished accusingly.

"He wasn't *rushed* here," Nate told her, "but hurried here on his own."

"Why?"

He shrugged innocently. "To see you, I imagine." He turned and winked at Tom. "The rest is up to you, buddy. Don't mess up. Come on, Jave. We'll find a room for Patty, then I'll buy you a Coke in the cafeteria."

"A Coke? How come *I* don't get plane tickets?"

KARMA WAS PACING the floor with Garrett for the third night in a row, thinking that she really didn't blame him for raising such a ruckus. She'd give anything for the freedom to scream at the top of her lungs as he'd done incessantly for time beyond measure. But she was the mom. She had to try to keep it together.

Only it had all dissolved on her. There was no laughter in her world, no happiness, no warmth, no comfort. She had Garrett, but he was as miserable as she was, and she couldn't seem to find a way to comfort him.

Christmas surrounded her—mocked her. She had a tree in the living room, gifts under the tree for the Nicholas children, for Chelsea, and a dozen things for Garrett. Carols blared from the radio and the television, and she had several floral arrangements around the room and a fruit basket from clients wishing her Happy Holidays.

The woman who'd once thought the Christmas holidays were a lot of hype punctuated by dollar signs finally believed in love and miracles and hope reborn. And now that Nate wasn't here to share all those qualities, their absence hurt far more than when she hadn't believed in them at all. Even Garrett seemed to want no part of her.

*I WANT NATE! Where is he? I thought we were finally all together, and I haven't seen him in days! I want a father! I can't face Malia and Chelsea tomorrow night without a father. So, where is he? What have you done with him?*

KARMA SAT in the rocker with Garrett, remembering the fun and excitement of the Christmas party. That reminded her of the little girl who'd been thrilled with the rag doll she'd been given by the Santa she didn't believe in.

She'd had such an admirable grasp on life, Karma thought. She'd known what was real and what wasn't, and she'd taken it all in stride. The hospital people, she'd said, were the real Santas.

Karma felt philosophy abandon her as she tried to cope with the probability that Nate was out of her life forever. As a profound sadness overtook her, she remembered that night in his bed, how tender he'd been, how changed she'd felt.

Then came the image of his grandmother's sampler on the wall. All Things Bloom With Love, it had read.

She sat up with a start. Garrett shrieked.

NATE SAT in the empty cafeteria and listened to the sounds of the cooler and the pop machine. His shift was over, Tom had left much earlier with Amy, and Jave had gone home to Nancy.

He was going home to emptiness.

Of course, that was his own fault. He would have been the first to admit it. It was beginning to occur to him that his decision had deprived him of Karma and Garrett anyway, though nothing horrible had happened to them. They were hale and hearty, only a mile away from him—and as beautiful and wonderful as Karma was, and as cute and endearing as Garrett was, some other guy with guts was going to make them a part of *his* life.

He'd been stupid and cowardly, and now it was probably too late.

Then he remembered Patty and the light he'd seen in her eyes when he convinced her she had another chance.

He sat up as it occurred to him that it was possible *he* could have another chance. Maybe he could decide to approach it a day at a time, concentrate on what he had instead of what he could lose, tell Karma he loved her and beg her to forgive him.

It was a lot to ask, but he had nothing to lose. Without them, he felt as if there was nothing left anyway.

He crushed the pop can in his hand, tossed it at the recycling box, and looked at the clock—12:45 a.m. He couldn't wake her at this hour. He'd go home, take a shower, and stare at the ceiling until eight o'clock.

BY THE TIME HE GOT HOME, he'd convinced himself that it was a dumb idea and she'd slam the door in his face. But he decided that he deserved that, and he wouldn't let it stop him.

He heard a baby screaming when he walked up the steps. Memories of Garrett, he thought. Wishful thinking.

It grew louder as he put his key in the door. He looked around. Not a soul in sight. It must be exhaustion.

He pushed the door open and knew instantly that the screams were real. And they were Garrett's. He felt simultaneous bursts of joy and panic. Was Karma here? Was something wrong?

"Karma?" he shouted, flipping on the living room light. She bloomed out of the darkness like somebody's attic angel in ratty sweats, her ponytail dragging, long, straight strands of hair hanging around her eyes and temples.

Her cheeks were pink and puffy, her eyes damp and tired. He felt their sadness like his own pain.

He stopped about a foot from her, both ecstatic and confused by her presence. Was she here for personal or medical reasons? Garrett was screaming, and she looked as though she might collapse at any moment.

"What?" he asked gently.

She swallowed, and it looked as though it hurt. "Garrett's been crying for four days," she said, her voice raspy.

Was that medical or personal? He still wasn't sure. He closed the space between them and took the baby from her. "Here, let me see him."

*AAAAGGGHHH! Aaagghh! Aagghh! Oh, hi. Well, it's about time. Where have you been? I've been calling for you for days! Look, are we all together, or what? Because there's a party tomorrow, or today—you've had me so upset I don't know if it's day or night—and if I don't have a father by then, I'm not going. Those girls are going to lord it over me again, and I'm just not up to it. So, what's it going to be?*

*Or is that the wrong approach? You like it when I smile, don't ya? How's that? And when I grab your finger. Feel that? I've been working out. I've got this new mobile, and I can almost reach it.*

*So what do you say? I know you're concerned because of that episode the other night, but, hey, I'm over that, and I promise not to do it again. I'm not going to be a reckless kid. I'm her son. How foolhardy do you think I'll be?*

*I can reach my toes now, and pretty soon I'll learn to count. I might go into accounting, too.*

NATE LOOKED AT KARMA as Garrett quieted, smiled and grabbed his index finger. "I think," he said, "that he just wanted me."

Karma watched her son at work and couldn't shake the feeling that he'd somehow intended this all along. All right. She was on his side.

She squared her shoulders and tugged on her sweatshirt, trying to lend herself some shred of dignity. When she'd decided to come here, she'd run out of the house without even a glance in the mirror.

"Well, he gets that from me, you know," she said, hope swelling in her because Nate's eyes were burning into her. But she also felt a painful lump in her throat. Could it be that she was simply seeing in Nate what she wanted to see?

Nate couldn't quite believe his ears. He opened his mouth to speak, and couldn't.

Afraid he didn't care, Karma pressed her case. "There's Christmas stuff all over the place, and *you*—" she stabbed a finger at him accusingly "—filled me with the spirit, and now it's worse than if I'd never had it, because you took it away! All the things I used to be able to do alone don't work anymore, because I got used to doing them with *you*. I hate my little house now that I've lived in this one, I can't eat my cooking 'cause you're not there to tell me how good it is, I can't sleep because you're not there to hold me. And because I'm not in that bed with your grandmother's sampler over it. All things bloom with love, remember?''

*EASY, Mom. You're going to spook him.*

SHE RESISTED the impulse to throw herself into his arms, to burst into tears. Instead, she swallowed and tried to make sense.

"Nate," she said reasonably, though her voice quaked, "we love each other. Don't you think if we try, we could both bloom? You'll grow to learn to cope with having a child, and I'll grow to be more understanding, more flexible, more..."

Nate looked into her anguished eyes and had to stop her with his fingertips to her mouth. "You don't have to be more anything. I'm the one who—"

He stopped abruptly as he realized what she was giving him. Another chance.

"You love me," he asked, "after I left you at your baby's bedside?"

Karma looked into his eyes and did see love burning there, she was sure of it. It was there when he looked at Garrett. And it flamed when he looked at her.

She sniffed and folded her arms. "That *was* pretty crummy." She glanced up at the vaulted ceiling. She felt a tear spill over and swiped it away. "Does this house come with you?"

Nate couldn't believe this, but he wasn't going to question it. He had to clear his throat. "Yes, it comes with me."

"Then, yes," she said. "I want you."

He pulled her to him, and she fell against him, sobbing happily, wrapping her arm around Garrett to enclose him in their circle.

"I'm sorry," Nate said. "I was being irrational, I guess. That scared the hell out of me, and in my business fear often means failure."

She hugged him hard. "We're going to be able to do this, I'm sure of it. With my organizational skills and your ability to make fun out of nothing, I think we can have a deliriously happy marriage, and raise a healthy, happy child."

*I'M NOT WORRIED.*

"AH, speaking of organizational skills," Nate said, kissing the top of her head. "Have you misplaced your car? I didn't see it when I drove up."

She grinned sheepishly up at him. "I left it at the park and walked a block. I was afraid if you didn't want to see me, you'd take off at the sight of my car."

He rolled his eyes. "I've thought about nothing but you and Garrett for days. I called, but you weren't home."

She nodded. "I turned the ringer off a few times when Garrett fell asleep out of sheer exhaustion. He's been horrid, and I've been like a zombie. Ah..." She drew out of his arms to go to the sofa, where she'd left Garrett's carrier. She pulled a long, thin box out of it and handed it to him, taking the baby so that Nate could open it. "Merry Christmas from Garrett and me."

Nate pulled the paper off and lifted the lid. Inside were a dog collar and a white envelope.

"Ah...what are you suggesting here, my love?" he asked.

She swatted his shoulder. "Open the envelope, you nit."

He did, and found American Kennel Club papers for a four-month-old harlequin Great Dane registered as Skywalker of Stratford.

"You can pick him up at the breeder's on the twenty-sixth," Karma said, her heart melting at the deep-down delight in his eyes. "We can give him a less pretentious name."

He wrapped her in his arms. "Thank you. It feels good to have you endorse my dreams." Then he put her away from him and went to the kitchen table, which was covered with gifts. He sorted through them and returned to her with one roughly the same shape her box had been. He took Garrett back.

Karma unwrapped it and found a legal-looking document inside. She read it and screamed.

"A year's rent paid on the office with the skylight in the Chambers Building!"

She hugged Nate fiercely. "Thank you! I've wanted that office for so long. I can't believe you remembered I said that. So . . . you endorse my dreams, too?"

"Completely. We're going to have a great time."

"I know." She leaned lazily against him, clutching the box. Her eyelids drooped heavily. "I'm so happy."

"You also look exhausted. Maybe we should go to bed," he said. "I had rather a big day myself."

*YAWN. Me, too. Crying that much is very tiring. I almost hyperventilated twice.*

KARMA leaned lazily against Nate as he walked toward the stairs. "What happened?"

He told her about Patty, and how she had finally resolved Tom's questions about the night of the fire. "So, when we get up," he said, "I have to get her airline tickets to Tennessee."

They reached the top of the stairs, and she turned to kiss him soundly. "So, you're the real Santa?"

He hugged her to him. "Santa isn't real, according to the little girl at the party."

"She said he was a front for 'the hospital people.'" She leaned back to smile at him, thinking that she hadn't known it was possible to be this happy. "That's you. The real Santa. So, am I going to be Mrs. Santa, or Mrs. Foster?"

"Well, how would it sound?" Nate asked, sitting on the edge of the bed with her and Garrett. "Karma Santa."

"I don't think so," she said.

"Right. Karma Foster."

"That's elegant."

*DON'T FORGET ME. Garrett Joseph Santa. I don't think that cuts it. I go for Foster.*

"GARRETT FOSTER," Nate said. "What do you think of that?"

Garrett waved both arms. They laughed.

Karma looked at Nate, her heart in her eyes. "I love it. And I love you."

*YES. It has a ring to it. "Garrett Foster pilots the first spacecraft to Mars." Or "Garrett Foster, Olympic gold medalist in boxing, flyweight division..." Or—this would be cool!—"Garrett Joseph Foster was elected fiftieth president of the United States by a landslide. Insiders attribute his success to the promise to make Christmas a yearlong celebration."*

"Yeah. I like it. Merry Christmas, Mommy. Merry Christmas, Daddy."